2190
EXTINCTION

A NOVEL BY
G. J. PAGE

PAGE PUBLISHING

Copyright ©2022 Gwyneth Jane Page

2190: Extinction

All rights reserved. No part of this publication may be reproduced, stored in a retrieval system or transmitted in any form or by any means – electronic, mechanical, photocopying, and recording or otherwise – without the prior written permission of the author, except for brief passages quoted by a reviewer in a newspaper or magazine. To perform any of the above is an infringement of copyright law.

Note for Librarians: A cataloguing record for this book is available from Library and Archives Canada at www.collectionscanada.ca/amicus/index-e.html

Cover & Layout Design:
Jenny Engwer, www.jennyengwer.com

Book Images:
Grass Sunset by TintaNegra, Shutterstock ID: 180218315
Silhouette City by Vadish Zainer, Shutterstock ID: 544599301
Hikers by Tithi Luadthong, Shutterstock ID: 1282908316

ISBN: 978-1-989302-12-5 (paperback)

PAGE PUBLISHING
www.gwynethjanepage.com

10 9 8 7 6 5 4 3 2 1

YEAR 2022

The climate change countdown clock in New York
gives us five years before the effects of
our destructive behaviour are irreversible.

Dear Reader:

This is our story. Yours. Mine. Not at the same time, of course. Yours is long before mine and is the reason for my scribblings. Could our history have been different? Well no, to be specific, it is my history, it is your future. History is of course the sum total of the decisions we make. My decisions were much more cataclysmic than yours. I still find it hard to believe that my choice of partner could mean the difference between the survival of the planet and its doom. But did I ever really have a choice? Maybe if your decisions are different then history can be re-written. Maybe I,ll write a different story. The choice is ultimately yours.

Emi

P.S.   I wonder if we,re related. Are you my ancestor? If I,m your great-great-great-granddaughter, what kind of life will you choose for me to have? Will you choose the one written here?

PROLOGUE
YEAR: 2122

Hayle groaned. She was only thirtieth in line but that meant twelve spots further back than yesterday. Still, she should be able to get *some* food. Rubbing her eyes to dispel the exhaustion, she stifled a yawn; lining up at 5 a.m., as she did most mornings, was taking its toll. Staring forlornly at the queue in front of her, she sighed, resigning herself to the fact that she would have to get up even earlier or she might not get any food at all.

The neatly laid out aisles that stretched to the back of the store were devoid of people shopping. Food on the shelves and serving yourself were things of the past. Anything available was locked in the storeroom behind what had once been the deli-counter at the front of the store.

She inched forward, eyes riveted to one couple going past with a whole loaf of bread, some rice — not real rice, of course, nobody could afford that — and a small bag of bruised apples. *What on earth could they have traded to get all that?* She couldn't imagine anyone with enough work to buy so much food. Her stomach growled.

'Leave some for the rest of us will ya,' grouched the pot-bellied man behind her as the couple quickly exited the store, shoving the items in their backpack.

'That'll last 'em for days,' interjected a scarecrow of a woman two spaces in front of Hayle. The woman reached the front of the queue and slid a pair of child's shoes across the counter. She was given half a loaf of bread in return. 'Is that it?' she asked the store owner, a thin, balding man with a kind face who looked more careworn than his years accounted for.

Mr. Brown nodded his head and called, 'next.'

'There should be rationing,' the pot-bellied man grumbled under his breath as another couple left with a half a loaf of bread.

Hayle approached the counter and put down her handful of worthless cash, hoping it was enough to buy something. Anything.

'Sorry, Hayle love, but we're all out. There's nothing left today.'

'But…but the lineup behind me is huge,' she said, glancing over her shoulder at the stream of people that snaked its way out the door and into the street. 'How can there be so little?'

'The Hyperstorm down south wiped out the crops. Evacuees have been arriving throughout the night. There's not enough to go 'round anymore.'

Hayle was shoved out of the way as the people behind her overheard the conversation and pushed their way forward.

'Open the storeroom!' someone demanded.

'You can't hoard for your family. We're starving!' said the pot-bellied man.

'Open up or we'll break the door down!' yelled another customer.

'There's nothing in the storeroom,' Mr. Brown tried to shout over the angry voices. 'If I had any food I'd sell it to you. Every day they bring me less. There's nothing out there to bring in.'

More people battled their way into the store, filling the entrance. Someone outside threw a rock. The front window shattered in a hailstorm of glass. Edging her way around the mob, Hayle squeezed through the open door and shoved her way through the crowd, desperate to get out before things escalated further. Hands grabbed at her, ripping her shirt, knocking her onto the hot, dusty pavement. She crawled away on hands and knees. Then somebody lifted her into the air. She screamed.

'Shhh. I have you. I'll get you out.'

Zed frowned as he picked up the monthly news bulletin. *Why did he bother?* Slowly exhaling between pursed lips he shook his head. He couldn't remember the last time he'd come across anything remotely positive. Today's headlines didn't look like they were going to alter his frame of mind. They read:

> Hurricane Rita Wipes Out Southern States
> Intensity of Hyperstorms Increase:
> Last Few Survivors Permanently Evacuated
>
> Another 500 000 Deaths in Europe This Week:
> Elderly and Infirm Victims of Toxic Food
>
> 2000 Farmers Declare Bankruptcy:
> Poisonous Soil Can No Longer Sustain Crops
>
> Mental Disorders Epidemic:
> Doctors and Scientists Explore Links to Food Toxins and Imprints
>
> Breakthrough Discovery of 2118 — Biological Dye
> Makes Imprints Permanent
> Supply Not Keeping Up with Demand

Zed lowered the paper. *What kind of world was he leaving for his son?* He gazed at Zachy, sleeping peacefully in his cot and allowed his mind to wander. He hadn't been prepared for the all-consuming love he'd felt for his son the first time they'd put him in his arms.

How could one person love another so intensely? Funny that Zachy's birthmark, a blue smudge covering the upper part of his right arm, was almost the exact shape, and in the same spot, as Hayle's tattoo imprint. It was as if she loved him so much she had passed along a branding mark that declared he was her child; like passing on his own wavy, brown hair or Hayle's blue eyes and straight nose. But even with all their love, what would become of this little scrap of humanity? He was forty years old. Average life expectancy gave him another nine years. Many children were left to fend for themselves, but the thought of this fate befalling his son before the age of ten was deeply distressing.

'Zed?'

'Hmmm, yeah, out here'

'Where?'

'Back yard'

Hayle appeared, shaking, her shirt torn and grubby. She threw herself into his arms.

'What on earth happened to you?'

'The queue for food…it turned into a riot.'

'You okay?' Zed enveloped her in his arms. He could feel the tension in her shoulders as she curled into him. He caressed her head causing them to be coated in a layer of fine dust. His fingers caught on a twig in her blonde hair. He untangled it and threw it to the ground.

'Just bruised I think,' she whispered as she rubbed at a spot on her knee that was beginning to turn purple. 'Mr. Brown said evacuees from the south are coming here.'

'Here? We can't feed more people here!'

She shook her head, tears welling. 'We need to move north. Try growing our own food where it's not so hot,' she said slowly between ragged breaths, articulating her thoughts out loud.

'But seeds cost a fortune. Don't think we could get any except on the black market.'

'We'll starve otherwise.'

'That's a bit drastic don't you think? Things aren't that bad.' Zed swallowed his words.

Wiping her sleeve across her face, Hayle took a big breath and closed her eyes. 'Someone grabbed me as I was trying to get away. Helped me to safety. He said to survive we needed to stay away from the food and medication being distributed. And avoid getting more imprints with the new ink. The things he said scared me.'

'But the medication and imprints are mandatory.'

'He was pretty convincing. And there's *nothing* for us here. It's hot and dry and the fields — what can we grow? Coffee beans! We can't *eat* coffee. Places that can still produce food don't ship it out. Why would they? If we want Zachy to survive and have some kind of a life we need to leave.' Her voice rose an octave.

'I know you're right but I hate the idea of moving again,' Zed gazed through the open door at his son. 'But for Zachy's sake —' he trailed off, concern deepening the lines of his face. 'This time last year we were eating tuna from the can and we thought that was bad. Now, I'd almost give my left arm for a few cans of tuna.' He frowned. 'Where do you want to go?'

'The guy I talked to was from New York. Maybe somewhere as far north as that. He said it's a *little* cooler and they don't get Hyperstorms. Plus there are a few valleys where rivers have less toxic water.'

'Sounds too good to be true.' Zed held Hayle more tightly, not wanting to get up and start the tedious process of sorting their possessions. 'But our car,' he grimaced. The car was old. He'd found it abandoned long ago and had managed to scavenge parts from other derelict vehicles and fix it. Cars were no longer made and the handful of spare parts available on the black market fetched a premium. Few could afford the newer hover technology and he was not one of those few. 'Sometimes I miss my old gas-guzzling station-wagon. It was a classic. The last of its kind.' Zed sighed.

They spent the rest of the day sorting their meager belongings, collecting the essentials: clothes, shoes, kitchenware, sleeping bags, first aid kit, camping gear. Now they'd decided to leave, Zed wanted to go as quickly as possible, before it was too late. He watched Hayle pick up the little wooden truck he'd made for Zachy just after he was born. He'd inscribed it 'For Dezmond, Love Dad.' But they had ended up calling their son by his middle name and it had stuck. He smiled. It was a frivolous thing to take but Hayle placed it in the backpack on top of the handful of tiny clothes. Zed tore the headlines from the newspaper, folded the page and shoved it into the outer pocket of his son's pack — it would be a good reminder of what they were running from. They left the bigger pieces of furniture for their landlord in lieu of rent; he could hock it in exchange for food or other necessities.

Early the next morning they put Zachy into the back seat next to the cooler of food and headed north. The sun was not yet over the horizon but already they were just one small family unit amongst thousands escaping the heat and violent storms of the south.

Zed, gazing out the windshield as he drove, watched as fights broke out and shop windows were smashed by those trying to grab the little that was left. He inched the car forward through the crowded streets, scared that if he were too aggressive they'd be singled out and attacked. Time slowed to a crawl. By the time they'd made it to the outskirts of town, unscathed, he felt like he'd been hunched over the steering wheel for days

Breathing a sigh of relief as they left town and headed out into the countryside, Zed remembered back to his childhood. The surrounding area had been green and lush, planted with a variety of crops. Now, all that remained was barren earth with a few crops here and there that could withstand the higher temperatures and contaminated soil. The devastation of the planet, when it had finally caught up with their careless ways, had been sudden. Catastrophic.

'Thank God we made it out! I was beginning to think we weren't going to.'

'We've a ways to go yet,' Zed glanced sideways at Hayle as they came to another town. Some of the buildings were in ruins and a handful of people were grabbing whatever remained in the shops.

They continued north throughout the day. The air blowing in through the open windows was hot and dry but it was better than nothing. The air conditioning had long since packed it in.

The congestion eased the further north they went. Not many people had vehicles. They were a luxury and replacement parts were almost impossible to find. Most people had to flee on foot so they didn't make it far, usually only to the next town, until they had to leave again.

'This is a *bit* better.' Hayle looked around as the late evening light bathed the surroundings in a golden glow. 'There aren't as many people in the streets. And there are *some* crops. A few towns still look lived in and haven't been looted.'

But the next place they came to appeared to be abandoned. She shivered; it was eerily silent.

'Maybe we should stop here for the night,' suggested Zed. 'It looks quiet and the buildings are mostly intact, so we'll at least have shelter.'

'Yeah, I guess,' Hayle looked around at the derelict town. It hadn't been smashed and looted; it just seemed as though everyone had agreed to leave all at once.

On the outskirts of town they found an old house that was still in decent shape. The weeds on either side of the gravel drive proclaimed that no one had lived there in a while. Zed knocked on the front door as Hayle retrieved Zachy from the back seat of the car. He opened the door and yelled, 'Hello.' He hadn't expected a reply so he wasn't disappointed. Venturing further, he pushed open doors and stuck his head into the rooms but there was nobody about. A fine layer of dust coated everything. These people too had taken what they could. They must have had a vehicle since the mattresses were gone. Just the bed frames remained. He flicked a switch but no lights came on. No surprise. Still, it was a roof over their heads and they could sleep on the couches.

Zed brought in the cooler and they shared the bread and cheese and washed it down with water from their canisters. Even if the water to the house was connected he wasn't going to risk drinking it; it was probably toxic. As the light faded from the evening sky they cleared up and then unrolled the sleeping bags.

It felt strange to break into someone's house and make camp there. Though he was exhausted from the long, hot day in the car, he knew sleep would elude him. He decided he would rather remain alert and ensure his family stayed safe.

'I'll keep watch, you and Zachy get some rest.'

Hayle curled up with her tiny son and was soon asleep.

Zed woke with a start. Dawn light streamed through the curtainless windows. He must have dozed off, too tired to stay alert. He gently shook Hayle awake and then made camp-style coffee. They shared an orange and had a slice of bread each with a thin layer of jam. Hayle had managed to make the jam out of over-ripe fruit — nothing kept for long in the heat.

The morning was unnervingly still. Hayle settled Zachy in the car as Zed hurried to pack up, trying to quell his growing panic. He glanced over his shoulder, feeling exposed away from the relative safety of the abandoned house, sure he was being watched. He needed to bundle his family into the car and flee. There had always been rumors that life in the north was less harsh; he could only pray they were true. As he started the car and slowly eased it down the gravel drive, a young woman ran across the rutted road toward them.

'Hello. Please, please wait!' she yelled, waving them down. Zed slowed the car to a halt and stuck his head out of the open window. 'Hi. Sorry. Didn't mean to frighten you,' she panted. 'You guys heading north?'

'Yep,' Zed's reply offered little encouragement to the young woman.

'Please, could I beg a lift?'

Zed glanced at Hayle, who scowled and shook her head. Zed looked back at the girl. She seemed harmless enough. Her long brown hair was tied back in a braid and her lightly freckled face was fresh and youthful. She couldn't be more than twenty. Zed's gaze shifted to Hayle and he raised his eyebrows. She shrugged her shoulders but still said nothing.

'I guess we could fit you in. Did you get left behind?' Zed indicated the abandoned house.

'I'm a scout. Trying to help those I can get to safety to valleys in the north. I'm Penelope Black, Penny for short. From New York.'

Hayle and Zed locked eyes.

'You seem kind of young to be out here all alone?' observed Hayle.

'There's a few of us around. But my transport was found. Destroyed by the Blues. I only just managed to get away.'

'By who?' asked Hayle and Zed, speaking at once.

'Are you okay? And who on earth are the Blues?'

'I'm alright.' Penny brushed herself down before squeezing into the back seat. 'The Blues. You know — people covered with imprints using that new Genedye. Can we get going?' She glanced over her shoulder through the rear window.

'I was hoping we were almost far enough north to stay put,' said Hayle. 'I noticed some people getting their whole bodies covered in imprints using that new ink. Don't like it myself but I got the imprint on my arm done with the government subsidy,' Hayle babbled, nervously trying to make conversation with their new companion.

'Good thing it's so small as the Genedye is *very* toxic,' said Penny, noting Hayle's imprint. She slumped in her seat, all the fight going out of her like a pricked balloon.

They headed north out of the derelict town and carried on through another long, hot day. Zed's heart sank as he stared silently out the window at the devastation. How were they going to survive? He'd no idea so many cities had been looted and left abandoned as people fled their homes to seek places where the soil was less toxic and fresh water flowed.

Just when he thought things couldn't get much worse, the car began to slow before coming to a halt.

'Damn it!' Zed got out of the car. The solar panel had been on its last legs for a while but it had been impossible to find a replacement. 'We'll have to walk with whatever we can carry. Damn, damn and damn!' He kicked at the nearest tire. 'Let's hope somebody comes by who's willing to give us a lift.'

'I'll help,' said Penny, slinging Zachy's backpack over her shoulder.

As they gathered all they could carry, Zed heard a noise. He looked up. Four menacing-looking men were coming toward them. They were tall and heavy-set, with immense arms, barrel chests, and dark blue tattoo imprints covering every visible part of their anatomy.

'Crap. Grab your baby and run! They want your stuff, not you. Run!' yelled Penny, snatching the bag of food beside her.

Zed grabbed Zachy, who had a firm grip on his little wooden truck, and ran with Hayle and Penny hard on his heels. They could hear the Blues shouting and destroying the car as they took everything from within.

Zed glanced back. A couple of Blues were chasing them. 'Run!' he yelled.

As they ran, Hayle fell headlong, hitting her head on a rock. Zed heard the impact and looked back horrified as the Blues closed in on her. 'Take Zachy,' he shouted at Penny, almost throwing the child at her.

He reached Hayle's side a moment before the Blues descended on them. As he bent down to lift Hayle in his arms he felt a rock come down on his head and all went black.

FORTY-EIGHT YEARS LATER

YEAR: 2170

Zach had no doubt he was nearing the end of his life but the fact that he'd lived to the age of forty-nine was miraculous. He nibbled his piece of toast. The small effort left him exhausted. Putting his hand to his stomach he lay back against the pillows as his insides clenched painfully, his toxic body trying to digest the miniscule amount of food.

His grimace turned into a hint of a smile as memories flooded his mind. Penny Black was the sole reason for his longevity. After she'd delivered him to his adoptive parents she'd continued to visit every few months, bringing what toxin-free food she could spare which was grown by the Fringe. Her visits had been a highlight throughout his life, not only for the diverse array of non-toxic food she brought but also for her kindness and compassion.

He was content to die. Life had become too harsh for him to wish to live — he was just another mouth to feed, taking precious food from his daughter. Although Dezerai would miss him, her fight for survival would take up most of her thoughts and energy.

He glanced down at the old newspaper clipping. He'd found it crumpled in the bottom of his pack when he was six. It explained why his parents had fled their home, sacrificing their lives to try to give him a better existence. It had been his first real awareness of the troubles that had engulfed them all.

Staring through the open window as the hot breeze ruffled the threadbare curtain, he frowned at the view — nothing but tall, dry grass; the only thing that grew in the desolate soil. The planet was so much worse off than fifty years ago when the newspaper headlines had been printed. *What kind of world was he leaving for his daughter?*

Dezerai poked her head around his bedroom door. 'Can I get you anything, Dad?'

He shook his head and patted the edge of his bed. 'What happened to you?'

'Got caught in another riot for food.' She looked down at her grubby, torn shirt and the scratches on her arm. 'Looks worse than it is. I'm alright,' she smiled. 'I managed to get some oranges for a change. They're so rare now I can't believe there were any left. And I got some deer meat, so it was worth the struggle.'

Zach moved his little wooden truck so she could sit down. He spun the wheels. It was all he had left from his parents. Now it was all he was leaving behind for Dezerai.

She sat next to him. 'I'm going to miss you,' Dezerai said, her eyes glistening.

'Promise me you'll survive this famine and I'll die a happy man.'

'I promise, Dad.' She swallowed audibly. 'At least I'll do all I possibly can,' she added, lips pressed together to prevent their trembling. Life was too uncertain for meaningful promises. 'With the food Caleb smuggles in I'm better off than most. And, as horrible as it is, things have to balance out eventually. There are so many deaths. At some point there *must* be enough food to feed those of us left.'

'One can only hope.' He reached for her hand.

Dezerai hung her head. 'Dad, there's something I need to tell you.'

'Sounds like something I'm not going to like.' His gaze fixed on the top of her head.

She nodded but didn't look up. 'I'm carrying his child,' she whispered.

'What!' Zach's face blanched. 'Carrying his child! You mean Caleb's — Penny's son's?' Zach's words came out in staccato clips.

Dezerai nodded again, her eyes focused on her hand resting in that of her father's.

'But the Fringe, they don't…intermingle. They keep themselves… they're still genetically pure.'

Dezerai shrugged her shoulders, looking down at the faded imprint that covered the upper part of her right arm — inherited from her dad — undeniable proof that she wasn't genetically pure. At last she looked up to meet her dad's eyes.

'He's already married. He has a family. What were you thinking?' Zach pressed himself further back into his pillows.

'I know. I —' she trailed off, unable to put her feelings into words.

'You'll have a tough time feeding two of you, even with his help,' he snapped.

'I'll cope. I always do. Don't worry about us. And I really want this baby. I'm certain it's a boy. I'm thinking of calling him Dez.'

Zach stared at his daughter. A myriad of emotions flitted across his face. She watched him come to terms with her news. Then he heaved a sigh and gently squeezed her hand.

'Dez. Hmm. I like that.' The corners of his mouth twitched up in a smile.

'Try not to worry, Dad. We'll survive.'

'I believe you will.' He held her hand, not wanting to let go and leave her to fend for herself. But he was so tired. 'Don't let on to anyone you're carrying a Fringe baby.'

'No, I won't.' She shook her head. 'We love each other, you know,' she added, giving her dad a hint of a smile in return.

Zach nodded. 'I've watched you two together. I wish you could be together, especially now. You're going to need someone.'

'We always knew it would never be allowed. He had to marry within the Fringe. That's just the way it is.' She shrugged in resignation, her expression unfathomable. 'And as leader he was expected to produce an heir. A genetically pure heir.' The tinge of bitterness in her voice was unmistakable.

'I wish I could be here for you for a bit longer.' Zach pulled his daughter into his arms. 'But I'm glad you told me about Dez.'

PART ONE

ONE
YEAR 2190

'Dez, what *are* you doing? I thought we were supposed to be hunting, you know, finding food so we don't starve. You won't catch much laying there.'

'Hey, Jax,' Dez nodded his head at his young companion. Jax was only fifteen but his thin frame and shock of sun-bleached blonde hair belied the reliable and grown-up character within. Mind you, they were all too old for their age; they had no choice in the world they lived in. At fifteen, Jax's life was probably already a third over.

Pointing with his chin, Dez indicated the swarm of people in the ravine below, partially hidden from view by the protruding rocky outcrop on which he was perched.

'Watching,' Dez murmured. His gaze shifted back to Jax. With a twitch of his head he indicated that Jax should also duck down out of sight.

Jax sprawled out next to Dez on the baked earth. A fine layer of dust covered Dez's dark hair and tanned, athletic build. It even obscured his genetic imprint — an indistinct blotch which, if one looked closely, was most likely an outline of an eagle in flight — that dominated his right bicep. Jax stifled a sneeze and wiped at his gritty eyes as the dust swirled, stirred by his motion. He turned his head to the scene being played out in the gully below.

'Blues! Here!' Horizontal lines of dirt ran across Jax's forehead, his brow deeply furrowed as he watched the rabble below. 'Getting a bit close don't you think?'

'Hmm. Yeah. Not looking good.' Was Dez's understated reply.

The crowd erupted into a hostile mob. With shaved heads and genetically inherited imprints from head to toe, the seething throng of blue-hued humanity was menacing. Dez closed his eyes and allowed himself a moment of refuge, cringing as the guttural cacophony re-ignited memories he preferred to suppress. The possibility of another attack was never far from his imagination. At least they were fighting each other and not the Network. He refused to lose more of his people but the thought of moving again was not something he wanted to contemplate. He swallowed the lump in his throat and forced his eyes open.

The raucous increased in volume, rising up to them on the hot, still air. Some of the Blues were knocked unconscious, their enormous bodies motionless on the cracked earth. Their blood seeped into the thirsty ground. One fellow, covered in snake imprints with a massive spike impaling the python tattoo on his bulging stomach, stood on a rock, frantically thumping his companions. Could he have found the waterhole and didn't want to share it with anyone or was he just enjoying the fight?

'We better head out,' Dez scowled as dust clouds stirred by the fighting obscured their line of vision. The dust was relentless. It was drier than ever. But there was no point expressing his fears out loud. What could anyone do about it? Nothing! 'I don't want to be found by the Blues in their current mood.'

Jax looked sideways at Dez.

'Is there *any* mood they have where you *would* want to be found by them? Don't they just have the *one* mood?'

'True,' smirked Dez as he cast a sidelong look at Jax. He enjoyed Jax's subtle sense of humour which lurked below the surface, ready to lighten the mood regardless of the situation.

'Wait,' Jax grabbed Dez's arm and pointed beyond the mob to where the billowing dust clouds were less intense. 'See, there.'

Dez brought his ancient pair of Zoomlenses to his eyes and trained them on the far side of the ravine. The woman was probably in her forties. She wore clean, well-made clothes, had perfect skin, no imprints, and glossy blonde hair. She seemed physically fit and well nourished and not as though she had to spend time exposed to the elements or searching for her next meal.

'Looks like someone from the Fringe.'

'The Fringe! Seriously? Can I look?'

'Sure.' Dez passed over the battered Zoomlenses.

'Wow!'

'I haven't seen anyone from the Fringe since —'

'Uh-oh!' Jax slithered back out of sight as the mob below began to break up.

'Time to go,' stated Dez.

He and Jax headed for the trees.

Were things changing, getting worse, or was it just his imagination? Could they get any worse? It would be good to share his thoughts with Sam after tonight's meeting.

'Will she be okay?' Jax asked.

'She'll be fine. The Fringe know how to look after themselves and I doubt she's alone. Come on; let's move! We still need to catch *something*.'

'Please, not squirrel again,' Jax muttered.

'Hopefully not,' Dez frowned as they disappeared further into the forest.

'Some days I get so fed up with nibbling around all their tiny bones. Hardly worth the effort.'

'I'll try for rabbit. Their bones are slightly bigger,' Dez replied, his tone implying that he was only semi-serious. Being fussy about what one got to eat was not an option and they both knew it.

They moved at a brisk trot through the trees, avoiding the brittle, broken branches. Once in a while they paused and threw brown leaves across their track. At last they emerged on the far side of the forest and came to a massive expanse of dry grassland. The golden stalks of invasive grass swayed far above their heads. Using sticks collected from the forest floor to protect themselves from the villainous stalks, they pushed through, following the almost invisible footpath that had been trodden out over the years.

As the sun started to fade from the sky, they came to another valley and paused to signal to the security guards before descending into their adopted home turf. The landscape gradually changed. The grass grew green and soft — short and non-invasive, trees became lush; birds chirped, and bushes rustled as squirrels and rabbits ran for cover.

'I'll go catch those rabbits. Can you collect potatoes and veg from the garden and refresh the water canisters? With the meeting tonight we'll need enough to feed a few extras.'

Tom loved the thrill of the hunt; the skill it took to move silently through the forest when underfoot there was nothing but brittle twigs and dry leaves. He rejoiced in catching sight of a deer, staying downwind of it, and looking down the length of the arrow knowing you had the perfect shot. Then there was the satisfaction of providing something better than squirrel or rabbit for a handful of families at

Sector D. It was one of the few things in his life that gave him contentment.

Hunting also gave him a good excuse to escape into the woods for the day. Life was hard for everyone with the scarcity of food, the heat and the dust but at least most had some kind of shelter that was a place of refuge. His home was a prison. He couldn't bring himself to leave because he needed to be there for his mom but he hated each moment. Every day he dreaded going back home but at least today had been rewarding. He and Liz had managed to bring down a buck. Carefully rationed, it would help feed the families that relied on him for at least a month. Maybe the news would bring a smile to his mother's face. He missed his mother's smiles.

He and Liz, his hunting companion and best friend, hauled the carcass to the village butcher and went their separate ways. He dawdled as he headed to his shelter, dreading that his uncle might be there. *Why couldn't his uncle have died when the Blues raided their village? Why did it have to be his dad and sister?* He'd never liked his uncle but now his dad and sister were gone, his presence was unbearable. When he opened the door he never knew what to expect. He didn't understand why his mom didn't evict his uncle. Persuading her was impossible. He'd even felt desperate enough to try and enlist the aid of Sam, the village leader, asking if his uncle could be relocated to Sector C. But relocating people was complicated as it meant another village was honour bound to feed the extra person. Sam had been sympathetic and said he would bring it up at the Network meeting he'd headed off to a few days ago but, ultimately, the decision was up to Tom's mom.

Taking a deep breath, he let it out slowly and lifted the latch.

'Mom, I'm —'

The door swung open.

He stood petrified, his hand instinctively covering his mouth as he retched. He took a gasping breath and fell to his knees beside his mother.

'Mom, Mom, Mom. Please, wake up!'

His mind rebelled at the horror before him. His nose filled with the sickening stench of iron. He closed his eyes, taking refuge in the few seconds of eternity as he hid behind his eyelids. He opened his eyes. The scene remained the same. His breath caught in his throat and he gagged. Blood was everywhere; his mom a crumpled heap on the floor, the loose flowing style of dress she wore was torn, leaving one of her breasts exposed. A massive bruise was emerging from the huge bump on her forehead.

'Mom. Please. Wake-up. What happened?' He gently shook the inert form. He pulled her dress up to cover her breast and put his head to her chest. She was still breathing. The dull thud of her heart echoed in his ear.

Her eyelids flickered open. 'Get…help.'

Tom scrambled to his feet and ran from the house. *Where to go? Who would know what to do? Kay, the village healer.* He sprinted down the rutted lane, tripping over his feet he flew headlong, landing sprawled out in the dust. He picked himself up, not bothering to brush himself down or check if he was hurt. The hot air burned his lungs, his breathing came in ragged gasps. *Why did they live so far from the Sector D village? Why couldn't they be near everyone else?* His mom might bleed to death in the time it took to find Kay.

He arrived at Kay's shelter, barely able draw breath. He bent over, his hands on his knees, trying to suck oxygen into his lungs. Then he lifted his fist and pounded on the door. *Please let her be home.*

The door opened and Kay stood there, her half-eaten dinner behind her on the table. Babbling out his story, barely stopping to register Kay's expression of alarm, he turned and ran home. Kay knew where he lived; she would come once she'd grabbed what she needed.

When he returned home he collapsed on the floor next to his mom, his legs unable to support him any longer.

'Mom, Mom, Kay's coming. You'll be okay. She'll be here soon. Mom.'

Tom looked around frantically, not knowing what to do. He grabbed a blanket from the cot in the corner. — The cot where his uncle slept; currently a crumpled mess, as if his uncle had been thrashing about with nightmares. — Folding the blanket, he put it under his mom's head and then staggered out to the back yard to get water from the pump.

'What *happened*?' Kay appeared at the open front door as Tom knelt down to give his mom a sip of water.

There were blood stains on the floorboards, a chair was toppled over and the dinner table was shoved at an angle.

Tom shook his head. 'Don't know. I was gone for the day — hunting. Got back and found her like this.' He waved his arm to encompass the room, looking pleadingly at Kay. 'Looks like she fell. There's a big egg on her head.'

'You don't bleed like *this* from falling.' Kay knelt beside the prone form and gently started to examine her.

Tom turned away while Kay conducted her exam.

Kay ran her hands over Sara's head, neck, arms, and legs, feeling for any broken limbs. When she pushed aside the torn dress, she gasped and started to gently probe Sara's abdomen.

Hearing Kay's gasp, Tom glanced back.

'What the hell? What the *hell*!'

His mom's stomach was distended and covered in bruises. The bruises on her breasts slowly registered upon his mind — they looked like they were caused by the vice-like grip of fingers.

'She's miscarrying!' Kay glanced at Tom.

'She's what?'

'Miscarrying. The blood. It's from losing the baby.'

'Baby. What baby? What are you talking about? My dad died ages —' Comprehension suddenly crystalized in his mind and hatred, the like of which he didn't think could be contained within one soul, erupted deep inside him.

Kay looked at Tom. He was frozen to the spot, his body rigid except for his rapidly blinking eyes. His mouth hung open, speechless. But she needed help and there was nobody else.

'Tom. TOM! Get me another blanket and boil some water. I need to sterilise my equipment. Tom. NOW!'

'Oh my God. This can't be happening,' he muttered. Nodding mindlessly, he rose and did as he was told; went to his bedroom to get a blanket, passed it to Kay, went to the little kitchen in the lean-to at the back of the house, grabbed a pot, filled it at the pump and put it on the wood-burning stove. His foot tapped the floorboards until the water began to steam and bubble.

When he returned with the boiled water he found Kay was no longer there. Looking beyond the open front door, he saw her bent over double in the yard.

'Kay? I have the water.'

Kay stood, turned to face him, and shook her head.

'I'm sorry. She's...she's gone. I tried. But she...bled out in front of me. I...I couldn't stop it.'

'Gone? Gone where? She's right —' he turned to stare uncomprehendingly at the scene contained within his home. 'She's dead? She can't be dead!' *I didn't get the chance to tell her about the deer.*

The meeting room in the village of Sector A felt crowded, though only a handful of people were present. It was a small, one-room hut with a low ceiling and not enough of the mismatched windows. It had been the best they could do with the bits scavenged from the nearest abandoned city of Cinnati. As Dez had expected, most Network leaders from the outlying villages had come. Times were too tough to miss a meeting.

But life had been even worse when individual villages had tried to fend for themselves. Horrific raids had become commonplace as the Blues moved north, away from the intense heat of the south. Villagers had abandoned their homes; their proximity to the desolate cities inhabited by the Blues had made them easy targets. At length, the village leaders had agreed to help one another, resulting in the Network. They had found new valleys, further from the Blues. Storehouses of extra supplies were established. Guards were posted and Hoverbirds were used to relay messages. Some of the outlying towns still endured raids but there were few deaths anymore.

'Hey, everyone.' Dez raised his voice above the chatter. 'Now we've all eaten, I hope you're ready to get down to business. We've lots to discuss and I assume everyone needs to do some trading.'

There were nods of assent all around.

'Jax, do you want to start us off?'

'Sure.' Jax stood up from his rickety chair. 'Well, the storehouses are getting low on some stuff. If anyone is planning a scavenging trip to a city, look out for clothes. We've got rabbit jerky and some dried fruit we could trade. Oh, and we need shoes. Tires will do if need be.'

Jax extended his leg to display the worn, rubber sole of his sandal. The bottom was carved from an old tire and the top was made of thin rope crafted from grassland stalks.

'Can you make me a pair too? That's quite the fashion statement,' Dez laughed. He looked around the room. Many people had bare feet or had fashioned footwear out of animal skins and woven grasses. 'Right, who's up next?' asked Dez, as Jax took his seat. 'Sam?'

Sam stood to address the group. He was tall and lanky with a smile that made you want to be his friend. Dez and Sam had been buddies since they were toddlers; back when their parents were alive, before either of them had thought about having to be in positions of command. Sam was now Dez's right-hand man; he couldn't imagine what he would do without him.

'Not much new to report. Tom's having to go further afield to find bigger game and thought he saw someone from the Fringe. Not sure what's up but it seems odd.' Changing tack, Sam added, 'On a more personal note, Tom's been in turmoil since his dad and sister were killed. His uncle has moved in with he and his mom on a permanent basis. I'd hoped, with time, things would get better but — ' he trailed off and shrugged.

'Almost everyone here has lost a family member, if not their entire family.' Dez surveyed the room. 'I still have vivid nightmares *and* I live with the guilt of not being able to save my sister. So let me, or any of us, know if we can help.'

'Thanks, Dez.' Sam nodded. 'But I think the current problem is more to do with the uncle. Tom *was* wondering if we could re-locate him. But he's pretty bad news. If anyone has any brilliant, or not so brilliant ideas, please come see me after the meeting.'

Sam resumed his seat.

Emi, a lithe, dark-haired girl, stood to engage the group. As she did so, one of the legs of her chair came loose causing it to topple to the ground behind her. She grinned and laughed nervously, before picking it up and putting the leg back into its hole. 'Well, we feel like the Fringe are watching us but I can't imagine they're interested in what we're doing.'

'And what are you doing?' Dez's breath caught in his throat. He'd always felt drawn to Emi; she had a quiet, gentle nature but with an underlying inner resilience. He hadn't seen her in a while. She'd changed. He suddenly felt tongue-tied and happy that it wasn't his turn to speak.

'For a while now we've been trying to improve our health so we live longer. And I *think* it's working.' Emi grinned. 'Did you know people used to live to be eighty, ninety, even one hundred?' She paused to draw breath. 'Anyway. *We've* had our first *fiftieth* birthday. Jon's. So we're halfway there.' Emi announced before being drowned out as the room erupted into applause and everyone started to talk at once. Emi grinned and then laughed. Her eyes sparkled at Dez, obviously thrilled at being the one to share such great news.

Dez returned Emi's smile. Their eyes met before Dez cleared his throat and looked away. He regained his equilibrium in the buzz of chatter. 'All right, let's carry on shall we or we'll be here all night. Meet with the leaders you need to trade with.'

For the next hour everyone in the small, dimly lit room moved around, exchanging stories and arranging trades. It was noisy and hot but they were all in good spirits, cheered by Emi's news. Once trading was complete, everyone resumed their seats and waited for Dez to speak.

'Network improvement is the next subject. Given Emi's news, I think we should all learn from Sector B what they've done to improve their health and try to emulate them,' Dez suggested.

'I second that,' said Sam.

'I third it,' smirked Jax.

Dez smiled indulgently before turning his attention to Emi. 'Emi, is your village in a position to help the others?' he asked.

'I think so,' said Emi. 'It's simple stuff really. We now boil all of our water…even drinking water. We share more of what we have so our diet is more varied. Each family focuses on growing a few particular items, in addition to the basics, so that they have extra to trade. And we rotate chores so everyone can have a day to rest. That way we're not always exhausted and scavenging for food every second of every day.'

'Right. That's decided then,' Dez nodded. 'Emi, maybe we could meet tomorrow to make plans,' he said, trying to mask his expression and pretend an indifference he was far from feeling.

Emi nodded and smiled before fixing her eyes on her hands, cradled in her lap.

'Everyone else, unless there's something we've missed, that's it for tonight.'

As they stood to leave, the door was flung open and Abe almost fell into the room. His massive frame filled the doorway and his chocolate-brown skin glistened in the dim light.

'Sorry to interrupt,' he gasped. 'I've just had a Hover-bird in from Liz. The 'bird was damaged so the message is a bit garbled but I think Sam's needed back at Sector D. Tom's mom collapsed. Sounds like maybe she was beaten,' he blurted. 'And Tom's uncle …'

The rest of what Abe was about to say was lost in the resulting hubbub.

'Crap. I'll leave at first light.' Sam massaged his forehead. 'Dez, can you have our supplies delivered by Hover-bird? I won't be able to stick around to deal with it now.'

'Sure. It'll probably get there before you do,' said Dez. 'Too bad we can't deliver *you* by Hover-bird.' His mouth twitched up slightly but his eyes remained shadowed.

'If I could get some of these Hover*boards* working I could get you there a lot faster.' Abe picked one up from the stack by the wall and studied the bottom of it.

'Any idea what this is about?' Dez asked Sam. 'Who would beat up Sara...and why?'

'Wish I knew. Sara rarely leaves their shelter. When she does, she *never* looks up, just shuffles along, avoids people. I've tried talking to Tom but he doesn't offer much. Turns into an argument,' Sam shook his head and rubbed his eyes. 'He's still good about providing food for the village but Liz said he likes to go hunting on his own now. Ditches her more often than not.'

'But I thought they were best friends and —'

'She doesn't know what to think but she saw Tom talking to a Blue. Big guy covered in snake imprints.'

'Snake imprints? I —'

'She couldn't hear what they were saying but apparently, Tom handed over the game he'd killed and walked away.'

'Tom came face to face with a Blue and lived to tell!' Dez's eyes widened. 'Well, if you figure out what's going on, let me know *and* tell me if you need any help.'

'Will do.' Sam stifled a yawn. 'I wanted to chat about a few things but I'll need to get an early start so I guess it'll have to wait.' He stifled another yawn and clapped Dez on the back then turned to leave.

'Sam, can I join you tomorrow?' asked Zoe, a tall girl with short-cropped dark hair and a vine imprint that looped down her arm. 'I hate travelling alone.'

'Sure. You okay to leave around 4:30?'

Zoe nodded. Traveling with Sam would give her company all the way back home. Her village at Sector C was near Sam's. Sectors C and D were further south, closer to the abandoned cities that the

Blues inhabited. She dreaded the thought of being found by a Blue when on her own. Being with Sam wouldn't help much but the illusion of safety gave her comfort.

The group broke up. A few to get some rest in the guest quarters while others stayed to mingle and compare stories of the past few months.

Dez started to close up the meeting room. He cursed under his breath as he shoved the table and chairs back into place. He'd been looking forward for months to catching up with Sam.

'Good night, Dez.' Emi had quietly come up behind him.

'Emi,' Dez's heart skipped a beat as he turned to look down into her upturned face. He gave her a quick peck on the cheek. 'See you tomorrow then.'

'Yes, see you tomorrow.' Emi left the hut and disappeared into the shadows.

He stood fixed to the spot, gazing at the space where she'd been. The moonlight slanting through the windows played tricks on him; etching her image upon his mind — her chestnut hair; her upturned face. He exhaled and headed back to his cabin.

Who knew what tomorrow would bring.

Tom was living in a nightmare. His waking moments far worse than his dreams. His mind was numb. He shook his head to dispel the visions of his life paraded before him in his minds eye, he an unwilling spectator, not knowing which way to turn.

Kay had arranged to have his mom's body removed and Liz had arrived on his doorstep as soon as she'd heard the news.

'Tom, I'm so sorry.' Liz enveloped him in a hug.

Tom, taking a shuddering breath, clung to Liz.

'Do you want to come and stay with me?' asked Liz, taking in the bloodstained floorboards, the tatty curtains, the toppled over furniture and the cot in the corner. The misery contained within the four walls of Tom's shelter was palpable.

Tom inhaled before raising his head from where it lay on Liz's shoulder he muttered, 'I...I don't know.'

'Well, you can, any time.'

Tom nodded. 'I think I need to stay here for now. My uncle will show up eventually. When he does, I need to be here.'

Liz gazed at Tom, her forehead etched with concern and dread for what Tom must be thinking. 'Okay, but don't do anything stupid. Let Sam and Dez take care of things.'

Tom nodded, his shoulders slumped.

'Shall I help you clean?'

Tom looked around. The bloody scene that had transpired in his living room finally registering on his consciousness. 'I guess. But I don't think it'll help much.'

'Maybe not but we should at least try,' said Liz, hoping the practical activity would help dispel Tom's stupor.

Tom and Liz scrubbed and scrubbed, down on their hands and knees until their backs ached and their fingers wrinkled like prunes — but a rag and water were never going to get the blood stains out of the floorboards. They would be a constant reminder of his mother's fate.

Utter despair and restlessness became Tom's constant companions. He would sit for hours, staring at the wall, his mind going over and over what had happened, putting together the pieces of the puzzle that had previously eluded him. His mind churned endlessly, always returning to the one thought — he wished his uncle had died at the hands of the Blues. He became haggard, his expression haunted, his eyes glazed, his guilt over not being able to protect his mother impenetrable. When he could no longer face scrubbing the floor he went out into the woods — sometimes hunting, sometimes not — the need to escape overwhelming; hoping he would return home at the end of the day and life would be different.

Between Liz's visits the house remained empty and silent. She tried to convince him to live with her but he couldn't bring himself to make the move. Where his uncle had disappeared to, he didn't know — probably hiding with his friends in Sector C. Tom was sure he'd come whistling through the front door one day soon. He was uncertain if he dreaded that day or was looking forward to it. His home held nothing but misery now, and memories. He thought of burning the place down, moving in with Liz; instead he shut the door behind him, and headed back out into the forest, taking only his bow and arrow.

If only his uncle had died at the hands of the Blues.

TWO

Rez lay on his bed and stared into the darkness. He could visualise every crack and chip in the plaster, every scuff on the walls. But it was his. At least he had a roof over his head. He flipped onto his side. Were the Fringe watching them? What could they want with the Network? He tossed onto his other side. And then there was Emi; seeing her again had stirred feelings he preferred to suppress. Caring about people too much was dangerous.

He pushed himself up, sat on the edge of his bed and ran his hands through his hair. Maybe he should get up. The first tinge of daylight was starting to seep through the broken glass of the window — it would be good to walk in the stillness of the morning before the day grew too hot.

He put on his shirt and shorts and slipped quietly out the door. Not that there was anyone else to wake in his shelter, but he was in the habit of being quiet, it came with the fear of being found by the Blues. The raid five years ago had been devastating — all their meagre vegetable plots ripped out the ground, their stores plundered, so many lives lost, including that of his mother. And he missed his little sister, Isi, as though she had died yesterday. She'd been so weak after the raid that he couldn't save her. Isi had been the last of his immediate family. He tried not to hate but it was almost impossible not to despise the Blues.

Dez shook his head to clear away the dark thoughts, changed direction and headed for the stream. Emerging from the forest, he clambered over rocks, still warm with the previous day's radiant heat, and descended to the valley floor. The rock pools shone pink and silver in the early morning light. A breeze rustled amongst the trees; refreshing for the moment but already laden with the threat of midday's scorching heat. He stripped off his shirt and dove in, allowing the cool, clear water to soothe him.

This valley had been an amazing find. Until a few years ago they hadn't known such places still existed, but then they'd been too terrified to venture far. Those who left didn't return — it was assumed they were taken down by the Blues. He'd never been allowed to go far when his mom was alive.

He turned over and floated on his back, looking up at the endless blue sky spread out beyond the tips of the trees. The green of the foliage and the clear streams of this valley were incredible — how had it evaded the contaminated soil of the grasslands? It had saved his village; that and strengthening the alliance of the Network.

He flipped over and started swimming back and forth across the rock-pool, enjoying the resistance of the water and its coolness on his skin. Feeling his muscles tighten and his breathing improve, his mind strayed to Emi. What was she was doing at that moment?

He came up out of the water to find Emi watching him.

'Hey.' He wiped water from his face. 'You startled me. Thought I was imagining things.'

'No, I'm real enough.' She took off her shirt and waded into the water in her tube top and shorts.

'You know how to swim!' Dez exclaimed. Most people couldn't as it was a luxury few had time for in their struggle for survival. But his mother had taught him; it had been her favourite way to cool off.

'Well, I can paddle enough to not drown. Does that count?' She grinned.

'It's a start. Feels pretty good in this never-ending heat.'

'I'm so used to being hot that I almost forget how hot it actually is.' Emi immersed herself in the water. 'Can you teach me something other than the doggie-paddle? Then I could show the kids in the village. They'd love it if only as a way to cool off.'

'How about I start by teaching you to float. Turn over onto your back. I'll put my hands under you for support. Now put your head back. Legs and arms out in a star shape. Perfect.' He cleared his throat and looked away. Emi's wet tube-top had become slightly see-through. 'I'm going to let go. Ready?'

Why had he thought teaching her to float a good idea? He hadn't thought this through. He slowly lowered his hands away from her back.

'This is the most relaxed I've been in months.'

'Yeah, it's a nice spot.' Dez tried to sound casual as he rolled over onto his back to float beside her. This was better. Floating forced him to look at the sky. 'Coming here helps me cope.'

'Do *you* think we'll be able to change things? Are we fooling ourselves?'

'It's been ages since people worked together as we're doing. Wish my mom had lived to see the Network as it is now; it might have given her *some* hope.' Dez's voice became husky. 'Hey, how about if I go with you,' he suggested, wanting to change the subject. 'Er...I'd love to meet our first fifty-year-old.'

'Sure.' Emi turned her head to smile at him and then thrashed about wildly.

Dez stood and reached out his hand to steady her.

Finding a foothold, she wiped the water from her eyes and face and grinned sheepishly.

'You okay?' Dez held her arm until she regained her equilibrium.

She nodded, turning a slight shade of pink, and looked down to where his hand held her.

He let go.

'Lesson one, the key to floating is to keep your head back and your body up. Looks like we might need to have a few more sessions before you teach swimming,' he said laughingly.

'You might be right!' Her flush deepened. 'I better go and get my things together. You okay to head out tomorrow? I need to get back,' Emi said, her manner suddenly very abrupt.

'Yep, tomorrow works. Meet you outside the guest quarters, say around dawn.'

'Sounds good. See you then.'

Emi grabbed her shirt and vanished into the trees.

Dez, putting his hands to his face, fell backward into the water. Then, turning over, he continued swimming relentlessly back and forth across the pool.

Dez and Emi left early the next morning. They hiked slowly up the green valley, conserving their energy, enjoying the peacefulness of sunrise and the chirping of birds. The idyllic setting wouldn't last; within a couple of hours they would need to seek shelter to escape the heat.

Passing Jax in the fields they gave him a friendly wave.

'Hey, Jax.'

'Dez. Emi. How long you away for, Dez?'

'Not sure. A week, maybe two. I'll send a Hover-bird with a message if plans change.'

'Well, if you happen across the Garden of Eden or Planet-B, let us know.'

'This was the Garden of Eden. But if I find Planet-B I'll be sure to let you know,' Dez winked as he turned to go. 'See you soon.'

'Stay safe.' Jax waved good-bye.

Dez and Emi headed up the path that wound out of the valley and into the forest. They followed the trail through the trees, enjoying the early morning shadows and the slightly cooler temperature offered by the overhanging canopy.

'I'm not looking forward to the grasslands. Hopefully we can reach the other side before mid-morning,' said Emi. 'I know a good spot for a break once we're through.'

'Great. You okay to pick up the pace a bit? I'd like to cover more ground in the cooler part of the day. Won't last long.' He grimaced as he glanced at the sun which was beginning to rise above the treetops.

They broke into an easy jog, winding their way through the forest until they reached the outskirts of the grasslands. The dense menacing wall of grass swayed far above their heads. The long, sharp blades left no room for anything else to grow and were impossible to navigate without a compass. The only advantage to going through the tall stalks was they offered concealment.

'You sure you want to go through here?' Dez cast a doubtful look at Emi. He never came this way, preferring the longer route through the forest that skirted the grasslands. The Blues had never made it this far north so trying to navigate these grasslands didn't seem worth the effort.

Emi pulled a machete and compass from her bag and smiled. 'Yep.'

'You're prepared.'

'It'll knock a few hours off our trek. Are you game?'

'Lead the way.' He shrugged and bowed her forward with a grin. There was a first time for everything.

The sun continued its daily journey across the sky. Emi and Dez took turns hacking back the stalks as they cut the most direct path possible through the grasslands. Emi pulled at her sweat-soaked shirt and sprayed water from her canister onto her head and arms. The tall grass offered protection from being seen; it didn't offer relief from the heat.

At last the grass thinned and they emerged into another forest.

'Almost to our side now,' said Emi.

Dez scanned the area for unwanted company and suppressed a shudder. He felt more exposed at the edge of the forest with its dry, half-dead trees and thin foliage. The crunching of the crisp leaves underfoot seemed deafening in the silence.

'We'll stop in the middle of the woods where there's a spring and a cave. We'll be fairly safe,' said Emi.

'I'm ready for a break.' Dez took off his shirt, sprayed it with water and tied it around his head.

As the sun reached its zenith, the trees thinned and they were confronted with a massive cliff face.

'Finally,' said Emi.

'Finally what?' Dez looked sideways at her and then up at the grey wall of rock.

'This is where the underground stream is and the spring. The cave's up there.' Emi pointed up the vertical cliff that towered over them.

'How on earth do we get up there?'

'We climb of course,' Emi winked at Dez over her shoulder, before skirting around the boulders that hid the spring from view. She lay on the ground, cupped her hands and drank from the cool spring before splashing the crystal clear water over herself.

Dez lay next to her, doused his red face, and busied himself with filling the water canisters.

Emi, now in familiar territory, exuded confidence as she approached the sheer cliff face and started to climb. She found toeholds and pulled herself upwards effortlessly. Dez was sure she could have climbed the cliff even if she were blind, guided by the habit of finding safe havens and knowing how to reach them. Squinting into the sun, Dez's hands scraped against the rock as he followed Emi's every move. They clambered over the ledge, shoved past the protruding bush and collapsed onto the rough floor of the cave.

The cave seemed dim compared to the blinding sunlight. Once their eyes had become accustomed to the darkness, they rummaged around in their packs and shared what food they had. Sitting shoulder-to-shoulder, content to be still and quiet, too exhausted to bother chatting, they soon lay down and drifted to sleep in the relative coolness of the cave.

Emi stirred in her sleep, suddenly alert. The fine hairs at the base of her neck prickled. There was someone other than her and Dez in the cave! Slowly inching her hand out to touch Dez in the darkness, she rolled over, pretending sleep, until she could whisper in his ear, 'Dez, we're being watched.'

Dez jolted awake. He reached out and gave Emi's hand a gentle squeeze. Slowly and quietly he sat up, keeping his back against the rock wall, as he reached for the solar-torch clipped to his shorts. He flicked it on to high beam to blind whoever was watching them. The cave was immediately flooded with light. There before them was the Fringe member he and Jax had seen. He exhaled.

'Oh, it's you!' He dimmed his torch. 'You scared the crap out of us. Maybe next time declare yourself so I don't hurt you!' He relaxed back against the rock and took a deep breath.

Emi released his hand, leaving fingernail prints in his palm. The Fringe were known to be peaceful but they unnerved her

'I'm from the Fringe. I was on my way to your village to find you when, as — uhh — luck would have it, our paths crossed. You're Dez, leader of the Network? And you're Emi? Correct?'

'Yeah, that's right. And who are you?'

'Elizabeth…Elizabeth Canterbury.'

'So how'd you know who we are? Why are you looking for us? The Fringe usually keep to themselves.'

Dez's tone sounded clipped, harsh in the tight confines of the cave. Emi could feel antagonism radiating from him. She could only assume that being cornered didn't sit well with him.

'We're hoping you might help us,' Elizabeth replied.

'Help you! Do you mean *me* or the Network?' Dez frowned.

'You.' Elizabeth paused for breath. 'And *all* of the Network if possible. We desperately need someone who can persuade the Network to help us. I'm sorry I took you unawares but we couldn't wait any longer.'

'Wait for *what*?' said Dez. The dimness of the cave masked the flat stare of his narrowed eyes and the scowl lurking at the corners of his mouth.

'It's complicated,' Elizabeth said. 'I'm sure you've noticed how hot it's been lately. The planet's reached a critical time. We need to try and reverse the trends — NOW! Any later will be too late.' Her speech was matter-of-fact, almost unemotional. Almost! 'We'll soon not have a planet we can survive on.'

Emi's chest contracted in pain and she felt sick to her stomach as the significance of Elizabeth's words registered in her imagination. She grimaced and glanced at Dez, trying to read his reaction. Reaching out for his hand, she wound her fingers through his. This time she didn't let go.

'I thought things were getting worse but what can anyone do about it?' Emi's voice came out strangled.

'We think we've perfected a way to fix the climate,' said Elizabeth. 'But we need a workforce to help build The Cloud. It's how we hope to control the weather.'

'Seriously?' Dez glanced sideways at Emi as he tightened his hold on her hand. 'So either we agree to help or we consign everyone to death and the planet ceases to exist as we know it. Would that be an accurate statement?'

Elizabeth nodded. 'Obviously, saving the planet is to your advantage as well as ours,' was Elizabeth's weary response as she slid down the cave wall, crossing her legs and putting her elbows on her knees. She rested her chin on her hands, looking expectantly at Dez and Emi.

'You've taken us off-guard.' Emi's voice sounded flat even to her own ears. She shuddered. Was it merely the confines of the cave or was it Elizabeth's presence that made her feel like a trapped animal?

'Sorry, but I needed to impress upon you how dire the situation is.'

'Hmm. You've certainly managed to do that!' Dez held firmly onto Emi's hand. 'So what *exactly* do you want?'

'We hoped you might put a leadership team together. We'd take you to New York, where we're based, and educate you. You'd need a good understanding of what's been happening to our planet and what it'll take to change things. You and your team would become the leaders assigned to oversee the work that's necessary. It'll take years. We need to get started as soon as possible.' Elizabeth's eyelids drooped in weariness. 'For now I'd love to get some rest and then join you. If you don't mind?'

Dez and Emi stared questioningly at each other. Dez shrugged and gave a slight nod. He looked down at their entwined fingers. A smile flitted across his face — Emi hadn't tried to retrieve her hand.

'I guess. Arriving at my village with me and Dez will make your acceptance easier, but you've probably figured that out already.' Emi sensed things were about to drastically change and couldn't help feeling hostile toward this charming intruder. 'We'll head out around dusk. Better to travel later when it's difficult to be seen. The rest of the trip doesn't provide much in the way of hiding places.'

'Thank you.' Elizabeth tried to suppress a yawn. 'I would love to be able to sleep properly for a few hours. Being out here on my own has made me edgy. Maybe with you two nearby I'll not wake at every little noise.'

'I'll keep a look out,' Dez offered. 'I don't think I could sleep now anyway.'

Elizabeth lay down on the hard, lumpy surface of the cave and was soon asleep.

Emi waited and then followed Dez to the cave entrance. 'So, what do you think?' she whispered as she squatted down beside him. She looked out across the treetops to the dry grassland beyond. It seemed to go on forever. She was so accustomed to being hot that she hadn't paid much attention to the changes. The image of everyone dying and the world left as an empty globe with nothing moving upon it was too grim to contemplate.

'Hmm. Not sure. What she says makes sense, but —' he shrugged. 'What about you?' he whispered.

Sometimes she could almost visualise the world of her ancestors, a world known only through stories passed on. The other day, when out gathering food, she'd come across a flower she'd never seen before; it had smelled amazing. Had there once been an abundance of such things? If Elizabeth was for real, she hoped whatever they were planning would work and they wouldn't ruin it this time.

'Guess we'll have to wait and see. Listen and learn for now. Hopefully, she's telling the truth and doesn't have a hidden agenda. Although I can't imagine what that would be, so —' Emi stifled a yawn.

'Why don't you try to rest. I'll be alright for a bit.'

Dez positioned himself more comfortably on the ledge while Emi settled down near Elizabeth. The cave was well hidden. Even if the Blues had made it this far north and followed them, they wouldn't have much luck scaling the rock face. He didn't really need to keep watch.

Hours later, as the light was starting to fade from the sky and the heat became slightly less intense, Dez peered into the dimness of the cave. Elizabeth and Emi were sound asleep. He noticed that even up close Elizabeth had the perfection of a Fringe member — her skin, her hair, her shape — but his gaze was drawn to Emi.

He gave himself a shake. Time to wake them and get started.

Dez, Emi and Elizabeth reached Sector B without incident. Elizabeth's presence caused sideways glances as people huddled together discussing what might be going on. Since Elizabeth seemed friendly and open, Emi had no doubt she would win people's trust — she hoped their trust wouldn't be misplaced. Once people grew accustomed to having a Fringe member in their midst, she would call a meeting to discuss the future. Right now she needed time to adjust to the changes that were about to be thrust upon them. The timing was lousy; she'd been looking forward to spending time with Dez. Giving her head a shake she knocked on the door to the guest quarters.

Dez opened the door looking sleepy and disheveled. 'Hello,' he said sheepishly as he squinted into the bright morning sunshine.

'Sorry, am I too early?' she asked, taking in his shirtless state and tousled hair.

'No, it's okay, I overslept. Do you mind pouring the coffee while I throw some water on my face?' He ran his hand through his hair and disappeared into the bedroom. She heard the back door open as he headed to the pump in the yard.

Emi took a deep breath and closed her eyes, trying to calm herself. She rolled her eyes and exhaled before giving herself a shake. *What was she thinking?* He hadn't shown any interest in her. Good thing Elizabeth was about to join them so she didn't make a fool of herself. She headed for the little kitchen. The fire under the rectangular metal plate was banked-down and the coffee was percolating, filling the air with its pleasant aroma. She poured the coffee into three chipped mugs and used the tongs hanging on a nail in the wall to take the toast from the cooktop. She placed the toast on a cracked plate before putting everything on the table along with the jam.

Dez returned with his hair tamed, face washed and a fresh shirt on. Elizabeth arrived at the open front door at the same moment. Emi took a seat at the table, hiding her false smile behind her coffee cup.

'Mmm, is that coffee I smell?' asked Elizabeth.

'Yep, come on in. Good job we can grow coffee beans. Some mornings it's a lifeline.' Dez stifled a yawn. 'We don't have much else to offer — just toast and jam.'

'I brought a contribution. I had one small pot of honey left in my supplies.' Elizabeth handed over a jar of yellow liquid.

'Thank you.' Emi took the jar from her and held it up to the light. She removed the lid and inhaled. 'What is it?'

'Honey. Do you not have honey?'

Emi shook her head.

'It's a sweet made by bees.'

'Bees?'

'Ahh, how to explain?' Elizabeth trailed off. 'Can we leave it for another day and just have coffee?'

Dez gestured Elizabeth to a seat and proceeded to pass around the meagre breakfast.

'I heard you've had your first fiftieth birthday in the Network.' Elizabeth spread some honey on her toast and took a bite before continuing. 'That's exciting news. You've certainly made great progress all on your own.'

'We're not on our own. We have the Network.'

'I realise that. I meant progress without the help of the Fringe.'

'But I don't think we've *ever* had the help of the Fringe, have we?' Dez got up to get the percolator from the stove.

'According to our history books, back in the twenty-first century, the Fringe gave some of your ancestors a gentle nudge in the right direction.'

'What do you mean, "a gentle nudge in the right direction"?' Dez's forehead puckered in a frown as he refilled the mugs. He'd given himself the one with the biggest chip and the missing handle.

'We had scouts who helped the…uhhh…less toxic members of society escape.'

'Escape from what?' Emi purposefully stirred some honey into her coffee, keeping her gaze firmly fixed on the dark brown liquid swirling around in her cup.

'Government regulation and corrupt big business. Governments liked to think they still had power but in the end it was the worldwide corporations that ruled. It was in their best interest to persuade people to have imprints for identification and medication for behaviour modification. It was extremely lucrative. But it led to people turning out like the Blues.'

'So, if it wasn't for the Fringe we would be what — like the Blues?' Emi sloshed some of her coffee onto the table, her hands shaking, her eyes now fixed on Elizabeth.

Elizabeth shrugged and took another sip of coffee as she watched Dez and Emi process the information.

'Shall we go meet Amy and Jon? I thought they'd be good people to have help you.' Emi, knocked her chair over as she stood to go. She didn't care if she was being rude or that Elizabeth was still sipping at her coffee, she didn't want to hear any more. To have their lives determined by the Fringe of the past and to have any genetic resemblance to the Blues were ideas she didn't want to contemplate.

Dez hastily cleared the table and they followed Emi out of the shelter.

Emi led them to the opposite end of the village where a cute little cabin sat within a fenced yard. The place was pristine. The lawn was green, there were flowers either side of the front door and on the far side, along the fence, was a vegetable garden.

'This is nice.' Elizabeth looked at the neat garden bordered by herbs and edible wild flowers.

'Yes, they're amazing. They even dug their own well and use solar and wind power for everything.'

' Good to hear,' said Dez. 'Wish I'd kept in touch more but getting between the valleys for just a social visit is nearly impossible.' He smiled at Emi as she knocked on the door.

A middle-aged man with ginger hair answered.

'Please, come in.'

'Jon, this is Elizabeth, from the Fringe.'

'Nice to meet you.' Jon shook Elizabeth's hand and smiled politely as he darted a questioning look at Emi.

'Congratulations on turning fifty. That's quite a milestone,' said Dez.

'Thanks.'

'Fifty! That's almost unheard of within the Network, isn't it?' said Elizabeth.

'Until now.' Jon grinned. 'I'm the first.'

'You look fantastic,' said Dez. 'What's your secret?'

'Wish I knew.' Jon shrugged. 'It might have something to do with my imprint being pretty light. We've noticed those with bigger or darker imprints feel less well. But also, my family were always careful about what we consumed.'

Amy joined the group around the little dining table.

'Emi is the one we should congratulate. It was her idea to study who live longest and analyse what they do,' said Amy.

Dez smiled at Emi who flushed a light shade of pink.

'Well, hopefully turning fifty will become commonplace. Elizabeth is here to ask for our help…and maybe if we help them we'll get the chance to live even longer,' said Emi. 'Elizabeth, do you want to explain the situation?'

Jon and Amy listened in astonished silence as Elizabeth told them what was needed for the planet's survival and how they had reached this point. At the end of the monologue they looked at each other, nodded, and agreed to help. How could they not?

'I knew we all used to be pretty much the same but I wasn't sure how the differences came about,' said Jon.

'I still don't understand. Are you saying our ancestors were Blues?' Amy stared at Elizabeth. 'Are you kidding?'

'Sort of. Not exactly. Back then they weren't blue; nor as violent. They were just on their way to becoming what they are now. Most we couldn't help. We took aside the ones that we could and separated them into a different group. That group is now you, the Network.'

Emi, Dez, Jon and Amy stared at each other, speechless. Finally, Dez asked one simple question. 'Why?'

'Truthfully. I believe that even then the Fringe knew they'd need help and lots of it. It's not written in the history books as it's, of course, politically incorrect to start a group in the hope they'll breed and become a useful workforce.'

'I can see that,' said Dez dryly. He glanced at Emi. She was leaning back in her chair with fists clenched under her crossed arms. 'What do we think of that then, Emi?'

'I really couldn't say,' was Emi's restrained reply. She gave Elizabeth a cold, hard stare.

'Why didn't you take our ancestors with you to become part of the Fringe?'

'You weren't genetically pure. We couldn't risk having you mix with us. We needed to keep you separate but set you on a path that, over time, would help you to become relatively toxin-free.'

'Seems a bit harsh.' Emi tried to keep her expression neutral and her breathing even. She couldn't believe Elizabeth would utter such things out loud. But perhaps she looked on them as the cold, hard facts. This day wasn't going as anticipated. Life was going to have some surprises in it with the Fringe around. She wasn't sure she liked the thought. She glanced sideways at Dez, who looked dazed, and wondered if her face held the same expression.

'Depends how you look at it I suppose.' Elizabeth gave them a hint of a smile.

Amy looked down. 'I guess, in the long run, it offered us a brighter future than ending up like the Blues.'

'And the Blues, how did they — why are they the colour they are?' asked Jon.

'It was the imprinting. They used to have to re-color the imprints. And the Blues had a lot of them. Many were covered from head to toe with designs. Then a genetically enhanced dye was invented that illiminated the need for re-coloring, but it turned out to be a mutagen. Nobody knows why as the invention of the dye was top secret. It resulted in offspring being born with the tattoos of their parents, then ended up coloring their whole bodies. The additional unforeseen problem was the accumulation of the toxins, of which the skin dye was the worst. It damaged the brain. What we did might seem harsh but we saved you from that.'

A shudder coursed through Emi. If it weren't for the interference of the Fringe she could have ended up being one of the Blues. She stole another glance at Dez, whose eyes were hooded.

Dez turned to look at Emi. He cocked his eyebrow and shrugged, obviously not willing to vent his emotions in front of Elizabeth.

'Well, that explains quite a bit. I'm still not sure what to think.' Emi's speech was clipped, her voice an octave lower than normal. She cleared her throat and averted her gaze. *Had Elizabeth expected them to be grateful for their intervention? Sure, they hadn't turned out like the Blues, but she didn't fancy the thought of being bred to work for the Fringe.*

'It might be best if you keep that story to yourselves. I'm doubt many in the Network would appreciate our interference.'

Emi glanced at Elizabeth. It was as if she'd read her mind. She shivered. So much planning, such control.

'Yeah, not to worry. I don't think any of us want to share that bit of info. It might be harder to get people to li…agree to help you if we did.' Dez's voice sounded tight. His face was a blank mask.

'True. But you realise it's imperative you help us? We can't guarantee the survival of *anyone* if you don't.'

'So what's your next step?' asked Jon, trying to defuse the undercurrents of tension.

'I'd like to take Dez and Emi, and a few others, to New York to show you what we've planned.' Elizabeth smiled at Jon. 'I know it all seems very sudden but —'

'We'd be willing to join you,' said Amy.

'Looks like you have your first four recruits,' said Dez.

'If we don't agree to help then all our efforts to create a better life for ourselves will be for nothing by the sounds of it,' replied Emi.

What choice did they have?

THREE

They gathered in the village square, a big, open field where children could play in relative safety, surrounded by rough shelters that were the homes or small stores and businesses of the Network. A whirring sound, as of intense wind being forced into a tunnel, filled the air as the leaves danced on the bushes and trees and dust motes spiralled. The giant metal bird hovered over the village before slowly descending, coming to rest in the middle of the field. The propellers slowed and stopped. A door opened, a ramp lowered and a tall, well-dressed man walked out from inside the giant machine, a smile on his face as he waved cheerily at the crowd.

'Everyone, this is a Hovercraft. My husband, Peter, is the pilot,' said Elizabeth to the stunned audience. The children hid behind their parents, wide eyed. The parents, their mouths agape, held firmly to their children as they backed up a few paces.

Dez and Emi exchanged glances and went forward to greet Peter.

Dez pretended a confidence he was far from feeling. Elizabeth had mentioned they'd be taken to New York by Hovercraft, but that hadn't prepared him for the reality. He swallowed the lump in his throat.

'I've seen pictures of Hovercrafts in books we've scavenged from the cities,' said Dez, 'but had no idea they were so massive...nor that they still existed.' He ran his hand through his hair as his eyes strayed over the enormous machine. 'It's incredible.'

Peter shook hands with the young people and gave his wife a quick kiss. He hadn't seen her since she'd infiltrated the Network. 'I think you'll find the technology of the Fringe a bit more advanced than yours,' said Peter. 'If you're ready, we should get going. It's a long flight and occasionally we get sudden storms out east later in the day, especially during the summer. I don't want to get caught in one. It would make your first flight a little *too* entertaining.'

Elizabeth gave a Sat-comm to a young woman called Sal and showed her how to use it.

'This will enable you to contact us in New York if you need anything, or need to reach us.'

Sal turned the device over in her hand. Her face held a look of blank amazement. She looked at Elizabeth and then again at the Sat-comm resting in her palm. Her forehead scrunched.

'But won't you be far away?'

'Yes, but we have satellites…' Elizabeth paused and glanced at Peter who gave a barely perceptible shake of his head. 'It's too complicated to explain. You'll just have to trust me that it'll work.'

Sal nodded. 'Well, hopefully I won't need it. Don't see why I would.' She slipped the device into her pocket. 'Wish I was going with you. I'd like to fly above the world and look down on it like a bird. Never thought of anything more than living day to day.' She smiled at Elizabeth. 'Maybe one day I'll get to fly.'

Elizabeth smiled in return. 'Talk to Peter when we return. I'm sure something could be arranged.' She turned to join Peter at the base of the Hovercraft ramp.

Sal backed up into the crowd. 'Amazing,' she muttered under her breath.

Jon and Ami emerged from the crowd to join Dez and Emi for the trip to New York. They waved good-bye to the onlookers, followed Peter and Elizabeth up the ramp and took their seats next to the windows. The door closed, the whirring started and they watched the people below become tiny dots on a green expanse. As the Hovercraft rose further into the air the landscape below appeared two-dimensional. The village was a series of small dots and the valley an emerald swath with a meandering blue line running through it. The rest of the world seemed golden. The yellow was endless — extending in every direction as far as the eye could see. Green valleys were few and far between.

'Is it all just dry grass?' Dez unclenched his hands and took a deep breath. He was struggling to take in the magnitude of what he was seeing.

'A lot of it, yes. The only invasive weed that thrives in our toxic soil. Bloody grass — doesn't even have any nutritional value.' Peter cleared his throat and turned to look at Dez. 'Some parts are better, some worse and some…some are gone.'

'Gone?' Dez shifted in his chair as he darted a glance at Peter.

Peter turned back to face the front of the Hovercraft. 'Yeah. Extreme tides, rising sea levels , hyperstorms! Some places, like Florida to the south, are now under the ocean. The only good thing for us is that the warm inland sea in the south causes most storms to head that direction. Weather patterns changed. New York only gets an occasional storm.'

Dez nodded but kept his face plastered to the window as he stared at the landscape below, willing his heart rate to decrease and the knot in his stomach to subside.

'But wouldn't more storms be better?'interjected Emi, her voice coming out in a whisper. She cleared her throat. 'I mean for the rainfall.'

'I'm talking about severe storms. Hyperstorms. They're very damaging.'

'Oh. Guess we don't get those.'

'No. Being so far inland you'll only get the tail end as a torrential downpour. Your location's very fortunate. New York *can* get extreme weather fluctuations. A massive storm followed by months of dry heat. We have to create rain when it stays dry for too long.'

'You can create rain?' Dez turned to stare at Peter.

'We've learned to, yes, but only over a limited area.' Peter glanced at Dez.

'That's quite something,' Dez shook his head, at a loss for words.

'Yes it is. Bit of a game changer. At least we hope so.' Peter lapsed into silence. A while later he announced, 'We're coming up to the New York skyline. I think you'll enjoy the view out of the left side of the Hovercraft.'

Dez, Emi, Jon and Amy peered through the windows. The landscape below was no longer yellow. A massive river bordered two sides of an island, joining an expanse of water that stretched to the distant horizon. A massive wall surrounded the island, keeping it safe from the ocean, now so much higher than when the city had originally been built.

'How can there be fighting over water when there's *so much* of it?' Dez was completely dumbfounded by the sight of the ocean. His mother had shown him a map of the world once but, again, the reality was far different from his imagination.

Elizabeth looked out of the window. 'We can use the seawater by putting it through multiple filtration processes but otherwise it's still polluted. All the chemicals and plastics used…ended up in the oceans. We have seaweed farms cleaning the oceans…but there aren't enough.' She sounded almost bitter.

Dez looked up at Elizabeth and then returned his gaze to the spectacle outside; an intact city, the like of which he'd only ever seen in photos in books.

New York City was an island covered in buildings, solid looking structures that reached for the sky; towers of grey with a million windows reflecting the setting sun. Every building had a garden or glass house on its roof, except for the few bearing a big red X, such as the one they were approaching.

'An impressive sight, isn't it?' said Elizabeth.

They nodded, staring transfixed at the city below.

'I don't know what to say. I didn't know what to expect but… certainly not this!' said Emi.

'Definitely not!' Dez exhaled and ran his hand through his hair, his forehead furrowed. His world suddenly seemed small and insignificant.

'And you want us to help you? Shouldn't it be the other way around?' suggested Amy.

Elizabeth smiled. 'I can see why you might think that. But we do need you, honest.'

'Can't imagine for what,' muttered Dez under his breath.

'Once you've seen what we're doing here things will make more sense.' Peter set the Hovercraft down on the red X of the building. Exiting the Hovercraft, Peter and Elizabeth led the way across the rooftop to a pair of shiny doors that slid open as they approached. Inside was a small metallic room. They all stepped in and the doors closed behind them. Elizabeth pushed a button on a panel and the room started to move.

Dez clenched his fists and jerked back against the wall. Realisation dawned — they were trapped and at the mercy of these people they barely knew.

Elizabeth glanced up to see the frightened expressions on the faces of her guests. 'Oh, sorry, didn't think. This is an elevator; it moves us up and down inside the building. Easier than taking the stairs when buildings are this tall. No need to worry.'

Emi drew a deep breath. 'Right. Guess we better expect the unexpected.'

'It might help.'

'I think I was less surprised by the Hovercraft. At least I've seen pictures of those. Nobody ever thought to take a picture of the inside of an elevator.'

Elizabeth looked at Emi and laughed, the explosive noise of hilarity in the confined space easing the tension. 'No, I suppose not.'

'What's next?'

'Well, for now we'll show you to your rooms and let you get showered and changed. Fresh clothes will be delivered to each of you fairly soon. Then we'll have a meal and call it a day. Tomorrow we'll begin your introduction to our world.'

They set out the next morning with Peter as their guide.

Dez craned his neck upward, snapping his mouth shut as he took in the unimaginable height of the buildings. The sensation of being like an ant crawling along the ground was impossible to shake. Taking a deep breath, he lifted his chin and forced his fists to unclench as he walked between the towering walls of concrete and glass. His feet ached as they pounded the paved streets, set out in a grid formation, going off in all directions. The world suddenly seemed perfectly ordered — there was no room for chaos here. The threat of a raid by the Blues was something from another life.

'Welcome to New York City, a place of infinite possibility. It once had a reputation as a place of new beginnings, where people became rich and famous and businesses flourished. A hive of activity at all hours, with a buzz in the air that was apparently indescribable. We chose it as one of our two main locations because it's an island, hard to attack, surrounded by water — two vital elements of our survival. Our other location is across the ocean in the United Kingdom…also an island and hard to attack. Here in New York City every rooftop, except for the Hovercraft landing pads, is a garden or greenhouse. Every window that gets sunshine is a solar panel. All water comes from the river and is filtered. Central Park, which I'll show you later, was once just for recreation and is now very carefully managed farmland. We're completely self sufficient.' The pride in Peter's voice was evident to everyone.

'And the buildings, are they full of people?' asked Dez. So many tall buildings could surely house a multitude of people. Was the Network really crucial to the plans of the Fringe?

'They used to be. There are still plenty of people here on the island, and we live quite comfortably, but it can't last, and we all know it. Shall we go and see one of the gardens?'

They entered a massive concrete skyscraper and went up to the 70th floor in the elevator. Dez doubted he'd ever get accustomed to being trapped in such a small space with no control of where his body was going. He was thankful to step out onto the roof and enter a glass structure filled with a profusion of plants. It was hot and humid and lush. Most of the fruits and vegetables growing were ones he'd never seen before.

'So much food. Jax would love this,' said Dez.

Emi looked over at Dez and smirked. '*Everyone* would love this.'

'Through our experiments we've managed to purify the soil and the seeds and we only use filtered water. These crops are organic; no trace of chemicals or genetic modifications, and there hasn't been for quite some time. The whole of the island is now almost free of contaminants and we've enough food to sustain ourselves. We've also shipped seeds to the UK. They've abundant farmland and better than average growing conditions. The UK now has enough, with what we've sent them, to sustain their population. The problem is that the world is continuing to warm. If it gets any hotter the growing conditions necessary for plant life will no longer exist and we'll be unable to feed ourselves. Come, let me show you the labs where we conduct our experiments.'

'I've the feeling our time here is going to be information overload,' Dez whispered to Emi as they left the garden and headed back down to the street. 'I've already seen more different things in the last couple days than in the rest of my life put together.'

'Hard to believe they planned on needing our help from so long ago. I'm trying not to be creeped out by the whole thing but —' She shrugged her shoulders. 'Still, I can't see what choice we have,' said Emi, quietly.

'Yeah, I almost feel like I've been groomed to be a certain way and then watched to make sure I'm doing the right things.' Dez and Emi lagged behind the others. He slipped his hand into hers, needing the human contact.

'But I do *like* Elizabeth and Peter. It's the story of us being destined for this moment that weirds me out. I don't get why they bothered telling us.' Emi glanced at Dez and gave his hand a squeeze.

'I wondered that too.' He squeezed her hand in return before quickly letting go as they caught up to the others. They'd stopped in front of another towering building.

This time they remained on the ground level and entered through a secured door into an immense room. It was a hive of activity. Everyone wore gloves, goggles and jackets. A conveyer belt, piled with dirt, circled the room and passed through a machine. The dirt was then dumped into huge bins below the floor. At long tables in the centre of the room people studied the dirt and a variety of crops.

'This is where we de-contaminate the soil. It's one of the first things we learned how to do so we now have a goodly supply. It's what's on all the rooftop gardens and in Central Park, and we've sent a lot to the UK as well. We're quite proud of it.'

'It's certainly very impressive. But surely you can't bring *all* the dirt of the world into this one room for de-contamination,' observed Jon, his practical nature overriding his state of awe.

'No. This is just stage one. We recently discovered that by adding a micro-organism into the clean soil it was then able to neutralise the toxic soil mixed in with it. Once the process was perfected, the scale of what we can accomplish multiplied a thousand fold. We're now sending the micro-organism to the UK. They'll be able to use it to clean the rest of their island without anymore help from us.'

'I'm beginning to wish we'd brought Jax with us,' said Dez. 'But we might not have been able to drag him away. He'd have a million questions.'

'We'll need Network members here. Would Jax be a good candidate?'

'I guess. He's young but good at what he does. So, what does the big machine do?' he asked, wanting to change the subject and not commit Jax to living in New York if he didn't want to.

'It's a high intensity light that neutralises the toxins in the soil. The same thing would happen in nature if you gave it enough time; this speeds up the process. Shall we carry on? I'll take you to the Hudson River next, show you our water purification system.' Peter led them back outside into the blinding sunlight. 'I hope you don't mind walking.'

'We're used to walking,' replied Dez. 'Not much choice most of the time. We've some Hoverboards we've managed to salvage but that's about it.'

They set off toward the river, which they could glimpse beyond the seawall, between the buildings at the bottom of the long, gently sloping street.

'The world's certainly not what it used to be.'

'No, guess not,' Dez agreed, his mouth turning down at the corners. 'Don't suppose you've any books I could borrow? I've always been curious to know how we got to this point. My mom had a few old photography books and I used to stay up late, under my covers with my torch, mesmerised by the pictures. My mom would get so mad at me for using my torch…the solar cell only had a limited life,' he clamped his mouth shut. Why was he revealing intimate details of himself to these people? 'I…it'd be great to fill in the story that went with the photos.'

'The New York News is running a series of articles right now documenting our history. I could give you those if you like. They're a bit more condensed than reading through a bunch of books.'

'That'd be great. Thanks.' He nodded his head once in appreciation, forcing his shoulders to relax. 'So, can we really turn things around? I mean if you compare now with old photos it seems like things have gone too far to be fixed.'

'We think we can. It's taken this long of running experiments to even have a bit of hope,' said Peter as they emerged from amongst the massive grey buildings into parkland that bordered the river. 'This is one of my favourite developments as it solves two problems in one. We use the constant tidal flow of the river, along with the solar panels, to generate power for the city. We also use massive solar evaporators to take water from the river, condense it, and then send it through multiple filters to produce fresh water for the inhabitants of New York. We have a number of these stations around the city.'

'So, let me get this straight. You've managed to figure out how to clean the soil, grow pure crops, create clean power and water on a scale large enough to help the planet?' Jon was incredulous. His expression one of utter disbelief as he tried to take in the magnitude of the information being thrown at them.

'We hope so. But it'll take a lot of manpower,' Peter replied. 'The biggest hurdle is to control the weather. We need to be able to create enough cloud in certain areas that we can control rainfall and grow crops. And the cloud will help reduce the earth's temperature. If we can cut it by 4.5 degrees for twenty years, then we should be able to get back to stable conditions.'

'How on earth do you plan to do that?' asked Dez. 'Pardon the pun,' he grinned, the lightness of his tone masking his internal turmoil.

'I think we'll save that for another day,' Peter smiled in response. 'It's a rather long and complicated process.'

Dez sat cross-legged on his bed. He didn't have security clearance to access the digital records so the promised stack of 'newspapers,' had been printed off for him. He leaned over to switch on the solar tube and picked up the first paper. He flipped through the pages. Each paper featured an in-depth article about the world's history, starting in the year 1900 and broken down into 45-year segments.

OUR HISTORY: WHAT WENT WRONG?
PART ONE: 1900–1945

The first four decades of the 1900s were devastating. Sandwiched between two world wars were the influenza pandemic, the stock market crash and the great depression. The wars brought with them a time of intense innovation. Many items were created that people would later become dependent on. At the same time, as men went off to war, women took up the jobs at home and for the first time in history entered the workforce en-mass. By the time World War II ended in 1945 many men had been killed, women had become accustomed to working and having their own income, and a vast array of items had been invented that made life easier.

Dez put down the paper. What on earth was a stock market or a great depression? And how did a war happen that involved the whole world? Obviously reading the papers was only going to lead to more questions. He sighed and picked up the next newspaper. He would read the full article later, maybe it would answer more of his questions. For now he hoped the synopsis would give him enough of an idea to piece things together.

OUR HISTORY: WHAT WENT WRONG?
PART TWO: 1945-1990

By the 1950s, people were tired of doing without. As women stayed in the workforce, households had greater disposable income. Women were no longer in the home cooking the family meal so they needed foods that were simple to prepare. Fast-food took off with a vengeance. People wanted life to be easier so they bought appliances and cars; and they wanted to be entertained. As well, there was a population explosion (in this century the population went from one billion to seven billion) so they needed crop production to be more efficient.

None of this is really bad in and of itself. But as a historian, when you put the whole thing together, it seems to be the line in the sand where things truly start to unravel. The first couple of generations managed to find some balance between the more traditional lifestyle and the modern one, but then finally there came a time when the next generation expected things to be easy.

They had to work an extreme amount to continually improve upon their lavish lifestyle, they drove everywhere and got little exercise, they didn't want to put effort into good meals so they ate processed or fast-food and unless they were constantly entertained they were bored and unhappy.

Dez lowered the paper and stared unseeingly at the wall. Fast-food? He'd have to ask someone to explain the term to him. And seven billion people! That was impossible to contemplate. How do you entertain so many? And how can you be unhappy if you have everything you need? Sounds like a recipe for disaster. He shook his head in disbelief and picked up the next article.

OUR HISTORY: WHAT WENT WRONG?
PART THREE: 1990-2035

This was a time of immense change and truly the beginning of the end. It also brought with it the introduction of technology to the general public on a massive scale. Within these years we have the first generation that was completely dependent on the internet. There was less social interaction as people communicated instead via 'social media,' children played computer games instead of playing real games outside, writing and printing were no longer taught as people only typed, and their writing was automatically corrected by the computer. The lack of social interaction and the sedentary lifestyle, along with an abundance of junk food (full of toxins that people were yet to learn about) led to mental disorders. The mental disorders led to the rapid rise of the pharmaceutical age. As people became addicted to medications to try to cope, the chemicals leached back into the water (through excrement) and the food chain. At the same time, the number of pesticides used increased and animals were given medication to control disease. The number of toxins consumed by the average person was thirty times the recommended 'safe' level as put out by the government of the day. The percentage of population not able to function in society grew exponentially. By 2030 it was estimated that twenty-five percent of children had mental disorders.

'Twenty-five per cent!' Dez exclaimed aloud to the empty room. *Was this the generation that lost the ability to read and write after technology failed?* His mind wandered to his mom. Thank god she had always valued education. It was the primary reason they had ended up being leaders of the Network.

He threw aside the paper and scrambled off the bed, feeling the desperate need for some fresh air. It was great to learn their history but it was pretty depressing stuff, especially since he knew the end result.

He picked up his shoes and quietly let himself out of the hotel room and made his way to Emi's room, the plush, red carpet soft underfoot. He knocked and waited, resisting the urge to glance over his shoulder. The hair at the base of his neck prickled as he shuddered involuntarily. There was nobody there, he told himself. The door opened a crack to reveal Emi dressed in jammies that barely covered her torso. She smiled at him and flushed a light shade of pink. Dez blinked. She was adorable, even in her disheveled state.

'Uhh. Hi. I couldn't sleep. Feel like going for a walk?'

'A walk? Now?'

'Sorry, did I wake you? Nevermind. I'll go'

'No, it's okay. I wasn't asleep anyway. I just need to change.' She left the door open for him and headed to the bathroom to put on her shorts and a shirt.

Dez swallowed the lump in his throat and averted his gaze from her retreating figure. He ran his hand through his hair and took a steadying breath. Maybe seeking out Emi in the middle of the night when she was barely dressed and alone in a hotel room was another of his not-so-brilliant ideas.

'You okay?' Emi came back into the room and slipped on her new sandals.

Dez shrugged. 'Just wanted to be able to chat in private I guess.'

Emi looked around at her empty hotel room. 'We *are* in private.'

'I'd prefer to walk,' he said as he put on his shoes.

Emi raised her eyebrows questioningly and followed him down the hallway and out into the empty streets of New York City. The air was balmy and the city quiet. The buildings towering overhead were dark and lifeless. The city streets were meticulous, nothing was out of place even in the middle of the night. They turned right and headed for the river where there was still the feeling of open space. Dez led the way up the steps of the seawall so they could stroll along the top.

'So, what's up?'

'Just feeling trapped I guess and wanted to talk. Sorry to drag you out so late.'

'It's okay. Honest. I wasn't sleeping anyway and besides, it's nice out. I wish it was like this during the day. I'm starting to miss open spaces and trees.' Emi sighed. 'Everything here is so manicured — including the people.'

'Yeah, maybe that's the problem, how pristine everything is. Puts me on edge. The Fringe treat us as honoured guests, yet somehow I still don't feel easy.'

'I think we're all feeling like that. We're just out of our comfort zone.'

'True. They must desperately need our help but...' he paused, trying to gather his thoughts. 'They appear honest. I mean everything's shown to us, explained; nothing *seems* hidden, but still, I have a constant gnawing in my gut. I'm not sure if it's because I'm not accustomed to being told what's expected of me or if there's something else, but...' he shrugged. 'I can't put my finger on it.'

They stopped where the buildings behind them were shorter and didn't seem so oppressive. They leaned against the rail and gazed out at the moonlit river. It was slack tide and the water lapped gently below their feet, emitting the faint smell of seaweed into the sultry air. Dez stole a sideways glance at Emi. She wasn't perfect like the Fringe women were but he felt completely spellbound by her. The moonlight glinted off her hair as the breeze picked it up and played with it. He realised he could no longer imagine not having Emi to turn to. He had grown accustomed to her quiet calm over the last couple weeks. *Should he put his arm around her, or simply lean down and kiss her?* He inched closer so their shoulders touched.

'Maybe it's because everything's so planned, and has been planned for a long time, so it feels manipulative,' said Emi, snapping Dez out of his romantic reverie. 'Even *we* have been part of the plan, though we didn't know it. Our freedom was harsh, but at least it was ours.'

Dez gave his head a shake. 'And I'm supposed to ask all of the Network to give up their freedom to become a workforce for the Fringe? I don't know if I can do that.'

'Yeah, I know. But we'll explain things and then take a vote. You can't carry the weight of it alone. Nobody expects that of you.'

'I knew talking to you was what I needed. Thanks, Emi.'

'Sure, anytime. We're in this together.' She gazed up at him.

Dez thought for a moment that she was going to put her head on his shoulder; show some kind of gesture that hinted at being more than just friends. But she didn't. Emi turned her head to look back at the ribbon of light reflected on the river below. 'I guess we better get back. It's late and we have a big day tomorrow.' She sighed.

Dez hesitated and then turned to follow Emi, cursing under his breath. *Why hadn't he made a move? At least then he would know where he stood, instead of all this second-guessing.* 'Right. The Cloud! The thing we're supposed to help build to control the weather. I can't even begin to imagine what that might entail.'

'It does sound a bit overwhelming but I'm sure it's all planned to a 'T'.'

Dez laughed, a humourless sound breaking the stillness of the night. 'I'm sure you're right.'

Dez returned to his cross-legged position on his bed and picked up the next paper. He needed to distract himself from thoughts of Emi. He would never get to sleep with the image of her standing in the moonlight embedded in his mind.

OUR HISTORY: WHAT WENT WRONG?
PART FOUR: 2035 – 2080

The last article covered the beginning of the end. Life got worse after that, much worse. On top of the troubles with society, toxicity and mental health you now add a growing concern with climate change and the destruction of our oceans. The warming trend began to shift weather patterns. Storms or droughts intensified. Sea levels began to rise. Once vibrant cities became abandoned ghost towns as people fled their homes in search of greener pastures (quite literally). By 2080 things had reached a critical state. Climate change, combined with the toxic accumulations in crops, water and soil meant it was no longer possible to feed the world's population. Though the population was obese they were also malnourished. Many people started to not live past the age of fifty. Due to the toxicity of what they consumed they became infertile and the birth rate declined dramatically. The world population was cut in half, and then continued to decline from there, and society became divided into what eventually became the Blues, the Network and us, the Fringe.

OUR HISTORY: WHAT WENT WRONG?
PART FIVE: 2080 – 2125

The year 2080 was the start of Hyperstorms. The 2.5 degree rise in ocean temperatures was enough to shift weather patterns significantly and increase the categories they needed to describe the intensity levels of storms. The strongest storm being a Category 5 was a thing of the past, now they had Category 10. The state of Florida vanished, consumed by the sea. An inland sea almost joined the coasts in the southern USA, and most of the population moved north. Cities were abandoned and anything mass-produced by the global businesses ceased to exist. People had to learn to fend for themselves. Many couldn't and they didn't survive. By the end of this era the population had gone from ten billion to less that a billion. All of Australia, India and Africa became uninhabitable as temperatures soared and fresh water became almost non-existent. Technology failed, except for those pockets where the Fringe were now isolated. Those who would eventually form themselves into the Network had resorted to becoming subsistence farmers, trying to protect themselves from the Blues. And the Blues were violent groups, killing for a mouthful of food.

He may as well read the synopsis of the last article before turning out the tube-light. It would get him up to present day, to a time when he existed.

OUR HISTORY: WHAT WENT WRONG?
PART SIX: 2125 – PRESENT

The last few decades have seen a further increase in global temperatures. Sea levels have continued to rise, storms have become more violent, and arable farmland extremely scarce. During this era we, the Fringe, have used what little time we have left to try to come up with a solution to solve the world's problems. The main areas of concern are lowering the earth's temperature, increasing localized rainfall and producing toxic free farmland. Edward Black, mayor of New York, informed me that we have now invented the means to do all these vitally important tasks. As a historian, and a journalist, I can only hope that I live to see the changes and that the next set of historical articles I write are much more encouraging.

Well, that definitely explained the past. Putting down the paper he reached over to turn out the light. Tomorrow he would learn what he could do to ensure they had a better future, or any future at all.

The next day they were shown the mock up of The Cloud — the structure that would control the weather enough to change the Earth's temperature. Most of it went over Dez's head but he thought he understood the basics. Bodies of water, solar panels and condensers would create cloud cover over large areas — low, puffy clouds over thirty to forty per cent of the Earth's surface were needed to cool the planet. High, thin cloud would only trap more heat in. Heavier concentrations of cloud in specific areas would be vital to produce the necessary rainfall for crops.

By mid-morning his head was throbbing and he felt like he could not retain any more information. But all he needed to know was how to construct The Cloud and put the pieces in place.

'I realise it's been a long week with a lot to take in,' said Peter. 'We wanted you to have the bigger picture but ultimately you'll only need to focus on the sector you're assigned to so it won't be so overwhelming. Today we'll quit early and let you head back to your hotel to rest. We've an honorary banquet for you this evening at which you'll meet our city mayor, Edward Black. It's a formal event so you'll find new clothes laid out for you in your rooms.'

As they were heading back to the hotel they bumped into a tall, dark haired man emerging from one of the more opulent foyers. Even in shorts and shirt-sleeves, in the stifling heat, he looked immaculate.

'Edward!' said Peter. 'How fortuitous. I was just mentioning you to our guests,' he explained as he made the necessary introductions.

'Hello. I'm so pleased to meet you. I hope you've enjoyed seeing some of our city and accomplishments. It'll be wonderful to have you working alongside us. A necessity if we are to save our planet,' he greeted them formally, an odd expression flitting across his handsome face as he shook Dez's hand before turning and lingering slightly longer over Emi's hand than he had over the others.

'Nice to meet you. We're honoured to be here,' said Dez.

'It certainly been an interesting week,' said Emi. 'Your advancements and city are…well…mind boggling.' She flushed as she tripped over her words.

'Thank you. Glad we meet with your approval,' said Edward, with a slight catch in his throat as he straightened up to look into Emi's eyes. 'We're sure our plans will work with the manpower the Network can provide. We're thrilled you've agreed to join us.'

Emi broke eye contact with Edward and cast a quick glance at Dez. His mouth was turned down in a frown. 'Oh, I, umm, I don't think we've made a decision yet,' Emi replied quickly, as she stared at one then the other, noting the similar blueness of their eyes.

'Of course. I'm being presumptuous,' said Edward, calmly. 'Forgive me.'

'We'll take a vote after we've explained things to the Network,' stated Dez. He hesitated, sounding ungracious to his own ears, yet his desire to flee was almost overwhelming. He didn't want to become a puppet to these people.

Edward turned to Dez, his eyebrows drawn down. 'A vote?' His mouth became a thin line.

'Yes. A vote! I'm not a dictator,' challenged Dez. 'You're asking our people to completely change their way of life and work for you. I won't force them. We'll take a vote.'

'You realise you may be condemning the entire planet to extinction,' said Edward, his jaw clenched as he stared at Dez.

'They're good people. I'm sure many will vote to help you with your plans but I won't force them,' Dez replied, his voice controlled, his eyes glinting dangerously.

'I'm sure once we've explained the situation to them most people will want to help,' Emi said in a conciliatory voice, not liking the undercurrents she was sensing between the two men.

Edward turned to Emi with a tight smile. 'I do hope you're right.'

'We can't guarantee it, of course,' she smiled her reply, 'but it is in everyone's best interest to do what they can.'

Edward nodded. 'Yes, but that way of thinking has never worked in the past. That is how we ended up in this mess but I guess I was prematurely relying on the cooperation of everyone. I'll be very sorry if that turns out not to be the case.'

'We'll do our best to be convincing,' said Emi, bestowing her most dazzling smile upon Edward.

'Thank you,' he replied, his smile looking slightly less forced. 'If you'll excuse me, I have some urgent business to attend to. I look forward to your company at the banquet tonight.' He nodded his head formally in dismissal and turned back into the building he had just emerged from.

FOUR

Walking into her room, Emi couldn't believe her eyes. She'd never seen anything so beautiful. She had no idea clothes could even be so — what word adequately described the thought — the dress was simply breathtaking. Gently running her fingers over the shimmery fabric she lifted the garment by the hanger and spun it round. The skirt flowed in waves of blue and silver, longer at the back and shorter in the front; the bodice appeared blue one moment and silver another, and the entire gown was covered with sparkles, like stars thrown across the night sky. The material was cool to touch and softer than anything she'd ever known. Emi headed for the shower, impatient to change.

She luxuriated in the simple pleasure of allowing the warm water to rinse away the dust and grime of the city as she massaged the various lotions into her hair. After towelling herself dry she rubbed body oils into her skin until it left her feeling silky smooth and smelling heavenly. She donned the bathrobe hanging on the back of the door and wrapped the towel, turbanlike, around her long hair. As she emerged from the bathroom she heard a knock at the door and went to answer it.

'Hi, my name's Charlotte,' said a young, elegant looking girl with a small suitcase clutched in her hand. 'Elizabeth asked me to come and see if you need help with your hair and makeup.'

'Hair and makeup? How do you mean?' asked Emi.

'For the formal banquet tonight. Elizabeth thought you might need help.'

'Oh, well, sure. I guess so. Come on in.' Emi opened the door so Charlotte could enter.

'How beautiful.' Charlotte held up the gown and twirled it around. 'I hadn't seen it finished. You're going to look stunning.'

'I know. I mean, I don't know about the looking stunning part but the dress is amazing. I've never seen anything like it. I'm glad you're here. I'm probably a bit out of my depth on my own.'

'Not to worry. We'll have you looking absolutely perfect. You'll be able to hold your own in front of the mayor and his elite. Even if you don't feel it, just fake it. They'll be too wrapped up in themselves to notice the difference,' Charlotte advised, with a beaming smile and a wink. 'Besides, you've got me on your side, so what could possibly go wrong?' Her deep blue eyes twinkled with merriment.

'Well, I barely know you but that seems comforting all the same. Will you be at the banquet too?' asked Emi, sensing that this girl was her ally and her friend.

'No, I'm needed behind the scenes, making sure things run smoothly. I'll just applaud you from the sidelines. Shall we get started?'

'Sure.' Emi grinned.

Two hours later Emi stared in astonishment. 'Is that really me?' she asked as she gazed into the full-length mirror. Her hair hung in raven waves to her waist. Her highlighted eyes looked twice as big and glittered with blue and silver to match the dress. She dazzled from head to toe. She couldn't tear her gaze away from her own reflection. And the dress! *What would Dez think?* The gown fitted her perfectly in the bodice, emphasizing her slender waist; the skirt fell in shimmery lengths to just below her knee in front and to the delicate sandals that adorned her feet in the back. The one fitted sleeve hid her tattoo imprint, while the sleeveless side emphasized her toned arm. *Was the sleeve covering her imprint deliberate?*

'Well, what do you think? Are you pleased?'

'I don't know *what* to say. You've worked such a transformation. I wonder if Dez will even recognise me?'

Charlotte smiled and her eyes sparkled. 'Or maybe you won't recognise him.'

'I suppose he's going through some similar process right now isn't he?'

'I've no doubt he is. Now, I'll escort you to the banquet so you don't get lost? I'd really like to catch a glimpse of people's reactions when you enter the hall. You're far more stunning than even the elite Fringe members,' said Charlotte with a hint of pride.

'Thank you. I don't think I've ever been so nervous.' Emi cast a last glance at herself before exiting the room.

'You'll be fine. Just find a familiar face in the room, like Dez, hold his eye, smile and keep your head up. You'll blow their doors off. Don't let them make you feel inferior because you're not.'

'Thanks Charlotte. I don't know what I would've done without you,' said Emi, giving Charlotte a huge smile in gratitude.

They had reached the entrance to the banqueting hall. Doormen opened the double doors and Charlotte ushered Emi into the room. Emi felt so tense she barely noticed a thing; only that everyone seemed to be staring at her and was equally beautifully dressed. Then she found the one face she needed to see and locked eyes with Dez as her heart skipped a beat. His suit and tie made him seem older and almost like a stranger. The dark suit and blue tie mimicked his dark hair and blue eyes, while his white shirt highlighted his tan. He made all the other men in the room seem average, at least as far as she was concerned. She swallowed her nerves, smiled and made her way toward him.

'Dez,' she reached out to give his hand a squeeze.

'Emi?' he replied.

She broke eye contact and surveyed the room for Amy or Elizabeth. Charlotte had quietly disappeared.

Emi trembled as her anxiety rose. She'd smiled at Dez but he hadn't smiled back. She'd locked eyes with him and managed to get across the room without tripping over in her high heels but now she didn't know what to think. He seemed cool and distant. Not quite the reaction she'd been hoping for. Maybe he didn't like glitz and glamour — it would make sense since they'd never had nice clothes, make-up, perfumes and all the accoutrements. Was he just feeling uncomfortable around her all dressed-up? Like they were on show. She suddenly longed to be back at her village in her shorts and t-shirt. She thought of the swim lesson at the rock pools and the connection there had been between them. It had vanished now, buried under a layer of proper behaviour and etiquette. Relief washed over her as Jon and Amy approached.

Emi, you look amazing,' said Amy.

'Thanks, you too. That dress is absolutely perfect for you,' said Emi, as she admired how Amy's golden dress brought out the green of her eyes and the blonde highlights in her hair. The few strands of grey she'd previously had were magically gone. She glanced at Jon. He was having a hard time taking his eyes off of Amy. It was as if he'd never seen her before.

'This all seems a bit surreal doesn't it?' said Jon with a grin. 'Wonder where Peter and Elizabeth are?'

At that moment they came hurrying into the room. 'So sorry we're late and not here to greet you. Few extra things to take care of with Elizabeth being away for the last little while,' explained Peter. 'You all look fabulous by the way.'

'The new clothes were satisfactory then?' asked Elizabeth.

'They're wonderful. Thank you,' said Amy.

'Charlotte does a fantastic job of sizing people up and getting just the right thing. I can't tell you how many times she has helped me out when I've been too busy.'

'But we hadn't met Charlotte before. How did she…?' She was inturrupted as the double doors opened once again.

'City mayor, Edward Black,' one of the doormen announced. Edward's suit was immaculately tailored, emphasizing his tall, powerfully built frame. His handsome face exuded charm and confidence. Everyone in the room applauded and nodded their heads to him. Edward shook hands and briefly greeted people as he made a beeline to where Peter and Elizabeth were standing with the Network members.

'Mayor, this is Dez, Emi, Amy and Jon, our guests from the Network. This is Edward Black, city mayor and leader of the Fringe,' said Elizabeth.

Good evening. Nice to see you again,' he smiled at them, his earlier animosity vanished under a polite veneer. 'We happened to bump into each other on the street this morning as I was coming out of my apartment building,' he explained to Elizabeth.

A momentary look of surprise flitted across Elizabeth's face.

'I do hope this evening will entice you to join forces with us. It does offer a taste of how life could be if all goes according to plan.' Edward bestowed them with his most charming smile but his gaze lingered on Emi. 'Please, come, sit, and enjoy the dinner. All the food served tonight has, of course, been grown here in New York City. We hope it will be to your liking.'

Edward led the way to the head table. Emi tried not to gawp as she passed the tables covered with pristine white tablecloths, and set with gleaming silverware, china, crystal wine glasses with cloth napkins folded into them and flower vases of white roses. Scattered across the tables were silver and glass beads that reflected the light from the chandeliers overhead. Emi felt more and more out of her depth by the second. She longed to reach out and take Dez's hand but with his cool manner she didn't have the nerve. Instead she followed Edward Black to the head table and took her seat. She'd never been so relieved to sit down.

A waiter came up behind her, took the napkin from the glass and placed it in her lap. 'Red or white wine, miss?' he asked. Emi, having never tried either, had no idea but she dare not have red in case she got it on the gleaming tablecloth or her dress.

'White please,' she said, swallowing her nerves.

'Very good, miss.' The waiter filled her glass halfway and moved on. She reached out for her wine glass, willing her hand not to shake and spill the wine everywhere, and took a sip. It was cool and refreshing. Taking another sip, she studied the little menu card in front of her.

MENU

APPETIZER

Potato and Leek Soup

or

Garden Salad — iceberg lettuce, cherry tomatoes garnished with zests of carrot and cucumber

FIRST COURSE

Grilled eggplants topped with mozzarella cheese

or

House salad — green leaf lettuce, cherry tomatoes, sprinkled with feta cheese, cranberries and pine nuts

MAIN COURSE

Grilled chicken breast or Rib eye steak served with roast vegetables and scalloped potatoes

DESSERT

New York Cheesecake served with fresh strawberry topping

Emi's mouth watered. Four courses? Were they to eat all this? How to decide between the items listed in each course? This was certainly a very different world from the one she was accustomed to. She was suddenly ravenous and a little light-headed from the wine. She prayed her stomach wouldn't growl.

'Is the menu to your liking?' Edward asked.

'Oh, yes, thank you, very much so. The trouble will be in making a decision. We're not used to having a selection when it comes to food. You get what is available and are thankful,' Emi replied, flushing as she realised how ignorant she must sound. She didn't belong here. Her face burned a further shade of red. What was wrong with her tonight? She took another sip of wine to steady her nerves.

'Well then, as my guest of honour I hope tonight will be a special treat,' Edward whispered in her ear.

She smiled at him, having no idea of the effect she was having on Edward and on Dez who was watching the exchange.

'Do you eat this well all the time?' asked Dez.

'We don't go hungry but the menu is not usually this extensive.'

'Must be nice.'

'There's little to complain about, I must admit.'

'Surely you could have helped others before now? Most of the world is starving,' Dez said, his voice low, eyes hooded.

Edward levelled his gaze at Dez. 'We've enough to feed ourselves without going hungry. We don't have enough to feed everyone without first repairing the damage to the planet,' Edward replied, his voice even, his mouth slightly pinched.

'You could've —'

'Could I have some more wine, please?' interrupted Emi.

Edward glanced at her, his hostile gaze softening. 'Yes, of course,' he said as he waved to a waiter who immediately came to do his bidding. 'Forgive me. This is meant to be an evening of enjoyment. We'll refrain from any more talk of…plans.'

Dez clamped his mouth shut as he cast a quick glance at Emi.

She gave an almost imperceptible shake of her head and sipped from her wine.

'If you'll excuse me for a moment. It looks like I'm being summoned to take a call.' Edward stood and exited the room.

Dez and Emi stared at each other across the empty space.

'Wow,' said Emi. 'You two are like bucks fighting.'

'Yeah. It's…not going well. I don't like it.'

'*That* is perfectly obvious,' whispered Emi. 'But honestly, try to… stay calm. Nothing is set in stone yet and he can't *force* us to do anything. At least don't…provoke him.'

Dez nodded, taking a big breath. 'Right.'

Edward came back into the room, a smile hovered at the corners of his mouth. His eyes gleamed with pleasure as he resumed his seat next to Emi.

Time seemed to stand still as a series of speeches, toasts, elegantly presented food, conversation and wine flowed past Emi. It was ages before dessert was cleared and a band struck up in the adjoining ballroom. People slowly filtered out to dance.

'Would you care to dance?' Edward turned to Emi with his hand out to help her to her feet.

Emi looked into his handsome face and startlingly blue eyes. 'No' was obviously not an acceptable response. She put her hand in his and rose from the table.

No surprise, Edward was a wonderful dance partner. He guided her effortlessly around the floor. She could feel the hard muscle of his arm beneath the immaculate suit and the warmth of his hand in the middle of her back. He held her close, maybe closer than was necessary, but at least she wouldn't trip over her own feet this way. She let him lead her, loving the feeling of the music and the rhythm of the dance. Glancing over Edward's shoulder she could see Dez dancing with Elizabeth. Given that he probably had no more idea than her what he was doing she was taken aback that he was on the floor at all.

The evening continued to go by in a blur, the dancing carrying on until the wee hours of the morning. She danced with various Fringe members, making small talk and never remembering a name. Time stood still and she felt like this one evening would go on forever. It was as if she had taken over someone else's life. And then, instead of another Fringe member, she found Dez before her asking her to take a spin about the room with him.

She nodded and smiled at him and let herself be led into the crowd of elegantly dressed people. She felt very aware of Dez's arms around her as he effortlessly guided her around the floor.

'You can dance?' she questioned lamely.

'My mother used to spin me round the room when I was little; taught me all the right steps,' he replied. 'I used to stand on her feet of course. I'll try not to do that to you,' he grinned down at her, laughter in his voice.

'Oh.' She had conversed easily enough with every other man, why could she think of nothing else to say to Dez?

'You okay?' he asked.

'The wine's gone to my head and my feet aren't accustomed to high heels,' she smiled up at him. His face was so close. She longed to kiss him but couldn't quite bring herself to make so bold a move. And until this moment he'd been aloof; the look in his eyes difficult to read.

'Want to go to the balcony, get some air, maybe take your shoes off for a while? You've been dancing for ages,' Dez suggested.

'Sure,' was the only response she could think to utter.

Dez put his hand to her back and led her out between the double doors to the balcony which overlooked the Hudson River.

Emi slipped her shoes off and breathed a sigh of relief. 'Thank goodness. I'm glad the Network doesn't have high heel shoes, they're like a form of torture.'

'That may be, but they do make you very tall and make your legs look great,' teased Dez.

'Gee thanks. But I think I'll keep with my regular height and average looking legs if that's okay by you.' Emi quipped in response. The old Dez had returned…her Dez. She relaxed.

'Hmmm, well I don't know. Given that I've none of the discomfort and all the benefit, I might beg to differ and think maybe the Network should introduce high heels,' he added jokingly.

'I could share the discomfort if you like and hit you with it.' Emi threatened him with the shoe.

'No, thanks for the offer, the spike looks like it could be quite painful.' Dez held his hands up to his face.

'My *point* exactly.' Emi grinned as she turned her head to look out across the Hudson.

It was dark over the river other than the glow from the moon and twinkling starlight. The breeze from the Hudson was refreshing, cooling Emi's flushed cheeks and causing her to shudder. Emi felt as if she was emerging from a dream.

'You do look stunning by the way,' Dez commented, his playfulness suddenly vanishing as he looked down at her with his lopsided grin.

Emi, conscious of his hand on her back, gazed into his eyes, trying to read his expression. He seemed casual but there was an undercurrent in the air. 'Why thank you kind sir.' She swallowed nervously. His face was close to hers. She longed to reach up and kiss his lips. She held her breath, not daring to move.

Dez leaned down and kissed her on the mouth. His lips were warm and soft, yet demanding. His arm tightened around her waist as his other hand reached up to cup her head. Returning his kiss, Emi wound her arms around his neck.

'I didn't think you noticed,' said Emi as she pulled away, breathless.

'Oh, I noticed! I was just stunned into silence and couldn't get a word out.' He placed his hands either side of her face before bringing his lips to hers. She could taste the fruitiness of the wine he'd been drinking.

'And I thought you didn't care, at least not like that, and I was trying to keep my cool.'

'Well, you certainly managed that. I thought you might actually hit me with the shoe if I tried to kiss you but…I couldn't *not* kiss you.' He held her close as he kissed her forehead, her cheek, her nose, and the corner of her mouth before returning to her lips. 'Now I don't seem able to stop.'

'Hit you? No, hitting you didn't cross my mind — at least, not really,' said Emi as she reached up and ran her hands through his hair. 'And stopping is not required,' she murmured.

'I was starting to be jealous of you dancing with all the other men, especially Edward Black.'

'That's good.'

'Good?' He brought his head up to look in her eyes.

'Sure, it caused you to make a move. Otherwise we might have been circling each other for years. Thank goodness for the discomfort of high heels.' She grinned up at him with a mischievous twinkle in her eye.

'Hmmm, maybe we *should* take a supply back to the Network with us, who knows how many romances we could start.'

'Probably not necessary. I would have kissed you even if I didn't have sore feet. Or, at least, I would have worked up the courage eventually…I think,' she said with a sheepish smile. Emi could barely contain her elation — he liked her and had made the first move. She didn't think she could have stood the not knowing for much longer. The agony of wondering and not being quite sure was like the pain of the high heels, a constant ache that you almost, but not quite, became accustomed to. 'Come on, we better go back in before we're missed,' she said, suddenly realising that the moonlight would soon give way to the dim light of pre-dawn. 'But I'm glad we've cleared the air,' she said as she gave him another lingering kiss.

'Do we have to? I much prefer it out here,' he said, trying to draw her back into his arms.

'Time to don the masks.' Emi let her face take on a carefree expression.

'I don't know if I'm that good an actor.'

'Trust me. You are!' She left him standing forlornly on the balcony, attempting to resume a neutral expression. Emi re-entered the ballroom feeling like she was back in control of her life and everything would be okay. Her high heels no longer hurt, she was walking on air.

There was a tap on her shoulder. Emi turned to find Elizabeth looking very grim.

'I've been looking for you. There's a call. They said they'd wait. If you'll follow me I'll take you to the Satcomm.'

Emi's joy turned to dread. Now what? Why would anyone be trying to contact her now — the sun wasn't even on the horizon yet? She lifted the receiver.

'Hello, this is Emi.'

'Emi. It's Sal.'

FIVE

Jax surveyed the storehouse. The daylight filtering through the vines cast a dappled green effect across the contents within. There were shelves to the ceiling, all stacked with clearly labeled supplies. But his smile turned to a frown as he glanced over his shoulder before locking up the storehouse. Why was he so jumpy? He'd been like this since Dez left. He and Emi had been gone for two weeks, and other than a Hover-bird delivering a message saying they'd arrived, they'd had no news.

The other leaders had departed. Most had reported in via Hover-bird that they'd arrived safely and their villages were happy to have the supplies so desperately needed. Jax sighed, at least their supplies were hidden in the storehouse. He was proud of his design for the storehouse. Built into the side of a cliff, with a rocky outcrop that made a natural ceiling, the front was made of saplings and disguised with vines and plants. There was one door, also camouflaged, which slid back on a track. He hoped that in case of a raid it would be too difficult for the Blues to find. He shuddered at the thought of the Blues; being attacked by them was his worst nightmare.

He'd yet to hear from Sam or Zoe. They had further to travel to get to the outermost villages to the south in Sectors C and D. It was too bad they couldn't take Hoverboards when they left or they would've been home long ago. Abe had since managed to perfect a few of the boards that they'd got from the exchange. Having reliable transport had opened up a whole new world and he liked that Abe joined him as he explored. He said it was a good way to test the Hoverboards but Jax thought that he just wanted the company. And given Abe's size, he'd be good to have around in case of trouble.

The hair at he base of his neck prickled as he looked over his shoulder again. This time he saw Abe zooming toward him on a Hoverboard, waving with one arm and holding a second board in his other hand. Jax smiled. He sighed with relief and waved back. But there was no answering smile.

Abe barely missed hitting a rock as he brought his board to a sudden halt.

'Jax! Thank God I found you,' he panted. 'Got a Hover-bird in from Zoe. Her and Sam were injured,' Abe blurted, stumbling as he jumped off the board.

'I was *just* thinking of them. What happened?'

Abe wiped his arm across his face but the sweat continued to drip from his forehead. He gasped out his news. 'The Blues! They were almost home. Zoe's not too bad off but Sam's apparently in rough shape. Zoe managed to get Sam to Sector C, but the Blues had already been through.'

Jax groaned, having no words to express the tumult of feelings coursing through him as he jumped on the Hoverboard, almost falling off again in his haste.

'Not sure about Sam's village. Haven't managed to contact them yet.'

'Just when I was hoping things were going to get better — ,' Jax trailed off, his voice hoarse with suppressed emotion. 'I *wish* Dez was back.'

'I've sent a Hover-bird to him at Sector B to let him know. Should be there by now. But I'll go and take help; don't think we can wait 'til Dez returns.'

Jax and Abe tore through the valley, skimming across the streams, narrowly missing rocks and trees, too distraught to be careful of their new boards. Rabbits scattered, and birds flew away, startled by the interruption to the peace. They skirted around the crops, wasting precious time — food was too valuable to ruin by blasting through with Hoverboards.

When they arrived at their village they jumped from their boards, grabbed them up and headed directly into the general meeting hut. The room was already full and felt hot and stuffy, even though the few mismatched windows and the door were open. It was loud with tensions running high. A couple of people were crying, heads in their hands, but most looked angry or frightened. Some were trying to form a plan as they talked over one another.

'Anymore news?' Abe yelled overtop of the noise.

'There was a second Hover-bird after you left,' Chi informed them. 'It was a short message. There've been quite a few killed in Sector C and a good portion of it destroyed. Plus the Blues took all the food they'd just got from trading. They need anything we can send.'

'Abe will lead a group to help. We could do some food drops using Hover-birds. I'll sort supplies to send from the storehouse and coordinate with Dez when he gets back. Who else is going with Abe?'

Expressions were grim as volunteers raised their hands.

'Right, well, gather supplies that might be useful — bandages, clothes, blankets, anything you can carry, then meet me at the storehouse for food,' said Jax.

Jax headed back to the storehouse. He entered the dim interior and proceeded to gather oats, dried beans, nuts, dried fruit and some jerky. They were the easiest things to carry. He hoped it would be enough.

Within a few hours of receiving the first Hover-bird they were ready to go. Each member of the rescue party had the bag of food provided by Jax, a thin sleeping roll, a water canister, a torch and a weapon of some sort to defend themselves with.

Abe arrived last, pulling a cartful of Hoverboards.

'I think I've enough Hoverboards for everyone if I take all but the one you have, Jax. It would get us there a lot faster.'

'Didn't know you'd managed to fix so many. Better have a bit of a lesson first as I don't think everyone's used them before,' said Jax. His first attempt at hoverboarding had given him a sore backside.

'Right. Grab a board and I'll show you how it's done,' said Abe as he jumped on a board and skimmed over the surrounding landscape. 'See, easy! Use your legs and feet to steer the board over the ground, don't lean too much, and make your adjustments small and fluid. To start moving you tip the front slightly upwards and to stop you flatten out and turn sideways. Got it?'

Everyone dropped their packs and grabbed a board from the cart. Jax held his breath as Abe and Chi almost collided, swerved to miss each other and finished up in the dirt.

'That was quite a show. You okay?' Jax was glad he wasn't the only one to have a sore backside while learning to hover.

They both stood up, looking sheepish, and brushed themselves down.

'All good,' replied Abe. 'Sorry, Chi.'

'Not to worry. It was my fault more than yours. Might have a few bruises before this day's over,' she said as she gave her backside a rub. 'I'll practice over here by myself for a bit so I don't cause any more accidents.'

'Abe, here's a spare Hover-bird to take, in case you need to send a message along the way.' Jax offered the package to Abe.

'Hope we don't need it,' he grimaced as he tucked the Hover-bird into his pack. 'Right, everyone ready to head out?'

Jax waved them off. He felt like all he did lately was say good-bye to people. But he knew it was better he stay behind. He walked back to the storehouse to lock up, his footsteps dragged and his shoulders slumped. Life was unbearable. He took a big breath, straightened his back and raised his head — he would not let Dez down.

'Please let the rescue team be okay,' he whispered as he headed home after locking up. The light of the late summer evening was starting to fade. The team wouldn't get far before nightfall.

Abe turned to retch onto the ground, but nothing came up. Just dry heaves. Why had he volunteered to come? It was like a re-enactment of what had happened to his family and his home all over again.

'You all right Abe?' asked Chi as she came upon him, bent over, trying to suck air into his lungs.

He nodded, shook his head, and nodded again. He wiped his sleeve across his face, straightened up and turned to Chi.

'I know. I'm sorry.' Chi frowned. Her eyes searched his. 'Maybe you shouldn't have come. Guess we didn't stop to think of…of what this would be like.'

'It's okay. It was my choice. We have to put a stop to this.' He waved his arm to encompass the destruction around them.

Chi scowled. 'You've got that right.' She turned to survey their surroundings. Every shelter in the village at this end of the valley was levelled to the ground — blackened ruins. The stench in the smoky air told the story. Most shelters had been burnt with the people still inside. Those that had tried to escape were lying in the dirt. Most dead, some severely wounded. The food that was meant to keep them alive had been their death sentence. Without their help, those left lying on the ground would die from starvation, too weak to seek help or to help themselves.

'Come on, we better get to work. These poor souls need us.' Chi put down her bag and started to unpack water canisters, food, bandages and herbal ointments. The smell of burning death permeated every intake of breath. Moments became infinite as they checked their immediate surroundings for survivors. 'Here, Abe, this girl's still alive.'

Abe gently lifted the little girl's head as Chi poured some water on a cloth and wiped blood from the young girl's face. Her eyes fluttered open and she screamed.

'It's okay. It's okay. They're gone. We're here to help. Shhhhh,' comforted Abe. 'Can you take a sip of water?'

The girl stopped screaming, her eyes wide with fear. She obediently sipped from the water canister. She had green eyes and a shock of red hair with a sprinkling of freckles across her nose.

'Can you tell if you're hurt anywhere?' asked Chi.

'I think just my ribs. They kicked me before they ran off,' she whispered, her eyes glistened with unshed tears as her body started to tremble. 'I…I —'

'It's okay. It's the shock.' Chi held the girl's hand. 'Can you carry her Abe? The others were getting a make-shift hospital together. We should try to get her to the shelter. What's your name?' she asked the little girl.

'Lea.'

'How old are you Lea?'

'Twelve.'

'Do you have any other family?'

'I d…did. My dad, Pat, and m…my little sister, Fie, but, but —' She inhaled a ragged breath as she turned her head and buried it in Abe's shoulder, finally giving way to tears now that comfort was offered.

Abe's shirt stuck to him where Lea's tears soaked through the fabric. He understood how she felt — the uncertainty of not knowing what happened to your family, the terror, the fear of loss, the despair. Holding her more tightly to him, he let her cry into his shirt, promising himself he would find out what had happened to her family.

They reached the first-aid shelter and left Lea on a cot being cared for by the first-aid team. The shelter wasn't much to look at but it was adequate given the circumstances. The first-aid volunteers had taken over the meeting hall of Sector C as the hospital. The timber walls were plain whitewashed boards. The floor had been scrubbed clean. Tables and chairs that normally filled the space had been moved to the side and spare mats or cots were placed on the floor for the injured to lay on. The volunteers were busy cleaning wounds, giving fresh shirts to those in need, and water to everyone who came in. Soup had been made and was offered to those who could eat.

'How are you feeling?' asked Zoe, who had volunteered to help care for the survivors that were brought into the shelter. Her own injuries were painful but helping others offered her a distraction.

'Safer surrounded by people,' Lea replied. 'I don't think I'm too hurt. When my ribs feel a bit better I'll try to help.'

'You're a real little trooper but don't overdo yourself.'

'No, I won't. I *have* to be strong...in case my dad or sister need me,' Lea added, valiantly trying not to cry again, her bottom lip quivering.

'Where were you when the raid started?'

'At home making dinner. Then I heard yelling and things being smashed. I *knew* it was the Blues. I left the food and ran. But some of them...chased me...threw me to the ground and...and...kicked me.'

'What about the rest of your family?'

'My dad and sister were working late out in the fields. If only they'd come home at a normal time instead of working until dark.

But…but my dad wanted to make the most of the late summer daylight. Wanted to make sure we'd have enough to eat this year. I'm *really* scared they're both dead. The Blues *always* rip out the crops and kill the workers. Don't they?'

'They usually take what crops they can, but workers often escape. Try not to worry too much just yet.' Zoe gave the little girl a hint of a smile.

'They're all I have left.'

'You poor little thing.' Zoe gently brushed the hair out of Lea's eyes. 'But I'm here if you need anything, even if it's just a hug or a shoulder to cry on.' Zoe gave the young girl another smile of encouragement before heading over to another patient who was calling out for her.

Lea turned her head into her cot. *Maybe tomorrow would be better*, was her last thought before she fell into an exhausted sleep.

After Abe had deposited Lea onto her cot, he and Chi had gone out to assist whomever else was left alive. It was a gut-wrenching task but he felt better for helping. Even if he only saved one soul it made up in some small way for not being there for his own family. His ancestors had been some of the very few who had managed to escape New Orleans when the first Hyperstorm had taken everyone by surprise with its ferocity. Over time, those who had escaped had then been killed by the Blues until there was only his immediate family left. He could still barely bring himself to think of that day. It was too hard to drown out the guilt. If he had been with them things would have been different. He was strong; he could have defended them. But he'd not been home. Tired of hearing his sister complain about being hungry all the time, he'd gone out to be by himself, wanting some peace and quiet. When he'd returned home, it was to a burned out building and silence. The destruction had been complete. His pain and guilt infinite. Now he put all his energies into helping others.

They found another survivor and Abe carried him back to the shelter. Then they went out again, and again and again, working in silence. Abe didn't think he could talk if he'd wanted to. His mind and his body grimly dedicated to the task at hand. As the day lengthened, his shoulders burned and his legs became leaden, as if he was walking through sand. His shirt adhered to his back and his eyes smarted as the salty sweat trickled down his forehead. Many times he wanted to quit, to turn and run and not have to be a part of the devastation.

If it wasn't for Chi he didn't think he would have been able to cope. Chi was amazing to watch as she comforted and soothed, cleaned wounds and gave out water and food. She had told him about her ancestors and how they had escaped Chinatown in San Francisco after the city had been levelled by a massive earthquake. With the rising tides, the Californian drought and the famine, it had been decided that re-building the city was not feasible. But surviving as a refugee at the time had not been easy. Chi had obviously inherited the inner resilience needed to be a survivor. He doubted she weighed all of one hundred pounds, she didn't look strong but she had an inner strength that he admired. At the moment there were smears of soot across her face and her clothes were covered in dirt and blood. The bandana tied around her forehead had turned a shade darker over the course of the day as the sweat poured off her and soaked the fabric. Yet she never seemed to tire or think about her own discomfort. Every once in a while she would look up at him and give him a hint of a smile. He appreciated the gesture, the fact that she hadn't forgotten him even when surrounded by so much pain and suffering.

They asked the name of each person they found conscious and reported it to the shelter as they dropped the survivors off so that family members would be able to find each other again. 'Abe, we should probably go get some food at the kitchen and rest for a while. We'll be no good to anyone if we're exhausted,' said Chi.

'What? Oh, right. I keep hoping that if I help just one more that they'll tell me their name is Pat or Fie. Y'know?'

'Yeah, I know. Check the register. Someone else might have brought them in,' said Chi.

'There are so many dead.'

'Don't give up. Not yet.'

Abe nodded, turned his face away, cleared his throat and coughed.

'I wonder if Dez has heard the news yet,' said Chi to change the subject to something slightly less raw. 'Emi's news was so encouraging. Dez must be learning lots to be gone so long. I thought he'd be back after about a week.'

'His Hover-bird didn't say much.'

'No, it sure didn't. But maybe his interest is more in Emi and less in health and he's keeping things to himself,' suggested Chi with a grin and a wink.

'You think he likes Emi?'

'Just a hunch. Women's intuition. But I wouldn't be surprised,' Chi replied. 'And they look good together.'

Abe nodded. His expression thoughtful.

'Come on. Time for food,' said Chi.

They entered one of the communal buildings that had escaped damage and had been set up as the kitchen. The aroma of soup made their mouths water. Overwhelmed with hunger, they grabbed a bowl each and sat on the grass outside the shelter. As she looked up from consuming her soup, Chi said, 'Abe, look, it's Zoe.'

Zoe was walking across the field toward them. She was limping, her arm was in a sling, she had bandages around her ribs and her face was bruised and swollen.

'Ah jeez, Zoe, look at you,' said Abe sympathetically. 'Makes me want to find the Blues and make them more black and blue than they already are.'

'Hey, Abe. Hey, Chi.' Zoe gave Abe a lopsided smile, the best she could do with her battered face. 'Thanks, Abe. At least I'm not dead. The damage had been done and most of the Blues had cleared out by the time we arrived. The few that remained mostly went for Sam, not me. Have you seen him yet?'

'Not yet. We've been trying to help the survivors. Where is he?'

'There's a shelter left in the woods that they didn't get to. We put him in there. He's conscious now but pretty broken up. I…don't know if he'll live. He's in so much pain. Do you think Emi's group could help him?'

'We're still waiting to hear from Dez and Emi. I'm hoping they'll bring some Network members from Sector B back with them since they know so much more about healing,' said Chi.

'It's weird, him being so silent,' added Abe. 'I hope we hear soon…real soon.'

'Real soon would be good.'

SIX

'Sal? What's wrong?'

'We had a Hoverbird from Abe saying there's been a raid. I wasn't going to bother you since you've a lot on your plate and the details were garbled — stupid Hoverbird,' Sal stopped to draw breath before adding, 'But I thought you should know that...sounds like Sam and Zoe were attacked on their way home. I think Sam's in bad shape. Apparently the Blues had already been through Sector C. We should send help,' she finished in a rush.

'Oh NO! Oh, Sal,' Emi replied, as dread crumpled her new world and threw it beyond reach. 'It's been so quiet lately — why now?' she whispered as she brought her hand to her forehead and closed her eyes momentarily to banish the images swirling in her mind.

'Don't know! The timing is pretty horrible. All the leaders away and the new supplies gone.'

Emi whimpered as she leaned against the wall for support. 'And Zoe, is she okay?'

'She was pretty beat up but I think she's okay. Guess they had most of the food already so they let her be after kicking her around. But there are lots dead and severely injured. We need you back.'

'Yes, yes, of course. I better go tell Dez and the others. I'll call you back as soon as I can.' Emi hung up. She put her hands to her face and moaned in despair. To go from such elation to such misery within a couple minutes. She took a steadying breath. And now she had to be the one to break the news to Dez.

She returned to the ballroom and scanned the crowd for Dez. *Was he still on the balcony?* She couldn't see him anywhere. A voice behind her made her jump.

'You look upset Emi. Can I be of service?'

'Edward! Oh, oh yes, please. I've just had a call — from Sal, from my village, there's been a...a raid...by the Blues. Many are dead. A couple of our leaders severely injured and all the new supplies we sent, gone,' Emi blurted, trying not to give way to her emotions.

'I'm so sorry. The Blues, they're barbaric. One day they'll kill us all with their savagery. Rest assured, we'll do all we can to help. Come let's find the rest of your team. We'll get you back as soon as we can and send food and some of our medical staff to help,' offered Edward as he put his arm around her waist, pulling her to his side, and guided her through the crowd.

'Thank you so much,' Emi looked up at him with a faint smile. She scanned the crowd again. Her eyes locked with Dez's. His face looked like thunder. *Now what?* She was suddenly aware of the weight of Edwards arm around her waist.

'Edward. Emi,' he said very formally as they approached.

'Dez. There's been a raid.'

'What? NO! Who, when?'

'On Sector C. Sal said Zoe and Sam were attacked on their way home but the Blues had already done their raid. Taken all the new supplies and left many dead. Sam's in bad shape! That's all I know. We need to get back. Edward said he'd help.'

'Thank you. That's very generous,' Dez nodded toward Edward, but there was no corresponding warmth in his eyes to match his words. 'We'd better leave as soon as possible.'

'Of course. I'll order a few Hovercrafts and load them with supplies and some of our best medical staff. It's three a.m. now. I'll need a few hours. We should have everything ready by morning.'

'Again, thank you. We'll be ready at first light,' said Dez, bitterly.

'I'll inform my medical staff immediately,' said Edward. 'If you'll excuse me, I'll make the necessary preparations,' he added as he removed his arm from around Emi. 'I'm so sorry the evening has ended like this.' He lifted Emi's hand to his lips. 'Excuse me.' He turned abruptly and left.

Dez and Emi looked at each other. Emi's eyes filled with tears. 'Dez, I — Edward was just —'

'Not now, Emi,' said Dez as he turned away. 'We better tell the others, then pack and try and get some rest. Tomorrow…today will be a long day.'

He was right. Now was not the time. People were dying. Everything else paled in comparison, but -

Emi returned to her room to pack. She took off her beautiful dress, showered and changed, and lay on her bed, staring at the ceiling. It felt like years since she'd been home, yet it had only been a week. *A week!* She allowed a couple of tears to slide down her face and soak into the pillow. *Was it only earlier this evening that she'd been so happy?* Life seemed like it was about to finally get better, and now, once again, it had been torn apart by raids — and irrational jealousy. She turned over and fell into an exhausted sleep.

The morning light was brutal. Memories flooded back. Emi sat on the edge of her bed with her head in her hands. *What would this day bring?* She pushed herself off the bed to answer the knock at the door and found Dez dressed and ready to leave.

'You ready?' he asked abruptly.

'Almost, just need to change,' Emi replied, feeling awkward and guilty being caught in her pajamas when she should be dressed and ready to go. Her people needed her. They were dying. She shouldn't be sleeping in a luxurious bed.

'I'll wait in the hall.'

'Dez…I —'

The door closed. She sighed and headed for the bathroom to change. She would have to talk to Dez later. Right now she needed to get her act together. She changed, grabbed her bag and stepped out into the hallway.

Jon and Amy were just coming out from their room when Edward joined them. 'All set?' he asked. 'I have everything prepared that I think you might need. If there's anything else, just let us know.'

'Thank you so much, Edward. You've been most kind,' said Emi.

'Yes, thank you,' Dez nodded his head but his eyes were still stony and he looked tired.

'Not at all. The least I can do,' Edward smiled graciously as he took Emi's bag, put his hand to her waist and guided her down the hallway to the elevator that would take them to the rooftop landing-pad and the waiting Hovercraft.

Once the four of them, along with the Fringe's medical staff, were all aboard, Peter lifted the Hovercraft into the sky and headed back toward Sector B. 'After I've dropped Amy and Jon back at their home we can fit in a few of your medical team. I'll deliver you to the site of the attack and stay to help in case you need more supplies,' said Peter.

'Thanks, Peter,' said Amy.

Emi remained silent and stared out the windows at the golden landscape below, lost in her own thoughts and dreading what was to come. It was hard to believe that just a few days ago they had made this same trip with the hope of making changes and planning a better future. Now they were back to trying to salvage what they could from the hopelessness that was left in the wake of a raid by the Blues. The story never changed.

They neared the valley and Amy and Jon prepared to disembark. Emi could see little dots on the village green. As the Hovercraft drew closer she could see the village medical staff ready and waiting to go. Edward must have phoned through to Sal to inform them of his preparations.

'Amy, could you put a message together and send a Hoverbird to Jax? Try and explain the last couple of weeks to him as best you can and tell everyone that I've gone directly to the raid site to help. We'll send an update as soon as we can,' Dez said. It was the first time he had said anything during the flight.

'Yes, of course. Stay safe. Let us know if you need anything else,' Amy replied before she and Jon disappeared down the ramp.

Sal, along with the medical team she had selected from Sector B, boarded the Hovercraft. The Hovercraft lifted off and headed for Sector C. They flew over the valley from north to south. The northern end did not look like it had sustained much damage. There were still small groups of homes and people moving about like tiny ants below. As they neared the site of the main village at the southern end they could see the charred ruins of the shelters; the thatched rooves and grass mats used for flooring would have caught fire easily; smoke permeated the atmosphere. There didn't appear to be much left intact; nor did there seem to be much movement.

'Not again!' Dez groaned as he pressed his forehead into the glass.

Peter set the Hovercraft down in a field on the outskirts of the blackened village. He couldn't get any closer as it would stir too much dust into the air near to where the survivors might be. Dez, Emi led the way down the ramp to where Abe, Chi and Zoe were standing, mouths agape and eyes wide.

'Dez? Emi? What the....? What...where...what's that?' asked Zoe as she waved her arm at the giant machine that had landed before them.

Emi would have found her look of stunned disbelief comical if the situation hadn't been so dire.

'Hi, Chi, Abe, Zoe. Oh God, Zoe, look at you,' said Dez.

'I'm okay. Looks worse than it is. But what *is* that? *Where* have you been?'

'Sorry to startle you,' Dez looked over his shoulder at the massive Hovercraft. 'Long story, but in a nutshell, we met up with the Fringe, they took us to where they live to show us around. They, uhh, need our help. I'll explain later. Then we got your news and they brought us back in the Hovercraft; fastest way to get here. We've brought some of their medical team with us to help and they've given us a bunch of supplies. This is Peter; he's our pilot. He'll get anything else we need,' Dez explained to his dumbfounded audience.

'Well, I have a *million* questions but for now they'll have to wait.' Zoe glanced with raised eyebrows at Abe and Chi who shrugged their shoulders in response. 'If you'll follow me I'll take you to the hospital shelters. Maybe you can help some of those that are beyond our abilities. We also need help looking for survivors and burying the dead,' she added grimly.

'How's Sam?' asked Dez as he ran his hand through his hair. He stifled a yawn. His weary gaze took in the forlorn look of the Network members who had come to greet them.

'Not good. We think he's bleeding internally. They beat him pretty badly and left him for dead. He's still breathing but I feel like he's slipping away.'

'Our medical team brought scanners and surgical supplies with them. If they can save him they will,' offered Peter, overhearing the conversation.

'Thank you,' Zoe turned to look at Peter. 'That would truly be a miracle,' she said as she led the way into the hospital shelter.

They stopped inside the entry. Dez groaned and brought his hand to his eyes. There were dozens of people laid out in row upon row, some on cots, but most were on blankets on the ground. Many of those closest to him seemed to have limbs that were at odd angles. All were either covered in blood or severe bruises and they were deathly white and looked as though they were barely breathing. He couldn't even begin to imagine the pain they must be in. How were they to cope with so many injured?

'These are the survivors that are in a less critical state. We think most of them will be okay, but many of them still need help, especially the setting of limbs. I'll leave some of you here,' Zoe waved her arm to encompass the scene before her, 'and take the rest with me to our other shelter where the more critical cases are,' she added as she turned to go.

'Those of you who can help here, get to work. Those of you with more advanced medical experience better follow Zoe,' said Dez. His mouth turned down in a grimace as he followed Zoe out of the shelter.

'Lord, what a mess,' stated Matthew, one of the Fringe medical staff. 'Right team, divide up and let's get to it. I'll go with Zoe to the other shelter. If the others are worse than this then we've no time to waste.'

Emi and Matthew let out simultaneous involuntary gasps as they entered the next hospital shelter. Sal turned away and brought her hand to her mouth before turning back and squaring her shoulders. Dez just groaned. There were far fewer people but they were in much worse shape.

Zoe guided them straight to a bed in the corner. 'This is Sam. Can you help him?'

'Can't promise anything but I'll do my best,' said Matthew. 'I'll need an assistant, the place sterilised and my hand scanner to see what internal damage there is. Then we'll see.'

'I'll help you,' said Zoe.

Emi glanced at Zoe and then at Dez. Dez looked too choked up to utter a word.

'You don't really look in any shape to help,' observed Emi. 'You sure you don't want me to help instead?'

'She's right,' agreed Matthew.

'I'll be alright and I'm not squeamish. Besides, we don't have enough people to go round so I'll have to do.' Zoe shrugged her shoulders and then winced. 'And I can't help haul survivors in or search for those further afield in my current condition, so …'

'Very well. Let's get started,' said Matthew.

Sal decided to head back to help those less critically injured. Emi and Dez left to search for survivors. Emi glanced sideways at Dez just in time to see him cast a last look over his shoulder at his friend as Matthew and Zoe prepared to discover the extent of Sam's injuries.

The extra help had freed Abe and Chi up to look for more survivors. They brought many in from outlying areas. In one of the fields, furthest out, they found a man, he was unconscious and looked severely beaten but what grabbed Abe's attention was his shock of red hair. He *must* be Lea's dad. But where was the little sister? They loaded the man onto the stretcher and took him in to the critical hospital. Abe went to find Lea.

Lea was sitting on a cot in the non-critical ward, looking very lost and sad. Her face brightened as she saw Abe walk in and then fell when she noticed his expression.

'Hi Lea. I think we've found your dad,' Abe said as gently as he could as he sat down beside her on the cot. 'He's alive, but only barely. Do you think you're strong enough to come and see him?'

'Oh, yes, yes please.' She got up and put her hand in his.

Abe led her to the critical ward and to the man with the bright red hair. He looked down at Lea questioningly.

'Daddy.' Tears welled in the corners of her eyes. She fell to her knees beside the cot and put her head carefully on his shoulder. The tears rolled down her face, soaking into her father's shirt, as she tried to control her sobs. Her breath came in shuddering gasps as she clung to her dad. He brought his hand up to rest it on her hair, and then his heart, beating erratically beneath her ear, stopped and he was gone.

Lea looked up. Tears continued their silent journey down her face. 'Did you…did you find my sister? She's all I have left?'

'Not yet. We're still looking. We checked all around the area where we found your dad and there was nobody else nearby. We'll keep searching, I promise. I'm so sorry,' said Abe as he picked her up and let her sob into his shoulder. 'I know. I lost my family in a raid. It's okay to cry. We'll keep searching for your sister. Maybe she got away and is hiding somewhere safe and sound. Don't give up hope.'

Dez and Emi worked tirelessly. They brought the last remaining survivors in, cleaned and bandaged wounds, fed those who could eat, buried the dead — so many dead. They worked silently, too overwhelmed for small talk. They ate when they could and caught cat-naps when absolutely necessary. Dez made sure people were sent to Sam's village in Sector D to see if they were okay. After a few days all the dead were buried and all the survivors were being tended to, the supplies had been unloaded from the Hovercraft and those that could got up and helped those that couldn't.

Dez finally had a chance to shower, change and sleep and then he went to find Chi in the make-shift hospital. He pushed open the flimsy timber doors to find Chi stooped over a patient who was resting on a blanket on the rough wooded floor.

'Has anyone reported in from Sector D yet? Are they okay?' he asked as she straightened up to face him.

'Yes, a couple days ago. Sorry, I thought you'd been informed. They must have thought you had enough on your plate. Sector D was raided as well and we have people there helping, but they're not as badly off as we are here…thank goodness.'

'Wish I'd been told. It would've taken a lot off my mind. Still, I'm glad it's been taken care of.'

'They've brought some of the wounded back here in the Hovercraft.' She waved her hand to indicate the extra people who were now crammed into the already crowded room. 'It was too difficult to spread out all the equipment and the surgeons from the Fringe,' Chi explained.

'And Abe…how's he holding up in all of this?'

'He's been a rock. Every spare moment he has he spends with a little girl named Lea who lost her dad in the raid. We're still looking for her little sister, Fie, hoping she's alive somewhere.'

'They're still looking for people?' Dez exclaimed, his eyebrows raised in surprise. 'I'd have thought everyone would be accounted for by now.'

'And most have. Just the little girl and a few others are still missing but we think they were burned in the shelters, whereas the little girl was out in the fields with her dad. He was found but she wasn't.'

'Damn Blues!' Dez growled as he slammed his palms on the table. 'Such needless waste of life.' Head bent, shoulders slumped, he stared at the tabletop and wondered if there would ever be a safe haven, an escape from the brutality of the Blues? He heard footsteps approaching, heaved a sigh and looked up.

Zoe came into the room covered in blood, her face frozen in shock.

'Zoe, what happened to you?' asked Chi, gesturing to her blood splattered clothes.

Zoe glanced down. 'I've been helping Matthew work on Sam.'

'And?' asked Dez, certain that he did not want to hear the answer.

Zoe gave her head a shake. 'I don't think it looks good. Matthew did all he could. But he said the injuries are too severe and Sam has been bleeding internally for too long.'

Dez closed his eyes and groaned. He slid down the wall, his forehead sank onto his crossed arms as his eyes fixed on a knot in the rough timber floor. 'But we grew up together and…I…we need him,' he whispered haltingly. 'Especially now.'

'He's in and out of consciousness, kind of ranting a bit sometimes,' Zoe looked at Dez as she choked back her emotions. 'I sat with him for a while but maybe if he saw you it might help him cling to life,' she added, her voice raspy with unshed grief.

Dez nodded as he got up to make his way to the recovery room. He paused, his hand on the door, 'Can he handle having visitors?' he asked, without turning back.

'I don't know. But I fear that if he rests he'll never wake up,' replied Zoe honestly. 'He's never conscious for long anyway.'

'Maybe if I just sit with him,' said Dez, his words trailing off. He pushed the door open with more force than was necessary, causing the entry wall to shudder under the impact, and headed off to the shelter where the more critically injured were housed. He found Sam on a cot in a corner. Sam looked deathly white beneath his tan but he was still breathing.

Dez sat on the floor next to the cot and reached out for his friend's hand. He felt the faintest pressure on his fingers and looked up to see Sam's eyes were open, pleading for understanding.

'Sam. Hi. I'm here buddy,' said Dez as he got the cloth in the bowl next to the cot and wetted Sam's lips. 'It's going to be alright. You'll be okay. The Blues are gone and we have the Fringe here helping us. It's one of their doctors that operated on you.'

Sam weakly thrashed his head from side to side.

'Shhhhh. It's okay. You just need rest.'

'Blues…Blues,' Sam whispered.

'Yeah, we know. They raided a couple valleys but they're gone now.'

'Blues…all the f…food. After m…meeting.'

'Yeah, they got all the food from the trading but it's alright now. The Fringe have given us lots of supplies, as much, even more than what was taken.'

Again Sam thrashed his head back and forth.

'Are you in pain? Can I get you something? I think the Fringe have something that helps with pain.'

Sam slowly shook his head.

'Set…up,' Sam whispered so quietly that Dez wasn't sure what he'd said.

'You want to sit up? I don't think that's a good idea yet bud. You need to recover. I'll go get you something for the pain,' Dez replied.

Sam shook his head. 'NO! Set…up, set-up!'

'Set-up? Take it easy, Sam. Go slow. I don't understand.' Dez leaned in closer to catch what his childhood friend was so obviously desperate to communicate.

'Set-up. Blues.'

'Do you want me to plan a set-up so we can kill the Blues?'

Sam shook his head and took a shuddering breath. 'Raid…set-up.' He drew a last gasping breath, his head lolled to the side, his eyes wide open.

'Sam?' Dez sat beside his friend, too dazed to move. His childhood playmate stared back at him from sightless eyes. Slowly he reached out and closed Sam's eyes. He pulled the sheet over his still warm body, got to his feet and left the room. He couldn't face looking at death any longer.

Dez found Chi and Zoe where he'd left them but Emi had vanished. Wasn't it a lifetime ago that he'd last seen them? He walked in and simply shook his head.

'He's gone?' asked Zoe.

Dez nodded in affirmation. 'I can't believe he's gone,' Dez ran his fingers through his ruffled hair. 'He was always so…there. In the end he was really agitated. I'm not sure if he wanted to sit up and start helping,' Dez shook his head. 'Like he was in any shape to help. Or if he was trying to say 'set-up.' But I don't know what he wanted to set-up. Then he died,' he babbled.

'I'm sorry, Dez,' said Zoe, her face drawn with exhaustion and sorrow. Zoe was a very resilient person but the last few days had taken a toll on her stamina. She shook her head and asked, 'What'll you do now? I mean for a leader? The village will need someone —' she trailed off. Dez glanced at Zoe and gave her a small grimace of a smile. She had obviously realised too late that now was not the time to discuss such things and had clamped her mouth shut.

'I don't know. I'll go to them in a few days but for now I think I want to go look for Fie. At least *she* might still be alive. I need to do something that has some hope attached to it!' He turned abruptly and walked out, slamming the door behind him as he went.

He collected a pack and water and headed out across the fields and into the woods beyond. His little sister, Isi, when she had been scared or frightened had found open areas in the woods that had been filled with ferns and wildflowers. She had said that they felt like a safe place when she was scared. He would see if there were any places like that here; maybe this little girl was the same.

Dez went further and further into the woods. He ducked under low lying branches and slashed at the undergrowth with a stick. The forest was filled with birch trees, so it wasn't overly dark; he would have been enjoying himself it weren't for the circumstances of his being there. He constantly called out Fie's name but never heard a response, just the chirping of the birds. Finally, he came across an open area filled with long grass, wild flowers and ferns, and again called Fie's name but there was no answer. He perched on a rock, sipped from his water canister and pulled at his sweat-soaked shirt, then wiped the perspiration from his forehead and flexed his weary feet. He wouldn't give up but it felt like trying to find a needle in a haystack. He returned his water bottle to his pack and wearily pushed himself to his feet. As he slung his pack over his shoulder he froze to the spot. He cocked his head — surely that was the sound of soft weeping and not the sound of a bird. He moved silently through the ferns toward the noise he could have sworn he'd heard.

SEVEN

'Hey Spike, that's mine,' Shade yelled, her hand shot out trying to grab the food before it got devoured by Spike. 'Give it back!'

'Nah. I want this one,' Spike replied to the large girl with spiked black hair and dark blue tattoo imprints that covered most of her body — the zipper imprints made it look like somebody was trying to unzip her skin to get to the slightly lighter shade of blue skin that was beneath. 'There's lots, get yourself another!'

Shade's fist shot out and punched him in the arm. His food dropped to the ground. 'I *said* it's *mine*!' growled Shade.

Spike looked down at his arm. It was going to leave a bruise, but since he was already black and blue it wouldn't be noticeable. 'Bitch! Not like there's not a whole pile of food right over there.'

'Get your own, asshole.'

'I did. Took yours. Ha!' sneered Spike, making the snake tattoos on his face dance.

'Tried and failed, more like,' said Shade, retrieving her food from the ground.

'Yeah, and you only got all this 'cause of the raid. Without the tip-off I got about the meeting and the food exchange you'd have nothin'.'

'Whatever. So you got tipped off. So what! We'd have raided Sector C or D anyway. They were due.'

'Yeah, maybe, but probably not at the right time. The tip-off is what got us all this.' He waved his arm, indicating all the food surrounding them. 'If it was up to you lot it would've been crops like normal,' said Spike as he hefted his bulk off the ground and lumbered over to grab another handful of the crispy, fried potatoes, before stuffing the contents into his mouth.

'Don't eat too many. Leave some for the rest of us. Food's still scarce, even with this haul,' said Shade, with a scowl that caused the zipper tattoos on her face to look like they were being pulled apart.

'Don't worry. There'll be more.'

'How do you know?'

'Because I still have this,' said Spike as he pulled something small and black from his pocket.

'What's that?'

'Dunno really.'

'Where'd you get it?'

'From the guy I met.'

'What's it do?'

'You talk into it.'

'Why bother? I'm right here and can hear you plenty fine.'

'You talk to people far away.'

'You're so full of shit.'

Spike shrugged.

'Let me try then,' she held out her hand.

'Nah. It ain't workin' now.'

'Like I said, so full of shit,' her hand dropped to her side.

CHAPTER SEVEN

'Fat lot you know,' Spike replied as he turned to go. He shuffled off down the dark alley, past the buildings that were now rubble and gazed around at the few that still stood with broken windows and doors long rotted off their hinges. Here and there were places that were more intact, but just barely. These were places where a Blue had tried to make a home for a while, probably because they had kids to look after, until the kids died — or the parents did. Mostly they lived underground, in old subway stations, basements or parking garages. Nobody stayed put for long. Once the garbage accumulated they needed to move on, find some new place in the city to seek shelter from the unrelenting sun.

Spike headed down the stairs of the parking garage. He lived two stories down with a few other people. It was his turn to cook. They all took turns, cooking the few things that their parents before them had cooked and taught them how to make. Nothing ever changed much. When they did a raid they had to take the food to the Exchange. A few people were in charge of creating their food. Some old abandoned warehouses had been made into food processing kitchens. He wasn't sure who ran the kitchens but he didn't care so long as he got something more edible than the crops he turned in after a raid. His meal tonight was chicken wings in sauce. He didn't think it was chicken. It was probably squirrel. He wasn't even sure what a chicken was. He really wanted deep-fried potatoes and onions but the Exchange hadn't had enough potatoes and onions to provide either. Maybe tomorrow Zara could make sausages…he always liked when others cooked. He hated cooking. Everything had to be cooked in the pot of oil or the frying pan over the open flame of the fire. It was a smoky, miserable job. Living with a group in the parking garage was the only way he could get other meals and some company and occasionally a girl. Zara didn't seem to mind, or Keyly. He sometimes heard other people grunting in the dark. The carpark was for group living; you put up with whatever. He'd even seem some kids born.

They didn't usually live long. Cried all the time and then died. Kind of a relief really as the crying got on your nerves, especially with the echo of the carpark. Not enough food to feed more people anyway so it was better they died. Besides, it wasn't much of a life…raiding the Network when food was scarce, occasionally killing those that got in the way, then just barely living until the next raid. The raids were exciting. Broke up the boredom and he could let out all his pent up aggression and frustration. He liked to kill when he was on the raids; it meant there was one less person that needed to be fed.

Nobody seemed to be around except Zara. That was good. He'd eat more and leave less for everyone else, if any. It was hard to stop eating once he got started. Guess he'd have to share with Zara if she stayed awake long enough or even noticed there was food. She was in her usual spot, sitting on one of the mats, staring blankly at the wall while her kid suckled her. She didn't seem to notice the kid, or his entry. She visited the dungeons regularly, traded her food for drugs. She often gazed blankly at the wall.

'Hey, Zara.'

She turned her head toward him but didn't reply, then looked down at her kid and shoved him off of her and onto the mat. The kid started to whimper but she didn't notice as she rolled over and passed out, her breasts still hanging out of her filthy shirt. The kid started to suck his thumb instead and stared at him with glassy eyes. It was amazing he was still alive. With his stick-like blue limbs and his distended belly he didn't look like he would last much longer.

He put some dried branches on the fire and poured the bowl of 'chicken' wings and sauce into the dented, handleless pot. He clenched and unclenched his hands, waiting for the wings to be cooked enough. He shook his fist at the kid as his stomach growled in protest at waiting. He kicked his foot out and sent the wood chunks the kid had been stacking flying everywhere. One hit the kid in the head and he cried.

Zara came to and yelled at him, 'Whatcha doin' ya idiot?'

'Nothin'. Stupid cow. Your tits 're out.'

Zara grunted, looked down and pulled her shirt over one bare breast before passing back out.

'Stupid cow.' Spike's blue lips pulled back in a sneer — if she wasn't awake then he wouldn't have to share. He reached out to stir the pot and bring the cooked wings from the bottom up to the top. He picked them out, one after the other — they burned his fingers and the sauce dripped down his hand onto his shirt. He spat the bones onto the concrete floor, satisfied at having all the 'chicken' to himself. It had been a good raid. The Exchange had been generous.

He looked down at his hands all covered in sauce and was about to bring them to his mouth and lick them clean when he looked over at Zara, passed out on her back, and grinned. He crawled over to where she lay and grabbed both her tits in his hands, leaving sauce all over her shirt and her one exposed breast. She didn't stir. The kid stared up at him. 'Can't say I didn't share. You'll get some sauce next time you're suckin' her tits kid,' he guffawed. 'Stupid kid.'

Spike smiled to himself. The last raid had been so easy. The leaders still away — slowly trudging their way home, the security lax, the extra food had already been delivered by those funny looking Hover-birds the Network used. He couldn't have planned it better himself. He'd enjoyed beating up the red haired guy. The spiked stick he carried was a handy weapon; deadly when he put the full force of his bulk behind it. The guy had put up quite a fight defending his daughter. Idiot. He should have known better.

He'd even managed to kill the blonde boy's uncle. Tom…that was his name. He'd heard someone yell out to him. He'd done it as a favour to the boy since he'd so willingly given up the deer he'd been lugging home a few weeks ago when Spike had been starving. Tom had been terrified, babbling about being the only person his mom had left and couldn't he have killed his uncle instead of his dad and sister. Spike had watched from his hiding place in the forest as the boy had returned to his shelter, his shoulders slumped and his head bowed as he went home empty handed. The man waiting for him on the porch had yelled at the boy about wasting an entire day and having nothing to show for it before he had sent him sprawling from a blow to the head. Spike didn't care too much about people but he figured the uncle deserved to die. His snake imprint stretched from ear to ear as his grin widened. The boy wouldn't have to worry about his uncle anymore. Best to keep the boy safe since he was good at hunting and willing to pass over his game.

He rubbed his hand across his belly, leaving the last of the sauce streaked across his already filthy shirt. He felt better now he'd eaten but he still wanted more. He needed to do another raid — a bigger raid. If everyone had clubs like his then they'd kill more people and take all the food instead of just what they could run away with. Yeah. He'd get a group together; they could all make spiked clubs, kill everyone. They could take over a whole valley. Nobody would want to raid until they were starving again, but when they were, then he'd make it count.

He shook the stupid device in his hand. If he could get it to work maybe the guy would give him another tip-off.

EIGHT

Dez fought his way through the forest toward the muffled sound. He was certain he was going in the right direction; the noise was definitely getting louder. It had to be someone crying and not the sound of an animal. He pushed through the last of the undergrowth and stepped into a clearing.

'Emi!' He came to a sudden halt.

Emi looked up and wiped her sleeve across her eyes. 'Dez! S... sorry, just feeling a bit all done and needed —'

'Do you want me to go?' he asked as he pushed his hair out of in his eyes. He rubbed at the back of his neck and looked beyond her before taking a step forward. He hesitated.

'No, no. I'm all cried-out now,' she sniffed. 'What are you doing here?'

'Looking for a little girl who's still missing.'

'Can I help?'

'Sure. Two pairs of eyes are better than one,' he said as casually as he could. He extended his hand to help pull her up from the ground. It dawned on him that it was probably the first nice gesture he'd offered since the kiss on the balcony.

Emi looked him in the eyes and then slowly extended her hand and hauled herself to her feet. Her reluctance to touch him was painfully obvious. He heaved a sigh. Was she too at war with herself, knowing the time to talk was not now but wanting to all the same? He felt completely drained by all the second guessing.

'Dez, I—'

'What? Let me guess! You're sorry you kissed me back now that there's the all powerful Mr. Black on the scene,' he said as dropped his arm to his side.

'No. No, not at all! It's not like that. He happened across me when I was upset after getting the call from Sal. He was *just* helping.'

'With his arms around you?'

'He didn't have his arms around me. Then or ever! He was guiding me through the crowd. Supporting me.'

'That's not how it looked. You immediately ran off, left me on the balcony and then came back in the arms of Edward Black.'

'That may be how it *looked*, but that's *not* how it was. Or is!' Emi said, her voice rising an octave.

Dez knew it was a stupid argument and one he didn't want to have.

Then Emi leaned into him, put her hand to his head and brought his mouth to hers. Amongst his jumbled thoughts he was sure it was all she could think to do to stop him saying more and fueling the idiotic argument even further. He let out a low moan and willed his trembling legs to be still as all the pent up tension in his muscles gave way. He returned Emi's kiss, wrapped his arms around her, crushed her to him and then buried his head in her hair. 'Sorry. I was…jealous. Didn't stop to think.'

'There's nobody to be jealous of.'

Slowly Dez came to his senses. Their argument had only lasted a matter of minutes but he realised they were selfishly taking time away from finding a lost, frightened, possibly injured, little girl. Minutes could be the difference between her surviving and not, given how long she had already been missing and exposed to the elements. He would never be able to live with himself if their delay was the reason for the girl's death. 'We need to find Fie,' he said, with a catch in his throat as he reluctantly pulled away.

'What?' murmured Emi, 'Right!' she shook her head and disengaged herself. 'Which way?'

He crushed her to him one more time before planting a hard, quick kiss on her mouth. 'Come on, let's go. We've got to be close.' He took her hand and pulled her after him.

They headed further into the trees, certain that a frightened little girl would want as much distance between her and the Blues as possible, even if it did mean going into the forest. Dez pushed through the undergrowth, constantly looking to right and left for some clue, something out of place — a broken branch, a bit of cloth caught on a tree, a footprint, a hollow where someone had bedded down for the night, anything that would give them a hint to where she could be.

They searched for hour after hour, occasionally stopping to listen, calling out Fie's name, hoping to hear a response. Dez was thankful for Emi's quiet support. He desperately wanted to find Fie alive. The thought of her perishing alone in the woods was more than he could bear — reminding him too much of not being able to save his sister. Fie was the same age as his sister had been when she had died. If Fie died it would be from the same cause — the aftermath of a raid by the Blues, slow starvation once all the food was taken. But as time wore on, there were still no signs of a lost little girl.

'I hope Fie has remembered the basic rules of survival,' he said to buoy up his own flagging spirits. 'Still, it's been a few days, she can't be in great shape at this point,' he added, his mouth turned down at the edges.

'No, I don't suppose she is,' said Emi. There was no point uttering lies and trying to give false hope. 'But we've all learned to be resilient.'

'Hope it's enough,' he said, his voice quiet as he rubbed at his face and continued to trudge through the forest. Even his feet felt heavy as he placed one foot in front of the other.

They kept hunting for Fie all afternoon and well into the evening but without finding a single clue to her whereabouts.

'It's starting to get dark.' Emi looked up into the sky beyond the treetops at the fading daylight.

'I think I'll bunk down in one of the clearings. It'll be too dark to see soon,' Dez said, his voice heavy with the weight of knowing that Fie would be lost and alone for another night. 'I'll keep looking in the morning. Do you want to head back to the village?'

'No. I think I'll stay,' she said as a slight flush spread across her cheeks.

They found a clearing in the woods and while Emi scratched out a dirt patch Dez found some dry branches to build a fire with. Once the fire was going they settled down and ate their food in silence.

Dez jumped when a twig snapped. He cocked his head and stared into the darkness, hoping against hope that Fie would smell the smoke or see the light from the fire, if she was nearby and if she was still alive. But a young doe walked by and Dez's shoulders slumped as he let out his pent up breath. As the night hours lengthened his eyelids began to droop — the last few days had been full of so much turmoil, and with the endless, hopeless searching Dez could feel the last of his resilience being stripped from him. He retrieved the blankets from his pack and spread them over the ground. After damping down the fire, he and Emi tried to rest, curled together for comfort. He knew now was not the time to resume their earlier brief passion as they needed to keep their ears pricked for the sounds of a lost little girl. He couldn't extinguish the last shred of hope that she was still alive by giving way to his own selfish desires.

Sometime in the small hours of the morning Dez awoke with a start. In the early dawn light, he could barely see beyond the embers of the fire. Had he heard a noise or was he imaging things? Perhaps an animal sniffing around to see what food they had. Quietly he got to his feet, trying not to disturb Emi, picked a stick from the fire and headed into the nearby forest in the direction of the noise he could have sworn that he'd heard. With the stick in front of him lighting his way, he waved it around, trying to find some clue, something out of place. He stopped to listen. There it was again…a rustling of leaves, yet there wasn't a breath of wind. He turned in the direction of the sound.

There in front of him was a little girl, no more than about six or seven, watching him, her eyes huge in her small face. She pressed herself up against a tree trunk, attempting to be invisible, her body trembling. She slowly sank to the ground, her legs out before her, her eyes never leaving his face.

'Hello,' he said quietly so as to not startle her. 'I'm Dez. I'm hoping you might be Fie as we've been looking for you for ages and want to take you home. Are you okay?'

She shook her head as the tears coursed down her face, creating dark patches on her torn and grubby dress. She looked down at her arm, cradled in her lap. His eyes followed the direction of hers. Her arm sat at an odd angle.

'Is it okay if I pick you up and carry you back to our camp. We have some food and water just over there.' He pointed through the trees in the direction he had come from.

The little girl nodded but didn't say a word. Her eyes were still wide with terror but he was obviously not the Blue she'd been expecting so she allowed her self to be picked up and carried back to where the embers of the fire still glowed in the early morning light.

Emi woke up to see Dez placing a little girl in front of her with her arm held awkwardly before her. She slowly sat up. 'Hi,' she said in a hushed voice. 'Can I look at that for you?'

The little girl nodded her head but stayed sitting where she was. Emi rummaged around in Dez's pack, found an old shirt, tore it into strips and formed a sling. She tended the girl as gently as she could, trying to not cause her even more pain. Meanwhile, Dez unearthed the spare water canister and prepared some food for her. Fie drank the water slowly as she had been taught to do when dehydrated. Bit by bit she consumed the food she was given. When she was done Emi gently wiped her face, arms and hands with a cloth to see if there were any further injuries beneath the grime. Other than a few scrapes from tree branches she seemed to be okay. Emi dug in Dez's pack and found his spare t-shirt. Gently she slipped Fie's dress over her head and put the t-shirt on the little girl — it swamped her but at least it was clean. After a while Fie crawled into Emi's lap and went to sleep. Emi and Dez looked at each other over her head, their smiles splitting their faces from ear to ear. They curled up in the blankets and went back to sleep keeping Fie safe between them.

The next morning they fashioned a stretcher out of the blankets and some branches and settled Fie as comfortably as possible. It was a tough walk back but Dez and Emi were so happy it felt like the miles flew by. As they entered the village a crowd gathered and news travelled quickly that the little lost girl had been found alive.

Abe pushed his way through the crowd. 'You found her. Oh, thank God. This way, this way, Lea's going to be so relieved,' said Abe as he led the way to the hospital where Lea was recovering.

They transferred Fie to a cot and after the medical staff had bathed and changed her, Matthew examined her with a scanner. 'We'll need to set the arm. I don't think there's any internal bleeding or she would not have survived. But the arm must be causing her immense pain. We'll get it taken care of right away.'

Can she see her sister first, just for a minute?'

'Yes, of course. I'll go get prepped. Bring her in as soon as possible.'

Abe went to get Lea. He carried her in and set her down by her little sister. Lea burst into tears. 'You're okay, you're okay. I thought you were dead. I was so scared.' Lea fell to her knees beside Fie's cot and gently put her head on Fie's shoulder, away from the injured arm.

Fie put her good arm around Lea and held on tight as tears slid down her cheeks. 'I thought…I thought you were dead too. I thought everybody was dead. I was so, so sc…scared. I thought I was going to be alone forever or, or die in the woods and no…nobody would ever know.'

They clung together, neither of them speaking. Finally, Lea raised her head from her sister's shoulder and brushed the hair from Fie's face. 'We'll look after each other and be okay.'

'Dad?'

Lea raised herself up further and looked at Fie as she shook her head but couldn't bring herself to utter the words. The tears streamed down her face, mingling with those of her sister as she embraced her once again.

Abe leaned over and enveloped them both in a big, gentle bear hug, understanding the turmoil of a family ripped apart. It could not be mended or put back together again. They could heal over time but they could never get back what they'd lost. They were so young, so little; his heart ached for them.

'We need to let Matthew take care of her now, Lea,' he said gently. 'We'll put her cot next to yours after. Come on, let me get you tucked back in. You still need your rest and to be strong for your sister.'

Lea nodded and allowed her self to be led away as Fie was taken to where Matthew was waiting. Abe went to seek out Dez and Emi.

He found them outside, near the hospital, sitting on the grass in the shade of a tree, trying to recover from their long walk carrying the stretcher.

'Can I talk with you two for a minute?' he asked.

'Yeah, of course,' Dez replied.

'Right. I've been thinking. What if I bring Lea and Fie back with me and kind of adopt them? Their dad's gone and their village mostly wiped out. A new place has gotta be good for them.'

'Hmmm, as long as they want to go,' Dez nodded. 'Might be good for you too…a new family of sorts,' he added. He glanced at Emi to judge her reaction as he draped his arm around her shoulder and pulled her more tightly into an embrace. 'Be good for everyone.'

'Thought you'd be cool with it. I'll talk to them soon, after they've recovered a bit, see what they think.'

Dez and Emi both nodded their approval.

'Would it also be okay, if Lea and Fie want to go, if I leave soon? I know there's still work to do here but if you think you can manage I kind of want to get them settled.'

'Yep, the worst is over for now, I hope. We'll make do without you,' Dez replied.

'Right. I'll go the hospital, wait 'til Doc's worked his magic. Thanks for going out for her. I thought to go but didn't want to leave Lea…I just couldn't.'

'It's okay, Abe. We understand. Thank goodness we found Fie alive. It's a miracle, given the circumstances,' said Emi.

Abe nodded and left.

Dez and Emi stayed in the shade of the tree, content that they had found Fie, tired from their long trek. Dez wound his arms around Emi and held her tight, grounded by the comfort after so much turmoil. Emi felt like an extension of himself. Gently he ran his fingers through her hair and rested his head on top of hers.

She leaned back and smiled up at him.

He was amazed to find such happiness amongst so much pain.

Abe returned to the hospital to wait. He slid down the wall at the entrance and sat cross-legged on the floor. The place was quiet except for the occasional groan from someone in a cot. The first-aid team moved silently amongst the patients in the dim light taking care of their needs. Abe rested his head in his hands and heaved a massive sigh. At least they had the help of the Fringe doctors this time. Occasionally he glanced at the doors that led to the room they'd sectioned off as a surgery, willing them to open. He knew the break had been a bad one but it felt like the surgery went on and on.

Finally, Matthew emerged from the operating room, his smock spattered with blood, his eyes shadowed with fatigue.

'We've set the arm and checked her over. There doesn't seem to be anything else significantly wrong other than minor dehydration. How she managed to find water and food with an arm in that state is beyond me, especially given her age.'

Abe nodded. 'Yeah, she's a trooper,' he said, too relieved to think of much else to say.

'We also found that she doesn't seem to have any markings on her body. She said Lea is the same. We were looking for bruising and fractures, thinking she might have been beaten. What we noticed, and correct me if I'm wrong, but we didn't see any evidence of faded imprints. Don't all the members of the Network still have old tattoo imprints? I mean you haven't been able to completely eliminate them yet, have you? You still have faint blue hues on some part of your body, correct?'

'Yeah, as far as I know.'

'Interesting. Well, we'll check Lea out tomorrow and then once the girls have recovered from their ordeal we may take blood samples and do some genetic testing. Try to figure out why they don't have the imprints. If that's okay?' Matthew asked, almost as an afterthought.

'I guess. Maybe. First I need to take them home and make sure they're going to be alright.'

'Home? Are they going to live with you then?'

'Yep. I've asked Dez if I can kind of adopt them and he thought it'd be good, as long as the girls are fine with it.'

'Good for you. That's very kind,' said Matthew with a smile. 'I better get back in there. Still lots of others that need tending. We'll bring Fie out soon and put her next to her sister.'

'Thanks, Doc. I'll go sit with Lea,' said Abe as he turned to go.

Lea and Fie recovered slowly over the week. It was amazing what rest, water and good food could do. Fie's arm remained in a sling with splints, but she didn't complain. Abe spent as much time with them as he could, hoping they would grow to like and trust him and get used to having him around.

At the end of the week he approached their bedsides and took a seat. 'I've something I was wanting to ask you and see what you think,' he said.

They looked up at him and smiled encouragingly. 'Hi, Abe, what's up?' asked Lea.

'About five years ago I lost my family in a raid, when I was only fourteen, so not a whole lot older than what you are now.' His gaze rested on Lea. 'And since you've lost your dad, I wondered…what do you say to coming back with me so I can look after you both?

There's not much left of your village anymore and I would care for you like you were my own little sisters. What do you think?' he said, his speech coming out in a rush. He held his breath as he waited for their reply.

Lea looked at Fie. Abe saw Fie give a small nod of her head. A smile hovered at the corners of her mouth. Lea turned back to Abe and answered for them both. 'We've been wondering what would happen to us. Coming to live with you would be nice. Better than anything else we've been able to think of.' Lea's eyes lit up and her mouth curved into a smile.

Abe's grin stretched from ear to ear. He took them in his arms and gave them a gentle hug. The girls hugged him back and smiled at each other across his back.

'Right. You okay if we head to Sector A tomorrow? I'd like to get you home. My shelter isn't much but our valley is nice. I think you'll like it.'

They nodded. 'Can…can we go back to our shelter before we go and see if there's anything left undamaged?' Lea asked in hushed tones.

'Of course,' Abe nodded. 'I'll go with you. Might be a bit upsetting for you but it would be good to look. Or I can just go if you don't want to.'

'That's okay, we can go too. It will be our goodbye,' Lea squared her shoulders as she let out a sigh.

'There's one more thing…and if you're not okay with it that's fine…the doctor, Matthew, whose been looking after you, noticed that neither of you two have any imprints. He wondered why and if you would be okay for him to take a blood sample to do some testing, see if he can figure it out.'

Lea glanced at Fie, eyebrows raised, her forehead furrowed. Fie lifted her shoulders in response but didn't say anything.

'Will it hurt?'

'I don't think so. Just a bit of a pin-prick with the needle. That should be all.'

'Hmmm. I guess. Matthew has been so nice to us, so — ,' Lea shrugged her shoulders and left the sentence hanging. 'Our dad didn't have any marks either.'

'Really! Right, I'll let Matthew know that you're okay with it as long as he's *extra* gentle with the needle,' Abe smiled at them as he ruffled their hair. 'You two rest now. I'll come back tomorrow to take you to your shelter and then we'll head out,' he added before heading off to find Matthew.

Matthew was just coming out of the operating theatre again, looking quite exhausted.

'The girls are okay for you to take that blood sample. We'll leave tomorrow, so maybe take care of it in the morning. They also said their dad didn't have any markings,' said Abe.

'Interesting. Thanks for asking for me. I'll take the sample back to New York and let you know what I find out.'

'Do you think you might find something that will take away the markings from the rest of us? Be nice to not have anymore. Takes a long time to get rid of things that have been passed on I guess.'

'If there's something in their genes that is cleaning up the imprint toxins, or somehow overriding the gene that carries the tattoo, and can be replicated and used for others I'll certainly try to find out. We've a great group of experts dedicated to research. If anyone can find something to eliminate the toxins it would be them,' answered Matthew.

'That'd be great. Thanks, Doc.'

Matthew nodded and headed wearily back into the surgery.

Abe wandered off to pack up for tomorrow's departure, deep in thought. It had been one heck of a week. The Fringe had been such a huge help. He couldn't believe how lucky they'd been to have them come along right when they did. They'd saved so many lives and provided lots of food. They'd even flown supplies out to rebuild the shelters. The medical staff had worked tirelessly and uncomplainingly in the rough conditions. He was sure nobody in the Network would mind helping them out now for whatever they wanted. He knew for certain that he owed them such a debt of gratitude. With Lea and Fie to look after it was like having part of his family restored to him and some of his guilt mitigated.

The next morning Abe took Lea and Fie to sort through the rubble of their home. As the girls picked through the charred bits of wood they found pieces of what had once been their beds, tables and chairs. They pushed aside fragments of crockery and other household items that were almost unrecognisable, not worth packing.

Fie gathered a handful of dry grass and brushed the ash aside. A tiny hand emerged as she swept at the grey dust. She reached down and pulled her doll out of the chaos. It was still in one piece, clothed in its little blue dress, hair tousled. Fie gently removed the dust from the doll. The cheery expression was timeless once the fine layer of cinder was brushed away. Fie placed her doll in her bag.

Lea routed around in what had been the kitchen and found an old iron fry pan and a few pieces of cutlery. She placed them in the bottom of her bag. She shoved aside a few jagged lengths of timber and made her way to the other side of the shelter where the bedroom had been. As she glanced down at her feet all covered in soot she saw the corner of a picture. She bent down and unearthed a partially charred drawing of their dad and mom. She placed it in her bag with the other meagre belongings, being careful so that it wouldn't be crushed.

Lea and Fie stood forlornly in the middle of the wreckage and looked around with eyes that glistened, their mouths clamped firmly shut. 'We're ready to go now, Abe. There's nothing left for us here,' Lea said stoically.

'You're brave girls,' he said, feeling very proud as he shouldered the small bags of treasures they had collected. He led them away from the destruction. 'Come on then. The Hovercraft is waiting.'

'We're going in the Hovercraft — that big thing that goes up in the sky?' asked Fie.

'We are. You okay with that?'

Lea and Fie nodded, their eyes as big as saucers. 'Oh, yes please.'

'Right you are, come on then.'

Peter lowered the ramp and they boarded the Hovercraft. The girls looked around them in wonderment. The inside of the flying machine was much bigger than they had expected. Even Abe could stand up to his full height. There were rows of comfy looking seats grouped in fours around a central table and beside each row of seats there were little oval windows. They quietly took seats next to the windows, facing each other across the table, as the Hovercraft lifted into the air. Lea and Fie immediately plastered their faces against the glass. 'Everything is getting so little. Are we really so small?' asked Lea.

'Guess so. From up here anyway. Never feel that way when I'm on the ground. Do you?'

They both looked at him and shook their heads and then pressed their faces back up against the glass, not wanting to miss a thing.

'There's an awful lot of yellow on the earth isn't there?' commented Lea after they had been flying for a while. Their burned out village had long since disappeared into the distance. Since then it seemed they had seen little other than the rippling fields of grasslands.

'Yeah, I guess a lot of the planet's too hot for the it to be any other colour.'

'We'll be descending soon,' announced Peter. 'See to your left.'

'Look, we're coming to our valley, do you see the green with the river running through it?' Abe pointed out the window.

'Oh, how pretty. So many different colours of green and the river looks big, even from here,' said Fie.

'It was a good find, a nice place to live. And we're further north — further from where the Blues live, so they haven't found us…yet,' said Abe, muttering the last word so the girls wouldn't hear it. 'I hope you'll like it.'

'We will,' they both stated at the same moment and then smiled at each other.

The Hovercraft landed and Abe led the girls off the craft. He shook Peter's hand and thanked him for the ride. Peter then turned to the girls and held his hands out, palms up. In each of his hands was a pin in the shape of wings. 'These are what pilots wear on their shirts. Maybe one day you girls could learn to be pilots,' he said as he smiled down at their upturned faces.

'Oh, could we?' asked Fie in a breathless whisper.

'Yes, when you're all grown up. I'll even teach you if you like.'

'Oh, yes please,' they said in unison.

'It's a date. Until then, look after Abe. He's a good guy,' Peter instructed with a grin. 'I'd best be off. Need to take more supplies back for the survivors. Best of luck Abe! You truly are a good egg.'

'Thanks, Peter,' he said with a wave as he turned and led the girls away. 'My place isn't great, but we'll fix it up and make it into a nice home for you both. I promise.'

'Can we help?'

'You bet. Couldn't do it without you,' replied Abe as he ruffled their ginger hair.

NINE

Dez made his way to Sam's village at Sector D, broke the news of Sam's death and helped decide on who was to be the new leader. They chose Liz. She was bright, efficient, kind but tough, and had worked with Sam, so knew how things were done.

'Congrats, Liz. I've no doubt you'll miss Sam a lot in the days to come but I really believe you're the right person for the job.'

'Thanks, Dez. I'll do my best. Try to be a leader that Sam would've been proud of,' Liz replied as she kicked at a pebble with her toe. They were standing in the shade of a tree just outside the tiny meeting hut of Sector D. She heaved a sigh of despair, shook her head and looked up at Dez, her eyes swimming in unshed tears. 'Although I feel pretty done-in at the moment. It's the shock I guess. Can't believe he's gone and suddenly I'm in charge,' she paused and then added, 'I really thought you'd pick Tom to be leader.'

Dez frowned as the dust motes caused by the motion of Liz's foot settled on their shoes. *It really was dry out. Could they change things?* 'I considered him. He's great but I don't think now's the right time, given…,' he trailed off. 'He had a chip on his shoulder before…and I need someone very levelheaded. Things are probably about to change quite a bit. It could be a big transition pretty quickly I'm afraid.'

'Why? What's up?'

'The Fringe want our help,' he stated.

'*Our* help! For what?'

Dez hesitated, hating to burden her so soon after picking her as leader. But, once again, he had little choice. 'From what I've been told…to…uhhh…save the planet and the human race,' he said with a crooked smile as he ran his hand through his hair. 'No big deal!'

'Seriously?'

'Yep, afraid so! Apparently there's not much time to waste.'

'Not sure what to say. But they helped us so much after this last raid, and the raid was so much more devastating than usual, I feel like we owe them something in return.'

'Yeah, quite a few Network members feel that way. I still feel reserved about committing all of the Network, but…'

'If they really need us, what choice do we have?'

'Exactly! I feel like I have a gun pointed at my head. I went to New York you know, their main city, learned lots, saw lots I've never seen before, but I still don't have a clear idea of exactly what they expect of us.'

'Guess they'll let us know eventually.'

'Since you're new to leadership I kind of wanted to give you a heads-up.'

'Thanks. It's a lot to think about,' Liz said. 'But we'll survive,' she shrugged her shoulders.

'One can only hope.'

'True.'

'Where's Tom by the way? I thought the leadership decision might best come from me rather than you having to break it to him.'

'Don't know. He's been acting kind of strange since his mom died.'

'Yeah, I can relate.'

'To be expected I guess — his behaviour I mean. But he's also been disappearing. I thought maybe he was out hunting. Sometimes he comes back with a deer for us to butcher. But if I ask him any questions he gets all surly — and I'm his best friend.' Liz explained. She paused for breath and added, 'And the last time he was missing was during the raid!'

'Hmmm!' Dez furrowed his eyebrows, the extra burden of worry etched itself on his face. 'Well, I'm extra glad we picked you as leader then. That seems kind of…'

'I'm not sure what to think. He and Sam were having quite a few arguments lately.'

'I wish I could've talked to Sam more before he died. In the end he was muttering things that didn't make sense.'

'Don't know what I'm going to do without Sam. Not sure I know where to begin.' Liz pushed the pebble around with her toe and stared at the ground. A few tears escaped, creating little splatters of dark on the dry, dusty ground.

'I'm sorry to put so much on you right away. Whatever help you need transitioning to leadership, just say the word.'

Liz nodded and rolled the pebble beneath her foot, creating patterns in the dirt.

'I wasn't sure if you knew or not — did you hear that Tom's uncle was killed by the Blues in the raid? His body was found on the outskirts of Sector C,' Dez said.

Liz's head snapped up, surprise stamped on her features. She brushed her arm across her eyes, trying to regain control of her emotions. 'He was the only family member Tom had left,' she stated. She paused to draw breath. 'Although, in all honesty, I doubt Tom will care.'

'No, I don't suppose he will.' Dez cleared his throat, the dust making it scratchy and dry. He gazed into the distance, but he didn't notice the landscape before him. 'When I was a kid, Sam, Tom and I used to hang out together, back when we lived in the same village, and I remember thinking, even back then, that his uncle was mean. I wondered if he was abusive. Don't know for sure. Either way, it was never a good relationship.'

'The whole family history is pretty rotten.'

Tom's uncle had lived with them off and on over the years. His dad had died in the last raid, trying to defend their crops. His mom had never recovered from the injuries the Blues had inflicted on her as she tried to defend her daughter. She didn't say much after the death of her husband and daughter. No one could figure out if she was unhappy, scared out of her mind, or both.

'Hmmm. If you see Tom, send him my way. I'll stick around for a couple days to help out,' offered Dez. 'What happened to his mom? I mean how did she die? Last I heard…'

Liz drew a deep breath and looked directly into Dez's eyes as she stated, 'His mom was pregnant …'

'Pregnant? Who…? Oh shit.'

'I don't think Tom knew…at least not until recently. She wore these loose dresses. I mean you do in this heat. They're comfortable. But — you couldn't tell. Then when Sam was at the leadership meeting, Tom found her collapsed on the living room floor…bleeding. Apparently she was about six months along. She miscarried and died from the blood-loss.'

'Crap. That *sucks*.'

'Tom said she had bruises that looked like…fingermarks on her breasts — her dress was torn —' whispered Liz.

'Oh God,' Dez ran his hands through his hair.

'Yeah. People heard Tom having a massive argument with his uncle. Then his uncle disappeared. And Tom …'

'How did I not know *any* of this?'

'Well, Tom has *always* kept things to himself. The rest of us could only guess at what was going on. Sam was trying to deal with the uncle before he left for the meeting, hoping the situation wouldn't escalate, but then there was the meeting and the raid happened and you were away…' she shrugged her shoulders.

'Poor Tom,' muttered Dez as he ran his hands through his already disheveled hair.

'I'll try to keep you up to date with things. For now I'll focus on getting the damaged shelters rebuilt,' said Liz. 'I guess more homes will be headed-up by the oldest child in a family! Poor kids!' Liz continued to push the rock around with her toe. 'Helping to save the planet will be a good distraction for everyone right about now,' Liz joked, trying to lighten the mood. She turned to leave, head down.

Dez watched her out of sight as she kicked the pebble along and wiped her arms across her eyes, one after the other. He turned away; shoulders slumped!

'Hey, Abe, how's things?' Dez knocked on the wall beside the open front door of Abe's cottage.

'Dez. Hi, come on in. Yeah, pretty good I guess. What do you think?' Abe waved his hand around at his freshly spruced up cabin.

'Much improved. The girls help you with all this?'

'Sure did. Smart little things they are. Loads of good ideas.'

'I'll say! The place looks great,' said Dez as he surveyed the tiny cabin. The walls and floorboards had been sanded back so the golden pine colour gleamed in the early morning light. The ceiling had been whitewashed, as had the table and chairs that Abe had restored. The long grasses that were now abundant on the earth had been collected, beaten until soft and then woven into a mat for the floor and a seat for the couch frame that Abe had built. 'Maybe they could come to my place next and give it a make-over,' said Dez with a grin.

'Could happen. They're pretty keen and it keeps them from dwelling.'

'How are they settling in?'

'Pretty good I think. Sometimes I hear them crying at night but that's normal I guess and they seem okay by day. Did you hear about them not having imprints and the Doc doing some tests to see why not?'

'Yeah, I heard. Any results yet?'

'Nah, not yet. But I'll keep you posted.'

'Okay, well I just ducked in to say we have a meeting coming up. Need to discuss what we'll be doing to help the Fringe.'

'Right. Count me in. They helped us so much it seems only fair.' Abe smiled at Dez.

'I've sent Hoverbirds to the other villages to let them know. Meeting's a couple weeks from now. The Fringe will be here too to tell us what they need,' said Dez, as the girls walked into the room. 'Hi, girls. Great job fixing the place.'

They beamed up at him.

'Thanks,' said Lea. 'Abe let us decide what we wanted to do and then he made everything or traded for it. It was so much fun.'

'Don't suppose you want to come fix up my place do you?'

'Oh, could we?'

'Sure,' said Dez as he winked at Abe. 'How about tomorrow, if you're not too busy?'

'Could we Abe, please?'

'Don't see why not,' Abe grinned at the girls and ruffled their hair.

'See you then,' Dez said as he gave them a wave good-bye.

They held the meeting in the dining hall. It was the only structure big enough to fit everyone. All of the benches around each table in the long, narrow room were full. The bright sunlight slanting through the windows reflected dully off the timber walls. The hall was hot and stuffy, crowded and deafening. Various members of the Fringe were there as well as the leaders from each village in the Network and the teams they'd picked.

Dez walked to the front of the room, stood on the temporary platform, brought his fingers to his mouth and let out a piercing whistle.

'Hey, everyone,' he said loudly as the room quieted down. 'Over the last couple weeks you've all received messages outlining the basics of what's happening to our planet and how we hope to save our world. The Fringe are here to fill us in on the details. We'll then take a vote as to whether we're willing to help or not and if so, discuss what it is we'll be doing. I'll now pass the meeting over to Peter and Elizabeth from the Fringe.'

Dez hopped down from the podium and went to stand beside Emi who was leaned up against the wall at the side of the hall. 'Here we go,' he whispered, as he linked his fingers through hers.

She squeezed his fingers and turned to watch the crowd as Elizabeth took the stage.

'Hello. My name's Elizabeth Canterbury. I, and my husband, Peter, are part of the Fringe leadership in New York. Our city mayor is Edward Black and we have a panel of twenty of us who work with him. I'll do my best to explain what we know. Peter will fill you in on what we hope to accomplish with your help. We'll, of course, answer any questions.'

A hand shot up at the back of the room. 'How many of us do you expect to need?'

'Well, everybody in one way or another. Some will stay in their villages, others will be out in the field and others stationed in New York or possibly even England.'

There was a general hum in the room as people shifted in their seats and exchanged glances.

'We'll answer questions later, for now let me explain. As you're more than aware, it's extremely hot most of the time. The earth is 4.5 degrees warmer than we'd like. Given the population has been drastically reduced, and we can now rely on solar, wind and tidal power, we're no longer polluting the atmosphere. However, we've not been able to undo much of the damage already caused, thus the world keeps getting warmer. We need to stop this trend and reverse it.'

The noise level in the room increased as people exclaimed over the idea of controlling the earth's temperature. Benches scraped and people fidgeted. Trying to survive from day to day had filled their every waking moment. Thinking on a global scale was incomprehensible.

'Quiet please,' Elizabeth yelled and then cleared her throat as people turned to listen. 'Again, as you know, a large portion of the world's soil is contaminated. Chemicals sprays used to protect crops made their way into the soil, accumulated over time, eventually causing the soil to be so contaminated that it could no longer produce anything. A further problem of the chemicals was for wildlife. Bees and other creatures that depended on crops, especially fruit blossoms and such, died in droves. Natural pollination almost ceased to exist. Thus again crops were threatened. This was the beginning of the world famine that hit in 2120 and caused the deaths of millions upon millions of people. We've found a way to make the soil healthy again.'

At this the room erupted into conversation. People talked over one another. Elizabeth was ignored — such concepts to big to grasp.

Dez watched as everyone digested the information. With so many people, and emotions running high, the hall was starting to get very stuffy, even though all the windows were open. He released Emi's fingers and made his way to the back of the room to open the door, hoping for a cross-breeze, even if it was a warm one. He returned to Emi's side and let out another piercing whistle before linking his fingers back through Emi's.

She smiled up at him and inched closer, shoulders touching.

Elizabeth raised her hands for silence. 'I know it seems insurmountable but if we work together it is achievable. Finally, there are the seeds themselves. The genetically modified crops that were meant to fight disease, and increase output efficiency, resulted in sterile crops. They didn't emit the correct amounts of oxygen and carbon dioxide into the air that was necessary for atmospheric balance, and when the crops were ploughed back into the ground after harvest they did not replenish the earth. So we need to plant clean crops — crops that help replenish the atmosphere, sustain wildlife and us. Lastly, the Blues will want what we have but if they destroy what we create then they'll destroy us all. We'll need heightened security.'

Again the room erupted into conversation. Peter and Elizabeth exchanged places. As Peter faced the audience he took a sip of water from the glass on the table beside him. His throat was parched. The cross-breeze was minimal and the room was becoming increasingly stuffy. Peter put up his hands to silence the crowd, the sweat stains under his arms evident, but there was little he could do to lower his body temperature. The sun would soon start to set and give them some reprieve from the heat. 'I'm sure you all have lots of questions. Elizabeth has filled you in on where we're at and how we got here,' said Peter as he stopped to take another sip of water. 'Now I'd like to outline our plans.'

Dez and Emi watched as the crowd settled down to listen. Almost everyone had water with them and many had cloths they were using to wipe away the sweat. If anything was going to make them want to help the Fringe it was the rising heat in the dining hall. Life had always been hard for his people; it was almost impossible to imagine it improving — or getting even worse. He wiped his sweaty palm on his shorts and then grasped Emi's hand once again as he smiled and winked at her.

'I won't bother getting too detailed,' said Peter. 'Most of you only need worry about the area you're assigned to. Climate control is our first priority. The basic idea is simple but *critical* to our survival. We need to produce clouds and rain. Clouds block the sun giving the earth a chance to cool. Rain also cools the ground and provides nutrients for the soil. We need help building condensers and solar panels that when combined can put clouds into the sky. That is project one — known as The Cloud.' Peter paused to take another sip of water but this time the audience remained silent, wondering what else he had to say.

'The *second* project is creating pure soil,' he continued. 'We've developed a microorganism that when put into the soil, spreads and eliminates the toxins. We need to take it far as possible to create as much clean soil as we can. The *third* project is producing clean crops. We have toxin-free seeds. Once we have healthy soil, and rainfall, we'll need to plant the seeds. Again, as far as we can reach.' Peter took another sip of water and glanced over at Dez and Emi. It was difficult to gage from their expressions what they thought of the reaction of the people in the room. They stood shoulder to shoulder, hands held fast, a united front. But were they united *with* the Fringe or against them?

'Finally, we need security. Everywhere. We've chosen secure locations for The Cloud. However, if things get any worse, the Blues will venture further in their desperation to find food. If they destroy one of the main Cloud structures, it may be too late to reverse the earth's heating phase and we'll perish,' he stated, as he downed the last of his water. 'We'll now take questions.'

The first hand shot up. 'How long will this take and how long until it's too late?'

'It'll take three to five years to get everything functioning and to start having an effect. We probably only have fifteen, maybe twenty years before it's too late.'

'That's cutting it a bit fine don't you think?'

'I do. But it's taken until now to figure out how to do everything on the scale that is necessary.'

Another hand shot up. 'You've said what you expect us to do but what'll you be doing?'

'Many of us'll be working alongside you. But we have one more project that is vitally important. The re-populating of species that are almost extinct, such as bees, and re-introducing some that are already extinct.'

'How'll you do that?'

'We have the DNA of extinct animals. Scientists were smart enough to take DNA samples when they knew they were looking at the last surviving animals of that species. We've those samples and the ability to re-create those animals from their DNA. But it's a challenging process that'll take years.'

Another hand went up. 'Are you sure your plans will work and we'll all die if we don't do anything?'

'Well, there is one thing I've learned from living and that's nothing is ever certain. Having said that, we're fairly positive — unless the earth suddenly starts to cool on its own, which it's done in the past. But I think it would be too late for all of us even if the earth suddenly did start to cool.'

'Can we choose what we want to do?'

'Many can. You know your own skills. It's up to you to decide where you'd be most useful. Some we'll hand-pick for certain jobs according to their skills and our overall needs.'

'We're pretty used to looking after ourselves. Are we now just going to be working for you?'

'Some, yes. But for the most part, we'll train you and then let you be in charge of yourselves, much like you are now. It'll be a new beginning for us all. We'll have to check-in to make sure things are going as planned but we want co-workers not indentured labourers.'

'When and how are we to decide?'

'I'll ask Dez to fill you in on the rest. Dez,' said Peter as he stepped from the stage and headed over to lean against the wall near an open window.

Dez returned to the platform. Everyone was silent, waiting to hear what their chosen leader would have to say.

'I know it's a lot to take in. I was quite overwhelmed when I first met the Fringe and heard all that you just heard. I tried with the messages sent in the Hover-birds to give you time to think before tonight's meeting. Now we'll clear the room, bring in more dining tables and have dinner. Please take the time to discuss things and ask any other questions you have. Once dinner is over, the Fringe will retire and we'll further discuss the situation amongst ourselves. At the end of the evening I'm hoping to take a vote. Slips of paper will be provided. Please mark 'Y' for yes you're willing to help or 'N' for no, if you prefer to carry on as we are. There's a box by the door to put your paper in.'

'What if some want to help and some don't?'

'We would like it to be unanimous, but it'll be a case of majority vote wins the day. If you feel very strongly one way or the other and would like to discuss things further in private then please also add your name to the paper. Now if you'll help bring in the tables, we'll have a meal together.'

The room was cleared, more tables brought in and the food served. It was a very noisy meal as everyone chatted amongst themselves, many taking their plates and sitting at different tables over the course of the evening. Once the Fringe had left and they'd further clarified any remaining issues at the final meeting, they filed out and dropped their bit of paper in the box by the door.

Dez took the box to the table at the back of the room and started to stack the bits of paper into 'Yes' and 'No' piles. The 'Yes' pile grew; the 'No' pile remained empty. He looked up at Peter and Elizabeth, who had returned, and Emi, who had remained behind, 'Well, there you have it, an unanimous 'yes'. You can't ask for more than that,' said Dez, his innards doing somersaults as he contemplated the changes that were about to be thrust upon them. He was unsure if he felt elated or despairing but moving forward was his only option. Their course was now set — joined to that of the Fringe.

'I must say I'm relieved. Don't know what we'd have done if we had a lot of 'no' votes,' said Elizabeth

'So, now what?'

'Can we call another meeting for the day after tomorrow, give everyone a bit of time to digest this information, and then start assigning areas,' suggested Peter.

Dez looked up at Peter. 'This is all going to move very quickly from here on out isn't it?'

'Yes, I'm afraid it is. It would've been nice to have been at this point fifty years ago but we weren't ready.'

'It would've been nice to never have been at this point at all,' Emi chimed in.

'True,' agreed Dez. 'Right, well, I'll send a message to the guest quarters and let them know and see you the day after tomorrow, say here, at nine a.m.?'

They nodded their agreement and left. Dez locked up and as he turned to head back to his shelter he found Emi waiting for him.

'Well, what do you think?' she asked.

'I think life is going to be very different but that we don't have much choice. I hope it's true that they want to work side by side and not enslave us. They do obviously need us though, so if things are not satisfactory for the Network then at least I have negotiating power.'

'And we've a strong leadership team…and I know they're behind you one hundred percent,' Emi replied.

Dez looked down at Emi and smiled. 'I've missed you.'

'Same.'

'Do you want to come to my place tomorrow for dinner? Lea and Fie, with a *bit* of help from Abe, have fixed up my shelter. It's pretty nice now and I've some good food from the Fringe. I'm not a *bad* cook,' he said, giving her his lopsided smile.

'Sure,' she grinned in reply. 'You've got yourself a date,' she gave him a quick peck on the cheek and turned to head back to the guest quarters.

CHAPTER NINE

TEN

Emi was having breakfast the next morning in the guest quarters kitchenette when Elizabeth poked her head in the open door and asked if she could join her.

'Yes, of course,' said Emi, suddenly feeling like a bug caught in a spider's web. Why she couldn't say but there was no escape.

'Since the vote was an unanimous yes, I have something in particular I would like to ask you before we get to tomorrow's meeting,' said Elizabeth as she avoided any pretence of small talk and came straight to the point.

'Oh. Sure. Go on.'

'We'd like for you to come to New York to be fully trained in health, specialising in research. The Network trust you and we feel there'll be a need to look into the genetic differences between us and the Network,' Elizabeth stated.

'Oh!' said Emi, taken aback. 'I'd thought that I'd remain with the Network, working alongside Dez as one of the leaders.'

'Eventually that would be an option. But, you see, everything we do will affect health — the new soil, the new crops — and we need to study the effect it has on people. We know how all the contaminated crops effected people in the past…the end result. They developed health problems — vitamin deficiency, allergies, some quite severe. Kids started to have mental disorders — socially, or with learning, or behaviour, acting out, getting more violent. Turned out that the modified food, combined with pesticides and additives, inhibited certain brain functions. Not a lot, like with a stroke, but just a bit so that it was hard to trace. Over time it accumulated in the genes so babies were born with deficiencies. Add in the imprint toxins and medication and you had a population in a very poor state. When the famine hit, many died. The Blues are the remnant that never changed their lifestyle and so have inherited all the toxic genes. The Fringe are already healthy so we don't expect to change much. The Network is much better off than it used to be but there are still trace toxins in your body that make some of you ill or tired occasionally, correct?'

'Yes, I guess so, some more than others.'

'Well, we would like to finally get you back to being completely healthy. We're not only trying to save the planet but also the human race. The Network makes up a large segment of the humanity and, quite truthfully, your wellbeing is important to our work. We'd like to study the effect of reversing toxicity. As you're the leader of the group that's in charge of health for the Network we thought you the best candidate for further training.'

'Would you be bringing anyone else from the Network to New York?' asked Emi. The thought of being alone with these people, trapped in New York, gave her the chills.

'Yes, we thought Jax would be a good candidate for being trained in crop production and there's be a handful of others we thought could take up key positions.'

'How long would you need me for?'

'A year or so, maybe two, I would think.'

'A year!' she exclaimed, feeling the noose tighten around her throat.

'I realise it's a long time to be away from your home but you could come back to visit. I'm sure we can schedule an occasional visit using one of the Hovercrafts.'

'Can I think about this?' she asked, knowing she was just mouthing the words as a delay tactic. She needed to feel like she still had some vestige of control over her life.

'Of course. I just wanted to give you a heads up before the meeting tomorrow. We do need some key people in New York. We'll also have some of our Fringe members at the Network. A bit of a swap if you will,' Elizabeth smiled and took her leave.

Live in New York! Why, though they professed to working together side-by-side, did she feel that she was not really being given a choice. They expected her to co-operate with their wishes and say 'yes'.

What would Dez say when she told him? She had been looking forward to dinner with him, now she felt the time would be bittersweet. Their time together always seemed to be tainted by something.

Emi knocked at Dez's door. The door swung open and Dez bowed her in.

'Welcome to my castle, my lady,' he said with a massive grin.

'Thank you, kind sir,' she replied laughingly, happy to see him so relaxed.

He pulled her into the room, took her in his arms and kissed her firmly on the mouth. 'And what do you think of my humble abode?' he asked.

'I don't really know, I wasn't given much of a chance to see before being manhandled by the king of the castle.'

'So sorry, my lady,' he said as he spun her around so she could survey the room.

The whole place had been given a fresh coat of whitewash. The kitchen was fitted out with shelving and a wooden countertop and the table and chairs had been mended and sanded back to a lovely smooth finish. In the living room there was a new couch. It had a basic timber frame with woven grass for a seat and backrest. Above the couch there was a shelf with candles and a little wooden truck on it. Emi's eyes stopped at the truck. It looked like a child's toy, something left over from when Dez was a little boy. It appeared to be old and well loved. To the right she could see through the door to the bedroom; someone had made a bed frame and a new cover in dark blue for the straw mattress. She averted her gaze, the sight of the bed brought a slight flush to her cheeks. 'Abe and the girls did a great job. It's very homey…masculine but cozy,' she smiled up at him, her heart skipped a beat at the intimacy of the moment.

'Glad you like it. It's a vast improvement on the previous dingy grey colour don't you think?

And now if you'll take a seat, dinner is ready. Would you like some wine Peter and Elizabeth brought me a bottle. They make it, apparently.'

'Yes, please. I really enjoyed the wine at the banquet.'

'I'll say you did. That was quite a kiss you gave me on the balcony after all that wine you'd had,' he said with a grin.

'Are you hoping for a repeat performance?' Emi's lips twitched up in a smirk and her eyes had a mischievous glint.

'Hmm. Maybe.'

Emi took a sip of wine before she leaned across the table and gave Dez a lingering kiss.

'Mmm. Not bad for a warm up,' he responded. 'Now eat your food before the wine goes to your head,' he admonished her as he shook his head in feigned dismay.

'I thought that was the idea,' she replied, enjoying the light-hearted banter.

'Maybe a bit, but I don't really want you passed out on my new sofa.'

'Yes sir,' she grinned at him and gave a salute before tucking into her meal. Her mind strayed to Elizabeth. 'Actually I do have something I need to talk to you about.'

'Sounds serious. Is it something to do with the Fringe?'

'Yep.'

'Can it wait until later, or even tomorrow after the meeting? I'd love an evening with just you. Be nice to pretend, for a few hours at least, that everything isn't about to change.'

'Yes, alright, it can wait,' she said, feeling relieved at not having to ruin the evening with serious conversation.'This is *so* good. What is it?'

'It's called spaghetti. Elizabeth gave me the noodles, which they somehow create out of spinach and told me how to make it. It's a mix of deer meat, onion, whatever vegetables are available, and then you add in diced tomatoes and herbs…I used rosemary and some oregano which Elizabeth also gave me. The cheese for putting on top was made by Amy. Glad you like it as it was a bit of an experiment.'

'It's delicious. Nice change from squirrel or rabbit and plain old vegetables and potatoes. The wine's good too, not that I have a lot to compare it to, but I wouldn't say no to a refill,' she grinned at him with a twinkle in her eyes. The frivolous atmosphere was intoxicating. 'Thank you.' She leaned across the table and gave him another kiss as he refilled their wine glasses.

'You keep doing that we're going to have to move to the sofa. There's too much table between us,' Dez said with a grin.

'Sofa it is,' Emi agreed wholeheartedly as Dez took the empty dishes to the sink while she moved the glasses and wine bottle to the newly refurbished coffee table. The golden pine colour of the table gleamed in the candlelight as the light beyond the windows faded to dusk. The mellow atmosphere brought a smile to Emi's face.

Dez came to sit beside her. He put his arm around her shoulders and passed her wine glass with his free hand before taking his from the table. 'I feel so at peace when you're around. I missed you when you were back at your village.'

Emi leaned into him. 'Same,' she said as she planted a feather-light kiss on his neck.

'You keep doing that — must be the wine,' Dez said playfully. He grinned down into her upturned face.

'Can't help it,' she admitted unashamedly.

'It's been so long since I've had anyone to *really* care about.' His voice was husky as he tightened his embrace and ran his hand through the glossy strands of her hair. 'Not since my sister Isi died,' he paused before whispering, 'I always seem to lose the people I love.'

Emi sat back and looked at Dez, her expression suddenly serious. 'You're not going to lose me!' she said. She put down their wine glasses and turned back to face him. She saw fear reflected in his eyes. 'You're *not* going to lose me!' she whispered before bringing her lips to his, demanding a kiss in return that was more than just playful.

Her arms went around his neck. The Fringe and all its demands forgotten for the time being.

'Hey, sleeping beauty, breakfast is ready.'

Emi emerged slowly from her slumber, trying to remember where she was. The memories came flooding back. She grinned from ear to ear as she pulled her shirt over her head and followed her nose out to the kitchen. The smell of coffee and toast was heavenly. She was starving.

'We'll be late if you stay in bed much longer.'

'Not *entirely* my fault,' she said as she gave Dez a good morning kiss.

'Now, cut it out or we won't make it to the meeting at all,' he smiled down into her upturned face and reluctantly disentangled himself from her arms.

'Oh crap. The meeting, right! Ahhh, I really need to talk to you before we go.'

'The serious thing I put off from last night?'

'Yep, and I'm pretty sure you're not going to like it much.' She hated to bring the laughter and intimacy to such an abrupt end.

'Go on.' He passed her coffee and toast and jam.

'Well, Elizabeth came to see me yesterday, wanting to give me a heads up before the meeting, and offered me a position.' Emi stifled a yawn before sipping her coffee. She met Dez's eyes overtop of her cup.

'What kind of position?' Dez asked, doubt creeping into his voice, causing it to drop an octave.

'They want me in New York doing research; learning about how the new soil and crops will affect human health and how our genetics are different from theirs. They figured that since I'm the leader in charge of health for the Network, I'm the best candidate for training.'

'That *is* fairly logical. What's the problem?' Dez asked, his eyebrows drawn down in a frown.

'They want me to stay for at least a year!'

'A year?' Dez's face fell.

'I know. That was all I could think as well. Elizabeth did say I could hitch a ride in a Hovercraft occasionally when I wanted to visit home.'

'In that case I expect to see you every second day,' he said, giving her a half-hearted smile as he reached for her hands across the table. 'Life seems very unfair sometimes.'

'Agreed. We'll just have to work something out,' she said as she moved around the table to sit in his lap and wrap her arms around him.

'So, what did you say — to Elizabeth, I mean?'

'That I wanted to think about it. But quite truthfully I don't really feel I'm being given a choice. I'm expected to co-operate. She was just being polite giving me the heads up. Didn't want me to be assigned my role in front of the whole room at the meeting today is my best guess.'

'Crap. I had the feeling this would happen,' his forehead creased with frustration. 'I wonder where they want me?' he murmured on a sigh. He could only assume that he would have as little choice over his own life as Emi.

'I got the impression they expect you to be here at the Network.'

'So much for not losing you.'

'You won't lose me. You haven't lost me. Not possible,' Emi replied. But she knew she was just mouthing words. Their lives were about to change dramatically and she had given up her chance of controlling her own destiny yesterday at breakfast.

The Fringe were in charge now.

PART TWO

ELEVEN

It had taken months, but finally people from both the Network and the Fringe were relocated to where they were needed. Modular housing provided by the Fringe housed all the new labourers. A vast army of people were assigned to building The Cloud. There were two sites so far, one just outside of New York and the other in England. The Network members that had worked on building shelters and with solar panels had largely been assigned to working on The Cloud. The Fringe in New York produced all the parts for the immense condensers and solar panels and the Network put them together according to the diagrams they'd been given. Someone from the Fringe came around at the end of each month to make sure everything was in place correctly.

Jax was in New York, lapping up learning about crops, yields and harvesting. He would be in charge of training others to oversee the planting when the time came. Certain plants, seaweeds, as well as trees, would clean the atmosphere better than others, so they were concentrating on developing these en masse. Eventually, it would require a huge amount of human effort to plant what was necessary. At present, he was studying how crops grew best, under what conditions, and which elements could be controlled and which couldn't. The rain from the clouds would help clean the atmosphere, but each crop required a different amount of hydration, so they had to study which ones to plant where, according to how big The Cloud in the area was. It was a very intricate plan and he enjoyed being taught what it was he could do to help.

Liz, since she was new to leadership, had stayed with her village. Things seemed to have settled down and even Tom was being productive and not quite so moody. He liked to construct things, so helping to re-build the destroyed shelters had given him focus. Liz said he still went off for days at a time on his own and never explained himself but he always came back with game for them to butcher. She tried to leave him be and not question him too much.

Emi was in New York, as she'd expected to be. She was not quite so happy as Jax to be there but knew her duty. Most of her time was spent in the various labs, learning how food affected human health. The more she learned the less she felt like she knew but it was fascinating. Occasionally, Jon and Amy would fly out to New York to meet with her. They were now the leaders of Sector B. If they were too busy then Sal would fly out to meet with her instead. She would teach them as much of what she was discovering as possible for them to take back to impart to others. She also sent food to help feed the village. Blood samples were taken from a test group of people before and after each delivery of food. The samples were then returned to her at the lab for observation. Every once in a while she would be flown to a village to do a talk about health. She often hoped that her visit would overlap with a visit to the same region as Dez, but it never did. When she had time to think she realised that she missed Dez dreadfully. They were able to chat via the Sattcomms they'd been given but it wasn't the same as being together.

Abe, since he had his two new charges, was allowed to stay in his home. He was now everyone's right-hand man. He took care of all the little things that so many did not have time for and kept in touch with everyone. Abe took over Jax's job of looking after the storehouse since Jax was in New York. He regularly checked in with Dez to see what things needed doing that Dez didn't have time for. He also kept in touch with Jon and Amy and occasionally went to see Emi. One day, when he was in New York seeing Emi and Jax, Matthew came to see him.

'Hello, Matthew,' said Emi as she let him into her apartment. She still wasn't accustomed to living in an apartment, high up off the ground, and having to 'buzz' people into the building and then unlock the door for them if she hadn't remembered to beforehand. Her place felt like utter luxury to her, but by New York standards it was fairly average. She had two bedrooms and a bathroom and an open living-dining-kitchen area with a balcony off the living room. She could still barely bring herself to stand on the balcony as it was so high up. Everything was done in what they called 'neutral tones' which she quite liked as they were fairly soothing. Her shelter at Sector B seemed as if it was on a different planet.

'Abe, I heard you were in town. I was hoping to find you here,' said Matthew, as he joined them in the living room and took a seat in one of the armchairs.

'Hey, Doc. Good to see you,' said Abe, smiling broadly at the addition to their little gathering.

'I've good news. It's taken a long time but I finally found out it's the girls' red hair and freckles that genetically override the tattoo imprint. I was able to isolate the freckle gene the girls carry and replicate it. I do believe I now have a vaccine I can give to people if they wish to rid themselves of the last of their tattoo genes. The freckle gene is very strong, completely eliminates the tattoo. Quite amazing really from a medical viewpoint.'

Abe's mouth hung open before he clamped it firmly shut. 'I'm not sure that I really follow you but…wow, that's great Doc. Amazing. The girls will be thrilled,' he said, nodding his head. 'I'd like to be the first to volunteer. Be good to not have my imprint, kind of tired of it,' said Abe, the pride in his voice shining through — his new little charges were the reason for this medical breakthrough.

'Does this mean we can replace our blue hues with freckles?' asked Emi with an impish grin as she got up to get a jug of water and glasses from the kitchen.

'Yes, you're likely to end up with a smattering of freckles, at least across your nose,' Matthew replied.

'I'd like that. At least I'd like it a whole lot better than my slightly blue arm. I'm happy to volunteer for a vaccine. A few freckles would be kind of cute,' Emi said, looking down at her blue arm as she placed the jug on the coffee table in the living room. She didn't *think* the ink toxins affected her much anymore but she was pretty tired of looking at the ugly blue blotch on her upper arm.

'Great. I'll bring it by tomorrow. It'll take about a month or so to completely reverse the effects of the tattoo gene. Once you two are clear, what do you think of coming to help me give the vaccine to those who want it in the Network? You'll be good models and I think more people will trust me if they can see how its worked. I thought we could start in Sector B as it's fairly central. What do you say?'

'Sure, as long as we're both free. How long would you need us for?'

'Depends on the turnout we get but I would think we could get most people done in a few weeks or so.'

'Can I bring Lea and Fie with me since it'll be for a few weeks? They're okay on their own if I'm gone for a day or two but a few weeks might be a bit long,' said Abe.

'Of course. Be good to have the original donors there anyway. Show that they're healthy and cute,' Matthew said with a smile.

'I'll check in with my lab…and Edward…and make sure it's okay for me to be away. I'd imagine it's fine. It's for a good cause after all and it'll be nice to be back in my village for more than just a day,' Emi grinned at Matthew. 'Plus I'll be able to take blood samples before and after the vaccine and see what the results are on people's health. We've never really known how the toxin works in the body.'

'I'll check in with Dez, but imagine it's fine for me too. I wonder if he'll want a vaccine?' said Abe.

'Be good to see him,' Emi said as a slight flush spread across her face.

'Great. I'll be back tomorrow with the vaccine and then I'll arrange for a Hovercraft to pick you both up in about a months time once the vaccine has worked it's magic…and I have produced enough for distribution,' said Matthew, taking his leave.

'I'm due to stock up the storehouses with some of the new crops so I can look after things while you're away, Abe,' said Jax. 'And I'll make sure Dez goes to get his vaccine,' he added, winking at Emi.

'It'll be good to be home. I feel like I've been in New York for so long,' Emi replied, turning a further shade of pink.

'Do you like it here, Emi?' asked Abe, gazing around at the comfortable apartment with it's modern kitchen, plush couches and unbroken windows with a view to the city of New York.

'Hmm. I guess. Work's great,' said Emi, assuming Abe meant the question in a more general sense. 'Genetics is fascinating. Learning about how the food we eat, and the water we drink, and the medications people take, affects the body is simply incredible. It's nice to know everything I'm learning will eventually help the Network. We'll be healthier and stronger and our children will have a better future,' she replied, her face lit with enthusiasm.

'Yeah, I could see that'd feel good to be part of.'

'And then Edward has been so good to me,' she added, looking away, her pink hue deepening slightly. 'I've this apartment, an abundance of food, decent clothes to wear,' her list petered out and her countenance changed — her list of benefits sounding false even to her own ears.

'I share an apartment with some other Network people. The clothes they provide are more for working in but they're comfortable. There's always something fun to do…and the food really is good,' added Jax, not noticing the change in atmosphere.

'What's the problem then?' asked Abe, directing his gaze at Emi, sensing the hesitation behind the list of benefits.

'Sometimes I feel like I've moved to a different planet. I guess I just miss what's familiar and being with people I've known my whole life. This all feels a bit…surreal,' said Emi.

'It's not home. But it's not for forever. It's not like we can never leave or we're going to live our whole lives and then die here,' said Jax.

'True. Although originally I was asked to be here for a year,' Emi hesitated. 'Well, that time's almost up and I feel no closer to leaving.'

'Can't you ask to be transferred back home?' asked Abe.

'No, I don't think I could,' she replied, shaking her head. 'I feel like that would be…selfish. The plan is for saving the planet and… us. If I'm needed here, then here is where I'll stay,' said Emi, shrugging her shoulders, trying to shed her feelings of discontent.

'Maybe you could visit more,' suggested Abe.

'Maybe,' agreed Emi, giving a half-hearted smile, knowing she was just mouthing words.

'Well, at least we'll have a few weeks back home soon.'

'True,' said Emi, the edges of her mouth turning up an extra fraction.

Dez wished that one of the things the Fringe had invented was cloning. He could do with at least three more of himself. He couldn't believe how much of his time was now spent travelling, checking in with different leaders and making sure things were running smoothly. He felt like a puppet on a string, always going to where he was politely asked to go. But being in charge and seeing every aspect of what people were doing, especially with the building of The Cloud, certainly gave him a bigger perspective on what they were trying to achieve and how complicated it was. But he missed Emi.

His most recent trip had been to England. Given that a year ago he'd never been outside the valleys he'd lived in, to then see New York and now England, was quite eye opening. The planet was vast. The Hovercraft trip had first taken him over dried grasslands and brittle looking forest; desolate cities that had once been home to millions of people and now were piles of rubble where nothing moved. Flying across the Atlantic Ocean had left him speechless and then, finally, they reached England. England was so different from New York, and different from anything he'd ever seen. The valley he lived in was green but it was surrounded by dry forest and yellowed grasslands. England was endless rolling green hillsides with pleasant stone villages scattered about. Some places were still abandoned due to the decreased population but again it was nothing like what he had become accustomed to. And rather than letting places go to ruin, the Fringe had simply knocked walls out and made the small houses which were attached together into bigger dwellings.

He'd loved exploring in his free time — wandering through the fields that were still home to cows or sheep, corn or wheat or laying under the canopy of a massive chestnut tree at the top of a rise, content to watch a squirrel busily gathering nuts, completely unconcerned with his presence. He appreciated that he no longer felt the need to kill and eat it. Occasionally, he'd come across patches of wild strawberries or bilberries, fruits he'd never tasted before, and enjoy the simple pleasure of picking and eating them, knowing with certainty that it was growing in uncontaminated soil. He longed to share the peace and tranquility of the place with Emi, sure that she would love it.

Dez had spent an entire month visiting with all the leaders in the various villages where projects were being conducted. Building The Cloud was the biggest project and its construction was almost complete. But there were other projects of growing seedlings, testing soil and water to make sure it was uncontaminated, building replacement parts for solar panels and machinery that was required to build The Cloud, and the list went on. There were so many people needed in so many different jobs. It was rewarding to see everyone working together toward the one goal and he knew his leadership was vital to connecting the groups into a cohesive whole.

He was looking forward to returning to England for when they started up their section of The Cloud, which should be fairly soon. But for now he was back taking care of basic home maintenance. The bit of downtime, and sleeping in his own bed was nice. He still appreciated his fixed-up shelter. Abe and the girls had done a good job. It wasn't very big, nowhere near as grand as the places he had seen in New York, but it was cozy and it was his. He heard a knock at the door and opened it to see Abe standing on his doorstep.

'Hey, Abe! I was just thinking about you. Come on in.'

'Glad you're back. How was England?'

'Amazing! I'd no idea there was still so much green left on the planet. Absolutely beautiful place!'

'Not all dried grassland like here then?'

'No. No grasslands. They've used the rivers and oceans to irrigate and keep it green, even with the lack of rain, although they get more rain than we do. Quite incredible really! The brilliance of the Fringe impresses me more all the time.'

'Good thing they had a plan,' Abe grinned. 'You not minding all the travel?'

'Sometimes, but England was good. The Network members assigned there are thrilled, so it was quite a pleasant trip, not really any issues to deal with. It was more a matter of showing my face, seeing what was going on, and letting people know that the whole project is one big thing. The good part of being a leader I guess.'

'Right, well I have some other good news,' said Abe with a smile. 'Doc has finally figured out why my girls don't have tattoo imprints.'

'Really, and, why?'

'It's their red hair and freckles. He says it's a strong gene and overrides the tattoo gene.'

'I wonder if others with red hair and freckles are the same? I never really paid much attention.'

'Don't know. I noticed your tattoo imprint is lighter than average. Do you have any red-heads amongst your ancestors?' asked Abe.

'I don't think so. Don't know why mine's lighter. Never gave it much thought. But then I don't know who my father was, so maybe it has something to do with his side of the family. My mom did tell me that I resembled him and I have a few memories of a man who came to stay with us for a while when I was little. But he vanished when I was about seven, just after my sister was born, so I can't really remember what he looked like. And I don't know if he was my father or not, I just assumed.'

'That might explain it but then he definitely wouldn't have had red hair,' said Abe, looking at Dez's dark brown mop. 'Anyway, Lea and Fie are a hundred percent red-headed. Somehow their ancestors always married other people with red hair and freckles. Liked it as a feature I guess. So their gene is very strong.'

'Interesting.'

'Anyway, the good news is that Doc has been able to make a vaccine so he can give the gene to others that want to get rid of their tattoos.'

'That'll be great. Love to be rid of the imprint toxins after all this time. Wonder how we'll feel.'

'Thought you'd like it. I volunteered to be first up for the vaccine. Thought you might like one too.'

'Sign me up.'

'Already did,' Abe grinned at him. 'Besides, Emi's one of the people passing out the vaccine,' he added with a wink.

Dez grinned back. 'You're more sly than you look. And when is the vaccine appointment to be?'

'Thought we could head over in a couple days.'

'Works for me.'

'Right…and I'm sure if it didn't, you'd make it work.'

'Yeah. Could be,' said Dez with a huge grin.

Abe, Dez and the girls arrived at Emi's village a couple of days later and were shown to their guest quarters. Dez had a room to himself. Abe shared a room with his girls, and there were quite a few other people in guest quarters waiting for their vaccine; too impatient to wait until it came to their village. People who knew Dez by sight, and hadn't seen him for a while, crowded around and asked questions on how the plan was going and where he'd been, what he had seen. Dez just wanted to go and find Emi.

'How are things coming along Dez?' asked Jon.

'Hey, Jon, really well. We're probably a few months out from launching some of The Cloud sites. It's really the glue that holds this whole project together. We'll be launching the sites one by one to be able to control the temperature as best we can.'

'I thought we needed to cool the planet really soon. Can't we get them going all at once, to get a jump on it, if we're running out of time?' asked Amy.

'No. Such a big project has never been done before. Only smaller prototypes were tested. We need to cool the planet by 4.5 degrees. If we cool it by only 2.5 degrees then it's not enough and if we cool it by 6 degrees then it's too much. So we need to be very precise in our control over, and our measurement of The Cloud and it's affect.'

'What happens if we go too far one way or the other,' asked Sal.

'If we're too cool, then we should be able to turn off some of The Clouds and adjust the temperature that way. Although I doubt that will be a problem any time soon. If we're too hot and cannot cool the planet enough then……' replied Dez, shrugging his shoulders and raising his hands.

'…..And what about all the people?'

'I don't know exactly. Most of us would live to our average old age of forty-ish but it would be increasingly unpleasant and the generations after us would live even less time, have a harder time surviving.'

'That's a bleak picture,' said Abe. 'I'd kind of like the girls to live and have an okay life. Life has already been hard enough for them.'

'Barring any major calamities, it seems like it should all work out. The Fringe are pretty brilliant; just hope they've thought of every contingency,' he added as he headed for the door, 'I best be off, I have a date with a wonderful new vaccine.'

'That's a funny thing to call Emi,' joked Abe, giving Dez a wink and a shove out the door.

Dez headed over to the new medical facilities the Fringe had helped them build in Sector B. The building was a single story wooden structure, painted white, with a solar roof. The windows were regularly spaced, large and matching. It reminded him of New York…a small portion of New York placed squarely in the middle of Sector B. The entire building was pristine and very well built. He pushed his way through the revolving front doors and followed the signs directing him to where the vaccine was being given. He found Emi with a needle in her hand and a line up of people waiting for their vaccine. He got in line to wait his turn.

Wow. Emi looked good. It had been too long since they'd seen each other. He allowed his eyes to drink her in. Living in New York had changed her. He noticed that her clothes were immaculate and her hair was longer, but there was something else, he wasn't quite sure what. Then it dawned on him — the blue hue of her upper arm was no longer there and she was wearing makeup, as many of the Fringe women did. She looked like a Fringe member. He quickly averted his gaze. Why had he assumed everything would be the same?

She must have felt his eyes on her, for at that moment she looked up and gave him a huge grin which he just caught out of his peripheral vision. He grinned back and gave her a wink. Emi turned a rosy hue and looked away. Maybe things weren't so different after all.

It was his turn. He took a seat and rolled up his sleeve. 'Emi, I was beginning to think we inhabited different planets.'

'Yes, it does seem a bit odd that we *hardly ever* seem to cross paths. I'm glad to see you now though.' She turned to a tray of small vials and placed one onto a needle. 'I'm going to take a blood sample before giving the injection so we have some before and after results to study. You'll have to see me at regular intervals for me to take blood samples to study over time.'

'Sounds good to me,' he replied with a smirk. 'I could hardly believe my eyes when I walked in, you look so…healthy.'

'Gee thanks. I'll try to not let that go to my head,' she said as she inserted the needle into his arm.

'Ouch!'

'Sorry, it stings a bit,' she watched the vial fill with blood before extracting the needle and then inserted the next one filled with a small amount of clear liquid.

Dez glanced at his arm, rolled down his sleeve and then brought his gaze up to Emi's. He found she was staring at him as if she was trying to eat him up with her eyes. She was so close he just wanted to wrap his arms around her. 'How long 'til you're off?' he asked with a catch in his throat.

'Only about another half hour to go,' she replied with a blush.

'I'll wait for you at the path to the upper fields then.'

She nodded and he got up and left. There was only so much one could say when sitting on a chair, getting a needle with a lineup of people close by waiting their turn.

He headed to the swimming hole for a cool dip and then sat in the shade of a tree to wait for Emi. Forty minutes later she was standing before him. She had changed into more casual clothing and looked a bit more like the Emi he remembered, his Emi. She held out her hand to pull him up. 'Want to walk?' she asked.

'I'd rather give you a big hug,' he replied as he took the proffered hand and pulled himself to his feet.

'Let's walk first.'

'You okay?'

'Yes, I'd just rather be alone for a bit.'

'We are alone.'

'Not alone enough,' Emi headed off down the dirt path, through the fields.

'Really?' Dez glanced around at the grassy fields stretching out before them, devoid of any other people. He followed after her, his apprehension rising. 'You sure you're okay? I mean, there's nobody in sight so how can we not be alone enough?'

'Sorry, I just feel the need for space,' she said as she looked left and right. 'I feel so confined, or controlled. It's not like I'm being watched all the time but at the same time — oh, I don't know, it's hard to put into words.'

'We did agree go where we're most needed.'

'I know. And sometimes I think I'm being ridiculous. But, still I have this gut instinct that — I can't really say what it is. It's just — wrong.'

'But everything's going so well. Is it because you're in one place, doing one job and you don't get to see the bigger picture, so you feel like you're trapped?' suggested Dez, hoping to dispel her fears.

'Sure. Maybe. But...I guess I feel like I'm being manipulated. How can we not have seen each other in so long, but others, like Jax or Abe, I can see anytime? All the travelling you do and yet we never cross paths.'

'Yeah, but Jax lives in New York and Abe is in touch with Matthew because of the girls. You're sure you're not just missing the freedom of your old life?'

Emi shrugged, displeasure etched on her face as she turned to face him.

They'd reached the end of the path through the fields and come up against an escarpment of massive granite boulders. Emi was familiar with the area; this was one of her favourite hikes. She started to climb, nimbly hopping from one boulder to another. Dez followed. Finally reaching the top, they collapsed under the shade of a tree in the meadow at the summit. 'It is beautiful here...and peaceful,' she said. She drank in the various colours of flowers in the meadow and the dappled sunlight shifting through the leaves of the tree.

'As for us seeing each other, well, if you feel you can't escape to come to me then I'll have to make sure I have more appointments in New York.'

'Somehow I don't think seeing each other in the city would be a good idea.'

Dez raised himself up on one elbow and looked down at Emi. 'Why on earth not?'

'Call it woman's intuition.'

'Come on Emi, this is too much. Nothing's going to happen to me…to us. I'm now…well…vitally important to the leadership of the Network and to the success of The Cloud and you're needed for ensuring the health of us all,' said Dez, starting to feel exasperated and resentful that she was ruining the short amount of time they had together.

'I know. Maybe I'm just being paranoid but promise you'll be careful,' she said as she reached up to run her hand through his hair.

He leaned down to kiss her, his lips warm and inviting, the stubble on his chin gently grazed her face. 'I will. We'll be okay,' he said, trying to lighten the mood and enjoy their few stolen moments.

'I know you're right. Sorry. Don't know why I feel so upset. Maybe it's because I haven't seen you in so long,' she said. She abruptly changed the subject, obviously trying to cool her overactive emotions. 'I wonder what it'll be like? Our future. It's hard to imagine a world that's different from the current burned-out shell…to have enough food, be healthy, to not be so unbearably hot, to regain the extinct species. It almost seems impossible, too good to be true.'

'It is quite incredible. But I've travelled a lot now. With everyone working together, it doesn't seem as impossible as it used to,' he said, relieved at the more optimistic direction of the conversation.

'But don't you ever worry that something will go wrong?'

'Yeah, sometimes, especially with The Cloud. The measurements are very precise — number of structures needed, where they're located, how long each needs to operate for and at what capacity. There's not much room for error. If one of the major facilities malfunctioned for an extended period, it would be almost impossible to then cool the planet the amount they figure is necessary to maintain life.' *Crap, why had he said that?* But he couldn't tell lies, not to Emi.

'That's not very comforting,' she said as her mouth turned down at the edges.

'No, sorry, didn't mean to frighten you. Don't worry too much, The Fringe are smart people and have spent the last few decades preparing for this time. Hopefully everything goes according to plan,' Dez smiled and leaned down to plant feather-light kisses on her forehead and nose. 'We're about to start building a major facility of The Cloud at the northern end of Sector A. It means I can spend more time at home. Maybe it'll make it easier for us to see each other if you can visit more often,' he said, trying to distract her from all the gloomy thoughts.

'I'll do my best,' Emi said with an impish grin. 'So what are the chances of forgetting about everything for a while and just enjoying the time we have together right now?'

'Sounds good to me. Count me in.'

TWELVE

Edward sat in the office of his penthouse, looking out over what had once been Central Park and was now an ocean of crops used to sustain the people of New York City. He had seen old pictures of the park and found it no less beautiful now that it was used for food production. They had kept the lake for irrigation purposes, the trees were now fruit or nut trees, and instead of grass there were herbs, berries and a variety of vegetation. There were still flowers, but they were ones that bees and birds thrived on, and many were edible. The careful selection of plants for Central Park had ensured that the local bee and bird populations had survived and that the view of the park from the surrounding buildings was quite breathtaking.

Sitting in his office looking at the view was one of his favourite places to be. It offered him a certain sense of peace, a reminder that things were unfolding according to plan. It also gave him a feeling of power. His family had owned this apartment for generations. It had been continuously updated over the years and offered a level of luxury not found in most other places. His family had been in a position of leadership for over a hundred years, since they had taken over from the government as it collapsed. The masses finally rebelling, having had enough of the government turning a blind eye to the dire situation their policies were allowing to continue. A government ruled by big business.

Maintaining control had been a challenge but the plan that his predecessors had put in place had been backed by the influential and the knowledgeable, as well as the scientists and the environmentalists. It had fallen to him, his generation, to take the strategies and put them into action. It was exhilarating to contemplate the future, to be the one who would once again exercise control over vast areas and numerous people. To rule New York was one thing, to have power over the world was something he had dreamed of since he was a child. The Fringe was a cohesive unit, united in ensuring their course of action was flawless. The Network had managed to clean itself up enough to be the workforce they needed for their game-plan to succeed. And the Blues, they were too stupid to think for themselves anymore; they just reacted to whatever was immediately in front of them; which made them very easy to manipulate.

His top priority now was of a more personal nature, the begetting of an heir. And preferably not just one but two or three — one was too risky. Why his father, Caleb, had only had him he had never understood. People who had known Caleb well had told him that he had not seemed to want to share his life with anyone, he'd kept things to himself, and rarely encouraged intimacy of any sort. That attitude had seemed to carry over into his home life as well as he could not recollect his father showing he or his mother much affection. His parents would often have muted arguments behind closed doors and then his father would take a Hovercraft and disappear for a couple days on his own. As he got older he would often wonder how his father could disregard his responsibilities as leader, even for a couple of days. Then, fifteen years ago, when he was fourteen years old, his dad had taken a Hovercraft and never returned. They'd eventually found the Hovercraft — it had crashed, nobody could figure out why. His dad had been an excellent pilot. But his body was not discovered with the wreckage. They could only assume he had managed to escape but had perished from injuries in the wilderness. After his father's death, he was recognised as sole heir, but since he was underage the board was meant to rule until he turned twenty-one, but his mother had convinced them that with her help he could assume the leadership. And so he had done so until his mother had died three years later from a brain aneurism and he'd been forced to assume all responsibilities. From the moment he took over, he'd been determined to be a better leader than his father had been. As he became an adult, looking back, he realised his father's loyalties had been divided. He recollected the overheard snippets of arguments which had caused him to wonder if his father had a mistress. Until recently he'd never been able to put the pieces together. The resentment festered.

He'd dated a few women over the years but had never found someone that he was drawn to that also had the right leadership abilities, which he would need in a wife. His mind strayed to Emi. She was not genetically pure as the Fringe women were, but she had a certain quality that he'd not found in anyone else. And he had to admit to being very attracted to her with a yearning he'd never before experienced. He found himself unable to concentrate sometimes, his mind filled with her image. He tried to bring his mind under control, but for once the ability eluded him. Instead he managed to see her in person, although he made it seem as casual as possible. He had the feeling that hurrying her would be a mistake. He could be patient and charming. He was sure she had the qualities of leadership he was looking for, plus the Network would follow her and together they would hold influence over most of the human race. Patience and kindness must win her eventually, and some degree of physical contact. He needed to devise a reason for another dinner and dance.

He picked up the Satcomm and pushed the speed-dial number for Charlotte.

'Hello.'

'Hello, Charlotte. Edward here.'

'Oh, hello, sir. How are you?'

'Very well thank you. I need you to do something for me.'

Well, that was as good as done. Now he must focus and get back to work. The building of Cloud III near the Network valleys was about to begin. As it would be the second biggest Cloud site on the planet it was vital that nothing went wrong.

He laid the architectural diagrams out on his desk and studied the calculations and predictions for temperature change, cloud cover, and rainfall. He hoped they'd not overlooked anything or been too optimistic in their calculations. If anything went wrong then his plans for ruling the world could come to nothing. He recalculated every equation and poured over the plans until darkness fell and most people had long gone to bed. Emi was finally pushed from his mind.

The Satcomm rang, startling him out of his concentration.

'Hello?'

'Edward. Sorry to disturb you so late. Matthew, here. I noticed your light on. I was just heading to bed, I haven't had a spare moment until now, when I thought you might like to know the results from the tattoo vaccine.'

'Oh, yes,' he replied, feigning interest. His forehead wrinkled, perturbed at being interrupted. 'How are things going?' his voice perfectly polite as he looked up from the papers covering his desk.

'Really well. We've managed to eradicate the tattoo toxins. One hundred percent success rate for all those who opted to have it! We're very thankful to have discovered those two little red-haired, freckled girls.'

'That is good news.'

'Yes, well, what's equally thrilling, from a medical standpoint, is that now most people from the Network will no longer have any trace toxins, and combined with eating our food they're approaching the level of the Fringe in health. We'll soon be able to reproduce with them, expand our bloodlines, and further ensure the survival of the planet.'

'That's fabulous news,' Edward said, his enthusiasm more genuine as his mind returned to images of Emi. 'Although, I'm glad their knowledge is not to our level or we could find ourselves taken over completely,' he added jokingly.

'That's unlikely,' Matthew responded, taking the comment seriously. 'They've a vast amount yet to learn. Some families still teach their kids to read and write but most can't. It's been quite fascinating living amongst them and seeing the differences in abilities.'

'Well, I'm happy to learn that at least their health is better…and that we retain the upper-hand. Maintaining control will be vital to our future.' He gazed out the floor to ceiling windows at the city skyline beyond. There was nowhere else like New York. It was his city. One day it would be his planet.

'Yes, sir. Not to worry. Everything seems to be going along better than we'd even hoped. The vaccine was an added bonus. Plus the Network are thrilled.'

'Well, thank you for filling me in,' said Edward, in a tone that implied he was impatient to be done with the conversation. 'I'll be having a dinner party in a few weeks time. Charlotte will be contacting everyone with the specific details soon. I hope you're free to join us,' said Edward, reverting to his usual charm.

'Thank you. Wouldn't miss it. I very much feel like celebrating.'

'Wonderful. See you soon then. Good night.'

'Good night.'

An improved work force; seeing Emi again — a toxin free Emi; a people who were grateful to the Fringe for something he had nothing to do with. Yes, it was all going very smoothly. One day soon he may very well rule the entire planet. It was an exhilarating thought! To think it had all come to fruition during his lifetime. He was no longer scowling.

THIRTEEN

Shade sat cross-legged on the concrete floor of the parking garage. The garbage was starting to accumulate in the corners and the warm air that wafted in every once in a while made her wrinkle her nose in protest. 'Ha, look at you! Idiot!' she said as she watched Spike trying to do up the zipper on his shorts; his huge, blue, hairy belly hanging over, blocking his vision as he struggled with the zipper.

'Not my fault. Stupid zipper's stuck,' he glowered at her as he yanked at the zipper.

'Ha!'

'I think it's broke. Now I'm gunna have to get a new pair, use up more of my rations for another stupid pair of shorts,' he kicked at a stale bread roll that somebody must have dropped days ago and was now like a rock.

'Didn't you just get a new pair?'

'Yeah. It's like they give us clothes that are no good so we have to use up our rations?' he complained as he slid down the wall next to Shade.

'Why would they do that?'

'Dunno. Just a thought,' he snapped.

'Ha. So you had a thought…just the one I bet!'

'I have thoughts.' His blue face took on an almost purple hue as his anger mounted.

'Like what?'

'I was wonderin' 'bout doin' another raid.'

'Wow, like nobody's ever thought of doin' that before! That's not exactly amazin' ya know,' her sarcastic tone full of condesention. Shade rolled her eyes as she stretched her legs out in front of her.

'I don't mean one of the little raids like what we normally do, you stupid cow.' Spike kicked at her foot with his.

'Ouch. Hey.' Shade kicked him back.

'I was wonderin' about doing a big raid…a really big raid,' he said.

Shade gave Spike a shove before getting to her feet. 'Fuck it's hot,' she said as she took off her tattered shirt to mop up the sweat under her mottled blue and black breasts. 'What da ya mean?' She looked down with a scowl that made the zipper tattoos on her forehead seem like they were being pulled apart.

'I dunno. Like maybe get a bunch of us together and take over a whole valley instead of just takin' the food. I hate livin' here,' he waved his arm to take in the bleak parking garage. 'And I'm bloody tired of bein' hungry all the time. Just havin' the food rations that the Exchange gives out.'

'You don't look like you're hurtin' for food,' Shade commented. She poked at his enormous belly, which was hanging out over his pants, as she gazed at his round face. She slid back down the wall as it was marginally cooler sitting on the concrete.

Spike's face turned a deeper shade of purple, his hand raised, ready to strike Shade in her 'too smart' mouth. He lowered his arm; he needed her as an ally. 'Do ya wanna hear my plan or not?'

'Yeah, go on then.'

'The Network always has food, right?'

'Yeah, so?'

'But when we do a raid, each shelter only seems to have enough food for a short amount of time, right?'

'Again, yeah, so?' Shade slipped her shirt back on over her head. It was inside-out, sweat stained and filthy but it was the only one she had.

'So they must store their food somewhere.'

'Hadn't thought of that.'

'Like last time, we got the tip-off they'd had a meetin' and swapped stuff and were stocked up on food, and we got way more than normal. So where's the food they're swappin' for kept?'

'You really are thinkin'.'

'Not as dumb as I look.'

'Good thing since you look pretty dumb.'

'You're a real bitch today.'

'Part of my charm.' Shade batted her eyelashes at him. 'Go on.'

'I wanna try to find the food stores and take over that valley.'

'But ya don't know where to look.'

'No, but it's gotta be somewhere and I'm gunna find it. Thought I'd get a few others to help out with the searchin',' he said as he started to fight with his zipper again.

'Count me in if ya want. Got nothin' better to do. I'll see if I can get a few others to help out. But how are we gunna get more food rations to be able to explore further?'

'We'll steal it.'

'From who?' asked Shade. 'Nobody has nothin'!'

'Yeah, that's for sure,' he said. The snake imprints on his forehead looked as if they were slithering into his hair as his brow wrinkled in concentration. 'Crap!'

'I wonder…could we break into the Exchange one night do ya think?' said Shade as the vision of a lot more food caused her to be more enthused with the idea.

'Yeah. Why not, they wouldn't be expectin' us, that's for sure,' replied Spike with a grin. The snake tattoo on his cheeks danced and stretched.

'And where we keepin' this stash of food,' asked Shade as she wiped her face with the bottom of her shirt. It didn't seem to matter how often she wiped the sweat from her face there was always more a second later.

'I dunno. Maybe we can store what we get in one of the abandoned places at the edge of town,' replied Spike as he finally managed to get his zipper done up. 'That way nobody will ever see us with the food.'

'All right. I'll get some helpers. So when we doin' this?'

'I dunno. Maybe in a week or so.'

'Works for me,' said Shade, with a shrug.

'I guess we'll need somethin' for carryin' food…and breakin' in.'

'Bloody genius, ain't ya?'

'Smarter than you, bitch.'

'Piss off, who asked you?'

Spike could just make out the shape of the Exchange against the black of the forest behind. The Exchange had once been a large restaurant in a manicured park; now it was a dilapidated structure surrounded by overgrown bushes and dark, menacing looking trees. There was no moonlight, only the faint glow of distant stars to navigate by. He squinted into the darkness, trying to see if there was a guard on duty. He could hear the tops of the trees sway in the warm breeze but there didn't seem to be any other movement near the Exchange.

A shape emerged out of the night and whispered his name. 'Spike, over here.'

'Shade?' he glanced around and finally detected the hand waving at him, the motion at odds with the surrounding stillness. 'I've got a metal bar and some sacks to put food in. How many did ya get to help?'

'I dunno,' Shade paused. 'There's a bunch of us.'

'We only get one shot at this so we gotta make it good.'

They crept up to the door of the Exchange, their ears pricked for signs of unwanted company. Spike raised the bar and smashed the window. The sound was deafening in the stillness of the night. Spike cringed as collectively they held their breath.

Then from behind they heard someone yell, 'Hey, you there. What the hell ya think you're doin'?'

A couple of the fellows at the back of their group spun around and went after the guy. The guard turned to flee, tripped over a tree root and sprawled in the dirt. They kicked him until he passed out.

Then they waited.

All remained quiet. Spike reached through the broken glass, undid the lock, turned the knob, and pushed the door open. It creaked on its hinges. He handed a sack to each person in the mob that Shade had gathered and they disbursed into the vast building to collect whatever they could. They quietly filled their sacks and met back outside the building in the dark, quiet night.

'All right, follow me. I found a building on the edge of the city. It's not great but it'll have to do. Let's go.'

They moved off, away from the 'park' and into the labyrinth of the city. They stumbled through the darkness of abandoned streets to avoid where people lived and fires glowed. As they walked toward the outskirts of the city there was less and less light. More of the city was ruined — an ocean of crumbling walls with weeds growing up where there had once been paved roads. Nothing else moved. There weren't even rats out this far as there was no food to be found. The complete desolation would be a perfect hiding spot.

They came to a concrete building that still had its lower three stories standing. Above that there were sticks of rebar reaching for the sky.

'Right, this is our new home. It's not pretty but it's too far out for anyone to care about lookin' for us.'

They hauled themselves up the stairs, too exhausted to say anything. The only sound was their laboured breathing, interspersed with a few grunts, as they carried their stash to the top floor.

'I've never bin so bloody tired.'

'Yeah, well, with the load you're hauling in front of you and the one added on your back it's not a surprise,' responded Shade.

'Piss off, who asked you?'

'We're all tired. But it's a good haul. Be nice to think of havin' this amount of food all the time,' said Shade as she dumped her bag on the floor.

'Yeah. If we can find the place I'm thinkin' of then maybe we won't have to be hungry no more.'

'What makes you think there is some great valley and storehouses full of food anyway? All these years of doin' raids and you suddenly come up with this thought out of nowhere. I mean thinkin' is not exactly your strong point.'

'You're such a bitch; you know that? Why do I talk to you?'

'Cause nobody else'll listen,' responded Shade with a smirk.

'Piss off.'

'No, really, why? I wanna know.'

Spike looked at Shade and relented. She really was his only friend. 'When we did the last raid, just before I attacked some red-haired dude, I overheard him sayin' to some guy about how it's good we only take a bit of food, and how we've no brains, we're too stupid to find the storehouses. His friend agreed it was a good job we're stupid and then ran off to protect his family, I guess. I was so mad at the red-haired dude for callin' me stupid. I showed 'im. Still need to kill 'is kid. Stupid brat escaped.'

'Didn't think it could be your own thought about the storehouses.'

'Shut up. Why do I talk to you at all?'

'I told ya already, remember, 'cause nobody else'll listen,' she said as she thumped him in the arm. 'This is such a hovel,' Shade scowled as she looked around at the concrete walls with their peeling green paint, the broken, grimy windows and the layers of dust and dried leaves that had blown in over the years. 'Why'd I let you talk me into this? It's gunna be even hotter here than in the garage.'

'Yeah, you might be nicer to me when you getta live in one of the Network valleys and have food all the time.'

'Maybe, but don't count on it.'

'Nah. I won't. Can't count on no one or nothin', that's my motto.'

'Good. I gotta lie down. Come on, let's see if there's a mattress or anything left in one of the other rooms,' she said as she exited through the doorless entry to poke around in what was left of the old apartment building. 'That was a bloody long walk,' she muttered as they explored the second floor.

'Better get used to it. Be more walkin' before we find the valley I'm lookin' for. The Network are smart. The storehouses must be hidden and beyond where we can normally get to.'

'Yeah, that makes sense. That tip-off about when to do the last raid sure put a fire under your fat ass.'

'You're not exactly a stick yourself yah know.'

'Never said I was but you don't seem to mind.'

'Nah, can't afford to be fussy,' Spike said as he reached out to grab her.

'Piss off.' Shade hit his hands away as she poked her head into another room. In the corner was a ratty old mattress full of holes. Shade collapsed onto it and stretched out.

'Thought that was 'n invite. I could come lie down with yah.'

'Well, it wasn't and I'm tired,' said Shade, making sure she sprawled out over the entire mattress so there was no room for Spike. 'What did the guy want in return anyway?'

'In return?'

'Yeah, you moron, you know…the guy who gave you the tip-off, what did he want in return?'

'Nothin'.'

'Really? Nothin'? You sure?'

'Yeah, really,' Spike glowered down at Shade.

'Why would he do that? Makes no sense.'

'I dunno. Maybe he had his own reason for wantin' the village raided.'

'Hmmm. Wonder why?'

'Dunno. Don't care. Got food and killed some people. That's all I care.'

'Yeah, that's you alright…eatin' and killin'.'

'I like to do one other thing. Sure you're tired?'

'Ah, all right. Come on then. It's probably the only way I'll get yah to shut up and leave me alone so I can rest.'

FOURTEEN

The guest list had been drawn up and the invitations sent. The Upper Floor, the best restaurant in New York had been booked and High Velocity, the most popular band, was to perform. Charlotte had promised Edward that it would be a night to remember and she'd personally delivered the new gown to Emi, who'd been speechless.

Edward didn't usually care for birthday celebrations, especially his own, but he was looking forward to tonight's festivities. The thought of dancing with Emi had been plaguing him for the last three weeks. How something as simple as a dance could torment him so was unheard of. He was appalled with himself, with his lack of self-control and inability to focus.

He showered and changed, donned his evening-wear and headed off to The Upper Floor. The restaurant had fantastic views as it took up the top floor of one of the tallest buildings in New York. The ambiance of the roof top dance floor would be exceptional on a night like tonight with the full moon.

There was a good crowd gathered at the restaurant when Edward arrived. Charlotte was the first to greet him with happy birthday wishes. 'I hope you're pleased, sir.'

'It's perfect and the place looks fabulous. Thank you, Charlotte,' said Edward as he took in the room and the attention to detail that she'd put into the decor. The theme was black and white — white table cloths, square black plates, alternating black and white napkins rolled into the wine glasses, white flowers and candles in black vases, and glass beads reflecting the twinkling lights overhead. 'You're simply irreplaceable,' Edward smiled.

'That's nice to hear,' she grinned in return. 'Dinner will be served at eight and the band will begin playing on the rooftop at nine-thirty.'

'Happy Birthday, Edward,' said Matthew as he approached them.

'Thank you, Matthew. So glad you could join us. It'll be good to celebrate together after all our recent successes,' said Edward. He was having a hard time relaxing and getting into the mood of the evening. He picked up a glass of wine as a waitress went by with a selection of drinks on a serving tray.

'I think you'll be very pleased with the results of the vaccine.'

'Well, here's to red hair and freckles,' said Edward. He raised his glass in a toast.

'I'll drink to that,' said Emi as she joined the group, glass in hand.

'Emi, my star patient,' said Matthew with a grin. 'You look stunning.'

'Thank you kind sir,' she gave him an impish grin along with a small curtsy. 'I must say it's much nicer having a blue dress than a blue arm.'

Edward turned to greet Emi; his breath caught in his throat. What on earth had he been doing that he'd managed to see so little of her lately? What had he been thinking? Somebody this beautiful and intelligent would not stay available for long. She truly was absolutely stunning. Her gown was a deep sapphire blue, the sequin straps over one shoulder attached to various places on the fitted bodice and then wrapped around her waist, before falling over the side of the skirt, where the slit beneath revealed her slender legs. 'Emi, you're positively...dazzling.'

'Happy birthday Edward, I can't thank you enough for the dress. It's simply amazing. I feel like it's my birthday rather than yours. Aren't we the ones who are supposed to come bearing gifts?'

He smiled down at her and kissed her on the cheek in greeting. 'It's quite alright. I also wanted to celebrate Matthew's success and I specifically asked for no gifts. If everyone here brought something I would have a mountain to carry home, and I walked over, so it would be quite troublesome, unless of course someone had bought me a Hovercraft as a gift,' he joked.

'I had thought to get you a Hover*board* until the 'no gifts' edict came out,' she replied with a laugh.

'Ah yes, I can just picture me zooming home on a Hoverboard, balancing ninety-nine other presents above my head. I think I would need lessons from Abe...it's Abe who's an expert on the Hoverboard, isn't it?'

'Yes, that would be Abe. I'm sure I could have persuaded him to throw in some free lessons.'

'Well, maybe next year for my birthday.'

'Perfect, nothing like planning in advance,' said Emi, looking slightly startled. 'And how are you Matthew? Having time off after the epic saga of passing out vaccines?' she asked, changing the subject.

'Yes, enjoying a bit of down time. I'm writing my report on the procedure and keeping track of the results, plus I still have some from the Network here in New York coming to see me, just not so many as at first. And how are you feeling, I mean you look absolutely fantastic, but how do you feel now you've had the vaccine?' Matthew asked as he openly admired Emi.

'Well, without trying to sound conceited, I feel as good as I look,' Emi laughed and then grinned from ear to ear.

'Discovering this vaccine will probably be the highlight of my career.'

'I can't thank you enough and I'm sure the Network feel the same.'

'As horrible as it was, if it wasn't for that raid, and those little girls being left on their own, we would probably never have made this discovery,' said Matthew, his eyes shadowed, troubled by the thought of the sacrifice that had been necessary to lead to the discovery. He cleared his throat and took a sip of his wine.

'If it wasn't for you…well, we would never have figured it out on our own,' said Emi.

'I hadn't thought of that aspect of it,' interjected Edward smoothly. 'The timing really was, as you say — the circumstances were most unfortunate with so many deaths, but I suppose the vaccine is some small consolation…'

'And how are Abe and the girls?' asked Emi, cutting across Edward.

'Abe tells me the girls are stars. Everyone's so thankful for the vaccine that they're showered with gifts — food, clothes, household items. Some of the fellows even came over and built them a swing-set in the back yard.'

'I'm so happy for them, poor little things.'

'Abe seems to be in his element. He loves those little girls. He's even added a bedroom for each of them onto his house. Although they still prefer to share and leave the extra room free for guests. I often stay when I go to visit.'

'Do you go often?'

'Whenever I get a chance. I've become quite fond of Abe and the girls, and they always make me so welcome. And Zoe is quite interested in medicine so she likes to meet with me…and ask lots of questions. We're planning on having her transfer here to study medicine. What do you think?' asked Matthew with a grin.

'That'd be wonderful. I'd love to have Zoe around,' Emi smiled. 'Can she be transferred here?' she asked Edward.

'I don't see why not,' said Edward.

Emi's eyes gleamed her appreciation.

'Shall we go into dinner?' He offered his arm to Emi and Matthew fell into step beside them. Charlotte had vanished behind the scenes.

The dinner was, of course, beyond compare. The food perfectly prepared and served with the best of wines, which were cool and soothing. Edward looked over at Emi and was happy to see her relaxed and content as the conversation ebbed and flowed around her. She obviously knew more people in New York now and seemed comfortable chatting with everyone at her table. She was liked and respected, an integral part of something vitally important to everyone present. Every once in a while her eyes would stray his way. He smiled at her and wondered what was going through her mind.

As dinner came to an end, the band could be heard beginning to play on the rooftop patio. People started to drift out of the dining room toward the music. Matthew held out his hand. 'Would you care to dance, Emi?'

'I'd love to,' she beamed up at him. 'Not that I'm much good. Never had any reason to dance, but I enjoy it all the same. I'll try to not tread on your toes.'

'My shoes are quite sturdy, and you're not exactly a heavyweight, so I'm not too worried,' he said, his eyes twinkled with amusement. 'Shall we?' he extended his hand to help her to her feet.

'Are you coming to join us Edward?' asked Emi.

'Yes, yes of course, as long as you save the next dance for me,' he replied, getting up from the table to follow the group to the rooftop. He was a bit piqued that Matthew was monopolising Emi so much, but then realised she would be quite comfortable with Matthew after spending a few weeks passing out the vaccine with him. He felt sure that he should not be too forward himself, he sensed that she would avoid him if he came on too strong. But the need for self-control was testing him to his limits.

The band was in full swing when they emerged onto the moonlit rooftop. The air was balmy and the night sky filled with starlight. There were high-top tables and chairs scattered here and there between potted plants and fairy-lights strung across the roof from wooden beams. Matthew and Emi went off to join in the dancing. Edward made his way to the bar to get himself a glass of wine and patiently wait his turn for a dance, chatting easily with his colleagues. As the song came to an end he didn't lose any time in claiming Emi. 'Excuse us,' he nodded to the others in the group as he put his hand to Emi's back and led her to the floor, feeling the warmth of her skin through the thin fabric of her dress.

'Are you having a good birthday?'

'Yes, very. I don't usually care for too much fuss. My birthday was just a good excuse really.' Edward put his hand to her back and pulled her closer to him to lead her around the dance floor. Her body moulded to his was an exquisite form of torture.

'What's the next step in your grand design for our salvation?' she asked.

'The building of Cloud III near the Network's valleys is the next major step. We have just begun, and I have Dez overseeing it,' he informed her, 'which is why he's not here tonight,' he added, the lie flowing smoothly from his lips. 'The Cloud is probably the single most important structure to our overall survival.' Edward was not sure how he could carry on this conversation when the rest of his senses were acutely aware of Emi's body pressed against his. He let his hand slip lower down her back and tightened his hold ever so slightly.

'And then what?'

'Once it's built we'll have enough Cloud cover to hopefully start making a difference to the earth's temperature. We'll continue making other Cloud structures once these ones are operational, but really these first big three are the key to everything.'

'What happens if one of them fails?'

'I dread to think. We've left very little room for error. I'm not sure the planet, or humankind, would survive if any one of the big three failed. The other smaller ones we have planned could take some of the load if they're built and functional but I would not like to stake my life on the outcome so to speak.' He inhaled the scent of her hair and longed to be somewhere alone with Emi.

'Why not make some of the other structures bigger, just in case?'

'Because they're so far away. Even with the Network helping we're tight for manpower. The further away everything is the more complicated it becomes. All the panels for The Cloud are made here, we only have so many Hovercrafts, and the further we have to send the panels, and people, the more time consuming it all is.' How on earth was he going to get Emi alone? He couldn't possibly lean down and kiss her amongst all these people — it would become a huge source of speculation and gossip. He didn't like people to be savvy to his personal life or innermost desires.

'We'll just have to hope nothing goes wrong.'

'That's one of the reasons I put Dez in charge. He knows the terrain, is well respected by both the Fringe and the Network and now knows the ins and outs of almost everything to do with The Cloud,' he said, this time telling the absolute truth.

'Well, if anyone can make something succeed it would be Dez. He's never backed away from a challenge in his life and everyone loves him,' said Emi, with a catch in her throat, her pride in Dez more than obvious to Edward's acutely attuned ears.

'I'm glad my decision has met with your approval,' he said, trying to maintain a light tone of voice.

Emi laughed. 'A great comfort I'm sure.' She grinned up at him, her face so close he could have easily brushed his lips against hers.

Edward's heart missed a beat. He desperately wanted to lean down and kiss Emi and having to refrain from doing so was becoming almost unendurable. Instead he held her even more firmly against him, his hand not quite on the curve of her buttocks as he glided around the dance floor with her. He wished the music would never end. He changed the subject, trying to reign in his emotions. 'This is far too serious a conversation for a party,' he smiled in return.

'Too true,' replied Emi. 'Shall we pause for a glass of wine?' she asked.

'Certainly, what can I get you?' He reluctantly let go of her as the music came to an end.

'Oh, Chenin Blanc, please.'

'At your service,' said Edward as he guided her to a high-top table and headed off to get their drinks.

'May I join you?' asked Matthew.

'But of course.'

'Enjoying yourself, Emi?'

'Yes, very much so, although, the perfection of everything here still surprises me. Maybe one day I'll get used to it,' she shrugged her shoulders. 'I was just talking to Edward about The Cloud. It sounds like quite the monumental project.'

'That it is. It's thrilling to be building it after all these years of planning.'

'Funny, to me it's this new thing, a new idea, but to you it's something that has been part of a strategy for years. It must be almost unbelievable to you to finally see it come to fruition.'

'It did, for a long time, feel like a pipe-dream, like it would never actually happen,' Matthew conceded. 'But we knew at the back of our minds that time wasn't on our side. Delaying much longer wasn't an option.'

'So, why wait to build The Cloud if you knew time was of the essence?'

'Because we had to make sure that the calculations were correct and…'

'Matthew, can I get you a drink?' asked Edward, interrupting their conversation as he approached the table with two glasses of wine, his mouth turned down slightly at the edges, not wanting to share Emi even for a moment, though they were surrounded by people.

'No, thank you. I'm going to head out soon, still pretty tired from all my late nights doing research and then passing out vaccines. Oh, hello Peter, hello Elizabeth,' said Matthew, turning to greet them as they approached the table.

'Hello Matthew, Emi. Happy birthday, Edward. Great party, Charlotte really outdid herself this time.'

'Hello. Thank you, and yes Charlotte's irreplaceable. How are you both?'

'We're well. Peter's being kept pretty busy with delivering Cloud panels to the various sites so I don't see much of him. Nice to have this interlude,' replied Elizabeth as she smiled up at her husband.

'I'll say. I'm actually so busy that we've decided to expand the flight school so we can train more pilots. One of our new recruits is Sal,' said Peter. He directed his comment to Emi.

'And how's she with piloting a Hovercraft?' asked Emi, her eyes widened in surprise at the thought of Sal in control of a Hovercraft.

'Peter tells me I'm a natural,' said Sal as she came up behind Emi.

'Sal. I didn't know you were here in New York,' said Emi as she gave her friend a hug.

'I arrived a couple of weeks ago but Peter doesn't let me have a moment to myself,' Sal replied with a smile at Peter. 'He is so busy and in desperate need of pilots that I'm in full time training.'

'This is such a nice surprise. I feel like it's my birthday,' said Emi. 'We really need to catch up. Peter you have to let her have some time off.'

'I don't think I'll be given much of a choice. Maybe she could take you for a flight and you can catch up that way.'

'I'd love to go for a flight sometime,' Emi responded with a hopeful glint in her eye.

'Well, she'll be fully qualified soon and then that will be a very real possibility since she'll need some practice runs. As long as you're a willing guinea pig,' said Peter, with a wink at Emi.

'I'd love to take you up flying but we should probably arrange a lunch-date first as my qualifications are still a few weeks away,' said Sal.

'That would be great,' Emi's face lit up with a smile. 'Did you know Matthew is planning for Zoe to come to New York as well to study medicine. Be good for Zoe, after the raid and all, be a good distraction. And I'll have a few of my old friends around, which'll be nice.'

'Sal mentioned she wasn't feeling too well,' said Peter. 'So we need her to see you for a checkup anyway.'

'What's wrong, Sal?'

'Nothing specific. Just kind of tired.'

'Come by my lab and I'll run some diagnostic checks,' Emi said, turning her head to include Edward in the conversation and finding him staring at her. 'Oh, dear. This isn't very fun birthday party chat is it?'

'I think maybe another turn around the dance floor is in order. Shall we?' Edward held out his hand to Emi, happy to be able to pry her away from the others again. He put his hand to her waist and led her to the floor, then took her in his arms, and smiled and then frowned. He was not very confident that his patience and self-control could hold out; there was something about Emi that was irresistible.

'Why the frown?' asked Emi. 'Too much business talk, per chance?'

'Oh, sorry, am I frowning? I wasn't aware,' he said as he smiled down at her upturned face. 'No, no, the business talk doesn't bother me but it does make me mindful of how much there is yet to do.'

'Well, I think we should forget about business for a while and just enjoy the music. It's your birthday after all.'

Edward's arm tightened around Emi's waist. He drew her closer to him, her body moving as one with his, as he effortlessly guided her around the dance floor. 'Agreed,' he said huskily.

The others watched as Edward and Emi circled the floor. 'I do believe that Edward might have found his future Mrs. Black,' observed Elizabeth.

FIFTEEN

They had been having a few technical difficulties with the New York Cloud and had sent Peter to collect Dez in the Hovercraft to see if he could sort out the problems.

'I sure hope it's nothing too major,' said Dez, his forehead furrowed. He puffed out his cheeks and exhaled loudly as he followed Peter onto the Hovercraft. 'I'm a little busy at the moment with trying to get Cloud lll put together on schedule.'

'I've no doubt,' Peter replied with a half-hearted smile of understanding. 'I need to fly into the city once I've dropped you off, but can come back to get you whenever you're ready to go.'

'Thanks, Peter. Much appreciated,' said Dez, as he really didn't want to be stuck at the New York Cloud for very long. The interruption was frustrating.

They continued to fly east over the golden landscape below. There was little movement except the slight swaying of the grass and the swirling of dust as it formed funnels in the air, reaching like fingers for the sky. 'Hmmm. We seem to have a pretty good headwind today,' said Peter, as he glanced over his shoulder at Dez. 'We're going to be a bit late.'

'Not to worry. It's not like I had a set time to be there.'

'My radar is showing some cloud accumulating to the southeast. If it turns into a thunderstorm I'll have to delay my return trip but I'll get back as soon as I can.'

Dez frowned and nodded. Thunderstorms happened from time to time and there was not much to be done other than wait for them to pass. They generally didn't last long. The rest of the trip turned out to be more turbulent than usual but Peter set the Hovercraft down near the New York Cloud structure without too much difficulty.

'See you later. Thanks for the lift,' Dez waved Peter goodbye and exited the Hovercraft.

Dez was greeted by one of the Network crew assigned to work on the New York Cloud. 'Thanks for coming, Dez. We're having trouble with some of the panels getting stuck horizontally. We haven't been able to adjust the angle so they can follow the sun and we're not sure where the problem is.'

'Right, lead the way and I'll see if I can get it sorted,' he sighed. This sounded more major than he would have liked. He was so busy, stretched to his limits, he didn't need any extra problems right now.

The solar array was as described. Some of the panels were horizontal while others were at an angle facing the sun. It appeared to affect every second panel.

'There must be a faulty connection on one of the relays. The problem is finding it. Damn. ' He let out his pent up breath as he ran his fingers through his hair. 'I'm going to need a few people to help me narrow down the options.'

'I'll see who I can find,' said the technician. 'Most people are working at the other end of the structure where things are still getting put together.' He headed off through the rows of panels to gather those who were closest. The breeze increased and twirled spirals of dust around him as he went.

Dez returned to inspecting one of the faulty panels. Engrossed in what he was doing he failed to hear the footsteps behind him.

'Dez. What are you doing here?'

Dez jumped and hit his head on the panel above him. He turned in disbelief as he rubbed at the top of his head. 'Emi!'

She stood there with a massive smile plastered to her face. 'Hi.' The wind picked up her hair and played with it, making it dance in front of her. Emi brushed her hair out of the way. 'Surprise.'

'I'll say. What are *you* doing here?' he asked as he enveloped her in a hug, hardly believing his good luck.

'Some of the installers weren't feeling well, so they called me out to see if I can find out what's wrong,' she said into his shoulder. Her last few words were lost in a sudden gust of wind. The rain started. It bounced off the panels.

Dez and Emi both turned to look up at the sky. The clouds were black with a blue-green tinge. The hair on Emi's arms stood up and her neck prickled. Overhead look ominous, the storm was gathering speed, the clouds swirled and the wind suddenly picked up to a steady howl.

'This doesn't look good. We better find shelter.' As he uttered the words the rain turned to hail.

'Ouch,' yelled Emi as they ducked under the horizontal panel.

'Shit, hail.' Dez pulled Emi in closer to him under the relative safety of the solar panel as the stinging hail became a pounding, bouncing cascade of pebble-sized hailstones. 'The control room, at the end of this row — run!'

They tore through the rows of panels, trying not to slip on the icy, moving ground, their arms above their heads to deflect the worst of the hail from their faces. When they reached the control room, Dez yanked open the door, grabbed Emi and pushed her inside just as the hailstones became the size of a man's fist. He slammed the door closed behind him. The interior of the control room was dim. The overhead lights usually self-adjusted to maintain a constant level of light but there was obviously a fault somewhere and the lights were stuck on their lowest setting. They were not normally needed as the solar tubes and windows usually provided enough daylight but as the storm intensified it was gradually turning day to night. The dimness of the interior became of little concern as the noise of the storm was joined by the sound of solar panels cracking.

'Oh God, no. Half of the panels are stuck. The hail will destroy them,' yelled Dez. 'I've got to try to turn them.' His frustration turned to anger at the thought of all the progress that had been made getting destroyed in a matter of minutes. He spun around and as he took in the layout of the control room he tried to figure out what he could possibly do to salvage things before it was too late.

'But there are people out there. The panels are all they have for shelter.'

Dez froze and cast a stricken look at Emi. 'I can't let…I have to try. We can't lose The Cloud.' He faced the control panel and frantically looked for some clue as to why the solar panels were stuck. He pulled the lever that turned the power to the grid completely off and then turned it back on. One of the connectors sparked momentarily. If it wasn't for the increasing darkness caused the storm, he would never have seen the tiny spark by daylight. He turned the power back off and yanked out the connector.

'Help me find one of these,' he yelled over the thundering storm as he held the connector up for Emi to see.

They opened the storage cupboards and pulled out boxes of parts. They glanced at the contents before thrusting them aside. Dez muttered under his breath and his hands moved frantically as he pulled out box after box. 'Damn, damn, damn.'

'Here. Is this it?' asked Emi. She held up a part in her hand.

Dez grabbed it from her and held it up beside the broken one. 'That's it,' he shouted in triumph. He spun around, took the few steps back to the control panel and inserted the new connector. Flipping the lever he turned the power back on. Above the roar of the storm he thought he could hear a slight hum that was not there before. Moving to the window, he peered out. It was almost as black as night outside but he could see the nearest panels moving, they were no longer fully horizontal. He punched a couple buttons on the control panel and watched as the panels moved into their vertical position. He cranked the lever on the wall to lower the storm shutters over the outside of the windows. Then he turned to face Emi.

'Dez.'

'Emi. I'm sorry. I had to.' They were the hardest words he'd ever had to say to her. 'If we lose half The Cloud we could lose the whole world,' he added, feeling the desperate need to somehow justify his actions.

Emi nodded and then shook her head. 'Oh God, Dez, those are our people out there,' she said, her voice hoarse with suppressed emotion, her eyes haunted.

They listened as the hail assaulted the roof of the little building, the only thing keeping them from being pummelled to death. The wind picked up to a shriek and rattled the shutters of their tiny refuge. Dez opened his arms and Emi stepped into his embrace. She buried her head in his shoulder and closed her eyes as a shudder coursed through her body.

Dez kept his arms wrapped around Emi, while outside the Category 8 Hyperstorm picked up momentum. He'd never heard anything so terrifying or felt so much power unleashed. He briefly disengaged himself to put the bar across the door. Thankfully, the Fringe built things to withstand the occasional Hyperstorm. He found a couple of emergency blankets, laid them out on the floor and drew

Emi down beside him. It was starting to get very cold. The control room was a concrete box. It offered little warmth when the sunlight was no longer streaming in. The massive hailstones continued to rain down. The outside temperature dropped precipitously and conversation was impossible over the deafening drumming on the roof. Emi shivered in his arms. He tightened his hold and ran his hand over her hair, offering the only comfort he could. There was nothing they could do for those caught outside in the storm but he knew Emi would be tormenting herself about her own safety while others from the Network died a horrible death.

Dez rested his head against Emi's and closed his eyes. His ears filled with the sound of the screaming wind and any items not fastened down smashing into the walls of the control room. Having Emi in his arms was his refuge. Then he found her lips on his, demanding a response, while her arms wrapped around him and her hands found their way under his shirt. He kissed her back and then pulled back to look into her eyes. With the dim light reflected from the control panel he thought he saw her fear and sadness mixed with guilt — but there was also a burning desire to seize life.

He kissed her then. He was finally alone with Emi, as alone as he could ever hope to be and she was all he needed to survive.

The world outside ceased to exist.

The Hyperstorm raged for forty-eight hours.

When Dez and Emi emerged from the control room the world was completely still and silent except for the relentless dripping. It was as if the screeching of the wind had stolen their hearing and replaced it with one noise — drip, drip, drip. The ground was covered in the massive, deadly hailstones and littered with debris — pieces of trees, odd fragments of buildings, the carcasses of animals, and the bodies of the Network members who had not been able to find shelter in time.

'We should have helped more get to safety. We should've got them into the control room with us. Why did we just leave them like that?' Emi whispered, the horror before them strangled the words as she uttered them

'We barely made it ourselves, Emi. We couldn't save anyone. We would've died trying,' said Dez, desperately wanting to alleviate the heartache he knew she was going through.

She nodded but didn't seem convinced, misery and self-reproach emanated from her eyes. Her job was to make people feel better, not allow them to perish while she saved her own skin. And to heap coals upon her own head she had made matters worse by finding pleasure in Dez's arms while her people died outside the walls of her refuge. Some would have been parents, have dependents. She had chosen to forfeit their lives for her own. But what made her so important? There was no child that needed her. She turned from Dez and headed out into The Cloud structure, stumbling over the two-foot thick mass of hailstones that carpeted the area, to look for survivors, someone to help.

Dez followed Emi out into the aftermath of the storm. They walked up and down every row of the immense structure searching for survivors until their feet ached and their hands were raw from digging through the icy hailstones. Every time they came across a protruding hand or a foot, they flung the stones aside, hoping for signs of life, but it was a fruitless exercise and they both knew it. They came to the end of the last row and surveyed their world. It became blindingly white as the sun emerged from behind the last of the clouds. There was nothing but the now vertical solar panels and the control room in sight.

'Come on, Emi. We can't...' Dez gasped. 'Crap, look at your hands,' he groaned.

Emi looked down at her hands. They were blue, swollen and raw, her fingers frozen in claw like shapes from trying to dig away the hailstones. ' I...I can't feel them,' she whispered as she looked back up a Dez with fear in her eyes.

'Shit. Come on, we need to get you warmed up.' Dez put his arm around Emi and guided her back to the control room. He could feel her body shaking uncontrollably and hear her teeth chattering. It was the only sound other than the dripping of the melting ice. He could not yet feel the suns warmth amid the frozen landscape though he knew the sauna-like conditions from the sun's heat combined with the water vapour were not far away. He did not want to have Emi out amongst the bodies when the temperature changed.

Back in the control room he wrapped her in the emergency blankets and routed around in the first aid kit for something that might help with frostbite. He found some ointment that was meant to heal the skin and some packs that became warm when you broke them. He carefully applied the ointment and rested Emi's hands on the packs as he gently blew his warm breath onto her hands to help mitigate the damage. It was the best he could do. Frostbite was not usually a problem they had to deal with.

He then looked in the emergency supplies for sustenance. He tempted her to have something to eat. He fed her since she could not move her hands and gave her something to drink so she didn't dehydrate. It had been a long few days. He held her until her shivering stopped and she fell into an exhausted sleep in his arms.

'I love you Emi,' he whispered.

Emi came-to with a start. 'Dez?'

'Shhh. It's okay. I've got you.'

Emi looked around at the bleak concrete walls and then returned her gaze to Dez. 'It wasn't just a nightmare?'

He shook his head and watched her closely for signs of shock.

'I've never been so scared.' She took a shuddering breath. 'The people. The poor people.'

'I know. But Emi, there was nothing we could've done.'

'I know.' She rested her head against his shoulder and glanced down at her hands resting in her lap. 'My hands; what happened to my hands?'

'We were trying to save people…digging in the ice. You wouldn't stop until we had searched the whole of The Cloud. Don't you remember?'

'I…I don't know. I guess,' Emi hesitated, shaking her head as if to try and clear her thoughts. 'My hands…they burn.'

'They'll be okay,' Dez said as he gently took her hands in his. He looked down at her swollen, angry hands nestled in his. His tougher skin and callouses from working outside on The Cloud had spared him.

'I…I need my hands…to…to do research and to heal people.' She looked up, despair reflected in her eyes.

'I know,' Dez swallowed the lump in his throat. 'I got you back here as soon as I realised and tried to warm you up. I'm sure once we're rescued, Matthew will be able to fix you,' he said, trying to sound far more positive than he was feeling.

She nodded, then looked around, comprehension slowly dawned. 'We're still alone?'

Dez nodded. 'I keep hoping to hear a Hovercraft. Someone has to come eventually to check on The Cloud. But…' he trailed off and shrugged his shoulders. Who knew what state the rest of the area was in, if any Hovercrafts were left undamaged or who was even alive. But he couldn't voice these thoughts to Emi.

'But you managed to save The Cloud?'

'*We* did, yes. Just in time. It has some damage, but nothing like what it might have been. At least we may have managed to save the planet,' he gave her a lopsided smile.

She nodded again and then snuggled into his arms. 'I love you.'

He kissed the top of her head and held her close. They waited for rescue and for their lives to be torn from them once more.

SIXTEEN

Emi had called Sal into her lab to run some tests. Blood work and scans were essential to establishing an idea of what her current health level was, and if Sal agreed to the vaccine, it would make for a great comparison to the end results.

'Hi Sal, come on in, take a seat. How are you?'

'Pretty good, just a bit off feeling sometimes for no particular reason that I can figure.' Sal glanced at Emi as she took a seat. 'Oh, Emi, look at your hands.'

Emi held them up. The swelling had gone away but some of the skin still looked angry and her dexterity had not yet fully returned. 'I know. It looks worse than it is and they're way better than what they were. It's a slow process to regenerate the tissue and the skin but Matthew can work wonders.'

'I'm surprised you're back at work already.'

'Working helps,' a smile hovered over Emi's face and then was gone. She had spent many hours with Matthew as he worked on rehabilitating her hands. His machines could regenerate her skin but it was up to her, and doing the endless exercises he had prescribed, that would make the difference to regaining full mobility. She had returned to work but she could still not undertake anything that required delicate handling. 'Anyway, today you're the patient. So, has the *off* feeling been getting more frequent or stronger?'

'I guess, maybe more often. Feeling a bit off is no big deal but I used to get on with things, but now…' she shrugged her shoulders.

'Right, well, first we'll do a scan to check your bone density, organ function and your brain activity. At least it only requires me pushing a button so you should survive my ministrations,' she joked. 'After that we'll do the blood-work. Although, it *will* be the first needle I've given so, hopefully, I don't stab you,' she smirked, holding her hands up for inspection.

Sal donned the paper gown and lay down on the scanning bed. As the lights came on she felt the bed warm beneath her; the lights were intense, even with the goggles on. Her nose pinched at the sterile smell. She closed her eyes and she took a deep breath as she unclenched her hands.

Emi input the various tests she wanted to run and watched as the results came up on her screen. She always found this part of her job fascinating. The first thing that jumped out at her was that Sal's tattoo imprint went deeper than most imprints. But why should she be feeling worse? Surely her imprint had always been like it was now. Maybe the blood-work would tell her something.

Emi turned off the machine and pushed the button to open the scanning bed. The room was quiet without the hum of the equipment.

Sal sat up, looking pale.

'You okay, Sal?'

'Not a fan of enclosed spaces,' she said, giving Emi a half-hearted smile.

'You okay with needles, because blood-work is next?'

Sal grimaced. 'Don't love them but…' She shrugged her shoulders. 'If you can do it, I can do it. Team effort for success,' she grinned at Emi.

'Alright, well let's get this done, then I'll enter everything into the diagnostic machine and by the time we're back from lunch, we'll have some results.'

Emi managed to insert the needle into Sal's arm without fumbling or dropping any of the vials. She breathed a sigh of relief — Sal had not winced as the needle was inserted so she assumed she had managed to not cause her too much pain. Her hand exercises were working. Once she had taken a few vials of blood, she sent Sal off to get dressed while she put the blood samples into the genetic analysis machines.

Sal came back in a cool cotton dress and sandals, her hair in a ponytail, and with a bit more colour in her cheeks.

'Ready to go? There's a cute little cafe around the corner that I thought you might like.'

Sal nodded and followed Emi out onto the busy New York streets. 'I can't believe how different it is here from where we grew up. It never crossed my mind that there was a city anywhere in the world that was still intact, nevermind thriving,' said Sal as she stared up at the building that towered overhead.

'It's a bit surreal. I'm *almost* used to it now,' Emi said. 'But I still miss home, even though it's so basic compared to here.'

'Miss Dez too, I bet.'

Emi flushed a slight shade of pink.

'I was supposed to fly some workers out to help build Cloud lll the other day but didn't feel quite well enough. I'm rescheduled for tomorrow if you want to tag along.'

'Love to. It's my day off. Be fun to surprise Dez,' said Emi, her face lit up. 'Thanks.'

'We happen to have a free seat and it's my first day solo piloting. You might be taking your life in your hands,' Sal cautioned.

'I'll take my chances,' Emi grinned at her.

'Those things pretty much fly themselves anyway. I would love to see the look on Dez's face,' Sal winked at Emi, causing Emi's flush to deepen.

They entered *The Perfect Spot* and were immediately assailed by the aroma of roasting vegetables and homemade soups. Sal looked around in delight. Each little table was covered with a different coloured tablecloth, giving the place a festive air; even the chairs were mismatched. Here and there were low tables with love-seats, inviting customers to curl up and chat for hours as if they were cozied up in their best friends living room. Each setting felt private and homey with potted plants — all edible of course — scattered around for screening. The centrepiece of each table was a candle surrounded by miniature hydroponic herbs. The hostess sat them at a table for two, poured them glasses of cold water and handed each of them a menu. They grinned at each other across the table. Not so long ago, such decadence was unknown to either of them.

'This all sounds so good,' Sal surveyed the menu, her mouth starting to water.

'I've been here a couple times. Edward's brought me after stopping by the lab to see how my research was coming along. The food's really good.'

'Edward Black. So what's he like? I mean I saw him at the party but I didn't really get the chance to meet him. He must be quite something given what this city's like.'

'Well, he's very charismatic and charming and he's the sort of person people want to follow. Exudes power, keeps things running smoothly and is still considerate…' Emi trailed off, flushing slightly. Edward had been so kind to her since her injury. He had made sure she received the best medical care and had arranged to have someone in to help her with bathing, dressing and cooking until she had regained the use of her hands. She was still amazed he could take care of any one person's individual needs when he had so much else to do.

'You like him?'

'He's impossible not to like.'

They paused in their conversation as the waitress brought their soup and salad to the table. 'Please use any of the herbs for garnish,' the waitress said. 'Can I get you anything else?'

'I think I'd like a glass of white wine, please. Would you like anything, Sal?'

'I'll have the same, please.'

'And I'm *starting* to be thankful to him for bringing me here,' joked Emi as she carefully picked up her fork and attempted to stab at the cherry tomato on her salad. It shot off her plate and rolled across the table to wedge under the rim of Sal's plate.

'Sorry, Sal.'

Sal laughed. 'Maybe pick it up with your fingers. Easier than using a fork,' she suggested. 'I won't tell,' she winked at Emi.

Emi grinned, picked up the tomato and popped it in her mouth. Using a knife and fork was still a challenge. She knew that spearing the cherry tomatoes was going to be beyond her abilities. She picked up another and rolled her eyes at Sal. 'I think handling the needle was easier,' she joked.

'I'm glad I'm not the tomato,' Sal smiled in reply. 'This wouldn't be too hard to get used to,' she said as she inhaled the steam coming from her cauliflower and cheese soup. 'I'm a bit tired of squirrel and rabbit, I have to confess. How do you like living here?'

'Well, working in the medical profession feels like something I was born to do. I'm meant to be here! I'm learning and helping people and…I can't really put it into words,' Emi said, her eyes lighting up. 'Speaking of health, can you tell me if you're doing anything different from the norm that might be affecting how you're feeling?' she asked as she tucked into her soup.

'Maybe I'm eating a bit less but I've been eating healthier food since coming to New York so…'

'Hmmm, wish I had your bloodwork from before, when you weren't feeling so bad. It'd be interesting to compare the results. I wonder if your body's going through some kind of detox.'

'Detox from what?' asked Sal, as she dipped her bread into her soup.

'Well, maybe from genetically modified food.'

'Is a lot of our food genetically modified? I don't think I'd know the difference. I always just ate whatever was available — it was either that or starve.'

'Some of our food would come from the genetically modified crops, and our soil was still somewhat contaminated, so we'd have been getting trace amounts of toxins and now you're having food which is one hundred percent pure, so maybe your body is just adjusting.'

'I guess that makes sense.'

'Or maybe, if you're eating less, you're not getting enough nutrients to boost your immune system. And have you thought about getting the vaccine and see if that helps.'

'It's just that my tattoo imprint has been in the family for generations. I feel wrong getting rid of it.'

'Well, my advice is to look forward rather than back and if you end up having children then you can pass on clean genes.'

'I hadn't thought of it like that.'

'I can give you the vaccine anytime. I'm sure you'll feel better,' said Emi. 'At least you will after your body has gone through withdrawal.'

'That was so good,' said Sal as she dabbed at her mouth with a napkin.

'I thought you'd like it,' Emi smiled at her in response.

The waitress cleared away their empty dishes. Emi gave her New York ID to pay the bill and they wandered back to her lab. It was hot out, as usual, but there was a good breeze off the river and they were in no rush. Sal was still in awe of how pristine New York was. She craned her neck to look down every street, taking in how clean everything was, how many windows were solar panels, the trees that lined the streets offering both shade and some variety of food. Everything that could be done to make the city liveable with their intolerable climate had been done.

When they reached the lab, Emi went immediately to check the results. It was as she thought, Sal's immune system was depleted.

'I think I should give you the vaccine today. As the toxins leave your body, hopefully, it will be enough of a boost to give your immune system a break.'

Sal held out her arm while Emi prepared the needle.

'I feel a bit more nervous this time having watched you with the fork and the tomato,' said Sal with a smirk, her eyes shining with amusement.

'No doubt,' Emi laughed. 'I'll try not to shoot you across the table.'

'Good job I'm not round.'

Emi shook her head, enjoying the light banter. 'Right, that's done,' she said as she withdrew the needle. 'We'll do a follow-up in about a month. Don't worry too much, I think you'll be fine,' she reassured Sal as she disposed of the needle. 'Guess I'll see you tomorrow for the flight.'

'Thanks Emi,' said Sal as she let herself out. 'See you tomorrow,' she called. The door closed behind her as she waited in the lobby for the elevator. She took the lift down to ground level. She extracted her sunglasses and hat from her purse as she stepped into the busy street and bumped straight into someone.

'Oh, sorry,' she exclaimed. 'I wasn't paying attention…'

'Hi, Sal. It's okay, no harm done,' Peter grabbed ahold of her to stop her from stumbling. 'Were you seeing Emi?' He craned his neck to look up at the medical building where Emi worked.

'Yes, getting some tests done, then we went for lunch,' she replied. She regained her equilibrium and finally looked up.

'Sal, this is Edward Black. Edward this is Sal. I don't think I ever got around to introducing you properly at the party. Sal's the person who has joined us from the Network to learn to fly the Hovercrafts,' said Peter.

Sal turned to shake hands and tried not to gasp. She must have been in a haze at the party, too overawed at her surroundings to not have properly noticed Edward. He was the best looking man she had ever seen. He took her breath away. Yet, there was something vaguely familiar about him. She held out her hand, trying to hide her response with formality. 'Hello, nice to meet you — officially.'

Edward took her hand in his, sending electric shocks up Sal's arm. 'Hello, Sal, nice to meet you too. I hope you're enjoying New York City.'

'It's amazing. I had no idea such places still existed,' Sal said, attempting to keep her voice even and say something reasonably intelligent. She felt like she was swimming through mud — her body and mind slow and unable to function properly. *How did Emi handle working alongside Edward?*

'They don't in most of the world. We were fortunate in being able to preserve what we had,' Edward replied, his smile further reducing Sal to mush. 'And how's Emi?'

'She's fine.' *She had to say more than that. It was so abrupt it sounded almost rude.* 'A little homesick. I think she's missing her friends,' she added in a rush.

'But aren't many of her friends here now?' asked Peter.

'Yes, but she probably misses Dez the most,' Sal said, the words tumbling out of her. 'I'm sure they'd be married by now if they weren't both so busy trying to help save the world. I was thinking that I...,' she glanced at Peter, then back at Edward. *Oh crap!* The hair on her arms stood on end and her stomach somersaulted. She felt she had just said something really wrong but she wasn't sure what exactly.

'Well, I wouldn't want Emi to be unhappy,' replied Edward, his earlier friendliness vanished into mere politeness as he cut across what Sal had been about to say. 'I could arrange for her to spend some time back home but I can't promise she'll see Dez. He's busy overseeing the building of The Cloud.'

'I'm sure she would be ever so grateful to get home for a while,' Sal responded, sensing that to mention the planned trip for the next day would be another mistake. Shit, this man really could put your brain in a dither. If Edward were to be romantically interested in Emi she would not stand a chance. Saying 'no' to him was not conceivable. *Poor Dez.*

SEVENTEEN

Emi gazed around her apartment for what seemed like the twentieth time. She couldn't believe she was this nervous hosting a dinner party for her friends, people she had known most of her life. She knew they would be happy to be there and would be content to eat whatever she placed before them. But she wanted the evening to be special.

She checked over everything again. The dining table was set with her new cutlery set, plain white dishes and the wine glasses that she had bought today for the occasion. She had candles for a centrepiece on the table and had others burning in the living room. She liked the effect; it gave her apartment a warm, homey feel.

The furniture Edward had provided was modern but inviting. Beyond her balcony the lights from other building twinkled in the dusk. The gentle breeze coming through the open window was pleasantly warm, without the scorching temperatures that daytime brought. And the aroma of the food she had prepared was making her mouth water. It was going to be a perfect. She smiled, heading for her bedroom to change before everyone arrived.

What to wear? She didn't want to be too formal. She settled on a pair of jeans and her white blouse, it was simple but nice. She put her hair up in a ponytail and applied some make-up. She had gotten used to wearing make-up now and liked the way it highlighted her eyes. Simple and elegant but understated.

She looked at herself in the mirror and laughed. What was she thinking? Nobody was going to care if she had nice clothes and make-up or if she was just wearing old ripped shorts and a shirt. How life had changed. And why was she so nervous?

She headed for the kitchen to pour a glass of wine when she heard the first knock at the door. She took a steadying breath before opening the door.

'Dez!' she said as she threw herself into his arms. All her nerves vanished.

'Hey. That's a nice welcome or do you greet all your guests that way?'

'Yes, of course. It's the New York custom,' she beamed up at him.

'In that case I think I might leave and come back in again.'

There was another knock at the door. Sal, Zoe, Jax and Abe arrived together. She ushered them in and gave each one a hug before closing the door. Moments later she opened the door to admit Jon and Amy as well as Tom and Liz. She hugged each of them in turn and grinned from ear to ear before turning to wink at Dez.

Her friends were here. Let the evening commence.

'Thanks Emi, that was magnificent.' Sal took her wine glass and headed for the living room with the others.

'No trouble. It's nice to have everyone here,' smiled Emi as she joined the group. They were gathered in her living room. The last couple hours spent around her dining room table, enjoying comfortable conversation and laughter over a sumptuous meal, had been all that she had hoped for and more.

She enjoyed cooking now that there was so much good food to be had. She had gone all out, making a couple of roast chickens with all the trimmings along with roast potatoes and seasoned vegetables. She couldn't remember the last time she'd been this happy. To have all her friends around, including Dez, and to be able to offer them a comfortable place to hang out, as well as dinner, had been unimaginable not so long ago. She felt like she could get used to living in New York; maybe even really enjoy it.

'This is almost like old times,' said Jax.

'Except the surroundings are a little more opulent and the food abundant…and there's wine,' observed Dez. He grinned at Jax's understatement and gave him a friendly shove in the shoulder.

'There is that,' said Jax with a laugh as he rolled his eyes.

'It's hard to believe the Fringe have been able to live like this all this time. I thought the whole world was a desolate wasteland,' said Liz. 'Wonder why they didn't contact us or help us earlier.'

'They've been so great since the raid though. I mean they've given us so much food and helped with re-building the shelters. We're way better off than what we used to be,' said Tom. He stared in appreciation at Emi's apartment and ran his hand over the soft fabric of the couch. He shook his head. 'So much luxury that I had no idea existed.'

'The Fringe have been very…helpful, but sometimes I miss my old life and working to be self-sufficient.' Jon glanced around at each person in the group. 'It's good to be together for a change.'

'I still find coming to New York a bit overwhelming,' said Amy. 'It's a different world from Sector B and even Sector B is not what it was. We're better off but…we've lost some of our freedom and there are *so* many people I don't recognise now,' she added as her mouth turned down in a frown.

'It's so nice that you're all here at the same time. I hardly know a soul in New York,' said Emi. She snuggled up to Dez on the couch. 'I've missed having friends around.'

'Well, speaking for myself, I must say there's nothing like being offered the position of medical guinea pig to entice a guy to see his girl,' stated Dez with a straight face and a wink at the group that Emi could not see.

'Yes, but medical research has to start somewhere you know. I need to compare your vaccine results to those of Sal, see if I can find what's different. I've studied her results for a couple weeks now and I just can't find anything specific for why she should continue to feel unwell, especially now that she's had the vaccine,' Emi replied defensively.

'No need to convince me, I'm a willing sacrificial lamb,' he said and pulled her in closer.

Jax smiled across at them.

Emi could hardly believe she had Dez to herself for a few days. And what made it even better was that it coincided with Edward being in England for a meeting, so there was no chance the two would cross paths. Even if Edward heard that Dez had been here it would be okay since Abe had brought Dez with him as part of her research. She looked down at her hands. They were fully healed now and she had finally been able to get back to doing the more intricate parts of her research. Thus, Dez being here should not raise any eyebrows.

'How's the flying going, Sal?' asked Abe, changing the subject to something more positive.

'I love it,' Sal smiled in response, her enthusiasm lighting up her face. 'Peter's a fantastic instructor and it's great being out of the dust and heat for a while.'

'I bet.'

'I feel like a bird when I'm up there…looking down. Makes me realise how very small we are, though I never feel that way when I'm on the ground.'

'It does change one's perspective,' Dez agreed.

'It's hard to believe we've destroyed the world so much given our relative size,' Sal shook her head. 'Thank goodness for the Fringe and their plans.'

'It's hard to get used to thinking positively about the future. Just surviving from day to day was as positive as I would ever let myself get,' said Zoe.

'Yes, me too,' Sal nodded at Zoe in agreement.

'Well, hopefully Matthew's vaccine works a miracle and one day you get to be a Hovercraft instructor for Fie and Lea, as they're both pretty keen,' said Abe.

'That would be fun. I could head up a whole division of female Network pilots,' said Sal with a grin that split her face from ear to ear before being replaced by a slight scowl as she shook her head and closed her eyes for a moment.

'Are you feeling *any* better since having the vaccine, Sal?' asked Dez.

Sal shook her head. 'Quite truthfully, no, not really.'

'Now that you mention it, you do look a bit pasty,' observed Emi. She stared across at Sal who had suddenly gone the colour of the couch she was sitting on — a shade of white.

'I'm not feeling my sparkling best in all honesty. Maybe I should go.'

'Why don't you lie down in the guest bedroom for a bit? If you want to stay the night you're more than welcome to,' offered Emi. 'I'll check in on you in a while.'

'Sure, thanks Emi. Sorry…don't want to ruin your party.'

'Don't be daft. It's all good.'

'So, any idea as to what's wrong with her Emi?' Jax asked as Sal vacated the room.

'No, I've run so many tests and I just can't figure it out.'

'Which is why you want to compare her results to Dez's?' asked Abe.

'Yes. I want to compare her bloodwork from before and after the vaccine to that of Dez and see if there is any difference that jumps out at me.'

'Why Dez in particular?'

'No reason really,' Emi replied, flushing a light shade of pink. 'There are a few others in the study as well,' she said quickly as she cleared her throat. 'The only thing I can see that is wrong is that Sal's toxicity levels have suddenly gone up. But I would have thought that after the vaccine they would have been lower. I can't figure out what has thrown her body out of whack.'

'Maybe Matthew should see her…run some tests,' suggested Zoe.

Emi looked at Zoe. 'I don't know why I didn't think of that. Thanks, Zoe.'

'I can book her in for tomorrow if you like. I'll be working in the office and I'm sure he would squeeze her in even if he is fully booked.'

'That would be great,' Emi grinned in appreciation. Emi had the feeling that Zoe had a lot more sway over Matthew than she let on, but since members of the Network and the Fringe were not permitted to be in relationships they had to keep theirs' quiet. One day, if the Network became genetically pure enough, the laws might change, but in the meantime their secret was safe with her.

The conversation ebbed and flowed as they shared their memories from the past and chatted about the future…now that they had a future to look forward to. Between the chit-chat and the laughter Emi poked her head into her guest room to check on Sal but she seemed to be resting peacefully. As the evening wound down Emi thought she heard a sound…a sound that did not fit with the fun time they'd just shared. 'Hey guys, shhhh…did you hear …?' she cocked her ear.

'Emi,' Sal called from the room, her voice raised.

'Coming,' Emi jumped up and rushed to the guest room. Sal was lying on the bed, her body shaking and a bead of perspiration on her forehead. 'I'm, I'm so co…cold,' she muttered between chattering teeth.

Emi reached out. Sal was burning up, her skin clammy. Emi stared, horrified as the shaking worsened. 'I'm calling Matthew. You need a doctor.'

She picked up the phone. 'Matthew, it's Emi. Come quick. It's Sal. Something's wrong! We're at my place.'

EIGHTEEN

Spike slammed his fist into the wall and then swore as the pain reverberated up his arm. 'I've walked in so many diff'rent directions for so long and nothing. Just bloody damn long, dry grass.'

'Yeah, it's kinda depressin',' Shade frowned and kicked a chair over that somebody had left in the middle of the room.

'Hey, watch-it, yah almost hit me,' yelled Keyly. 'And those chairs are the only place we have to sit, other than the floor.' She slid down the wall, her legs splayed out in front of her on the relatively cold concrete.

'Yeah, well, I found 'em so I'll kick 'em if I want.'

'Fine, whatever, just don't hit me with 'em.'

'What's wrong with you? You're real snappy.'

'Zara died.'

'What? When?' asked Spike, his head snapped round as his curiosity got the better of him. Not that he really cared.

'Couple days ago, I guess. I went to see her yesterday. She was my sister ya know,' replied Keyly. 'But she was dead.'

'What? I didn't know you were sisters. That sucks,' said Shade. 'How'd she die?'

'Dunno. She'd had a new imprint done. They always made her feel sick so she took more pills to stop puking. Maybe she overdosed or maybe she suicided. Who knows? Either way, she's dead.'

'What about the kid?' asked Shade.

'Yeah, what about the kid? It's probably mine and now I'll have to look after it. I hate kids.'

'Yeah, well if you hate kids you shouldn't make kids you creep. You had me, and my sister, and left her with the kid,' Keyly scowled at Spike, her speech coming out in short, angry bursts. 'I always wondered whose he was,' she muttered under her breath.

'Yeah, well I didn't know you were sisters did I. And I don't hate makin' kids, just havin' them 'round that bugs me,' he said as he kicked at the toppled over chair.

'You're such an asshole. Stay away from me from now on.'

'No problem, I've got Shade now anyway.'

'Shade too? You do get around.'

'And for your info, you haven't 'got' me,' Shade added in contempt. 'I've just slept with you a couple times to make you shut-up.'

'Stupid cow.'

'You should talk. So where's the kid?' Shade asked Keyly.

'Died.'

'The kid too? Why?'

'Dunno. Zara was still feedin' him…prob'ly didn't get enough real food. Or maybe it was her blue milk. She showed me once…her milk…turned blue after she got a new imprint. Maybe the kid didn't like blue milk,' Keyly shrugged. 'Better off, he wasn't goin' to have a good life anyway, especially if creep-o here had to end up carin' for 'im.'

'It's not like I wanted 'im dead, I just didn't wanna look after 'im.'

'Well, now you don't have to do you?'

Spike grunted.

'Don't worry Spike, the way you get around, you're sure to have loads more kids to not look after soon enough,' said Keyly venomously.

'Yeah, you are, sooner than you think,' said Shade as she rubbed her belly and winked at Spike.

'What? Really? Crap!'

'Well, said. Glad you're so *happy* about it asshole.'

'Why should I be happy? It's a crap life, crap world, and a crap place to raise a kid and then you die.'

'True,' Keyly nodded her head. 'Maybe overdosing was the better way. Doesn't have to put up with all this shit for a few more years.'

'Yeah, but what if we're about to find the valley and food and all that?' Shade asked. 'I mean the Network live way longer and better than we do,' she said as she looked from one to the other.

'Yeah, whatever, I was tryin' to make myself feel better about her suic...her dying,' said Keyly, as she started to sob, the pain of loss finally penetrating the barrier of denial. 'She...she was the only family I had, her and the kid, and now they're both gone.'

Shade and Spike stared at the floor.

'We're just gonna have to carry on lookin' ain't we. Hopin' that Spike's idea of a mother load of food is for real 'cause I don't wanna have no kid just for it to die a year later 'cause it's not got enough to eat...or I don't.'

Spike looked at Shade, slammed his massive blue fist into the door, yanked it open and walked out. Damn, why had he started any of this? He didn't want no kid and he was bloody tired of pushin' his way through endless dry grassland for no reason. He had been about to call it quits, but there's no way Shade would let him rest now, not since the kid was his. What was he gonna do? He was trapped, trapped by his own stupid idea.

What he really needed was another tip-off. But he had no idea how to find the guy and he wasn't sure he really wanted to — the guy scared him. He still had no idea why he'd been given the tip-off about the food drop last time. The guy had never asked for anything in return and he hadn't seen him since. But another tip-off about now would be nice, get everyone off his case.

He felt so angry. The food was getting low, the building was dry but not comfortable, and everyone was edgy since they hadn't found the food he'd promised them. They blamed him; everything was always his fault. Killing off some more Network people would feel good. Why should they have it so easy when his life was nothing but one hard time after another?

They couldn't go back to the parking garage to live. Everyone would know it was them that stole the food since they'd disappeared the night of the theft. Nobody in his wreck of a city ever showed any mercy. They'd be dead by tomorrow if they showed their faces. They could only return if they went back with more than what they took. Crap, what had he been thinking? Why had he suddenly thought it would be easy to get food? Just 'cause he'd had one tip-off didn't mean he'd get another.

Tomorrow he would go out on his own. Get away from everyone. He would take a few days worth of food, more than he really needed, and explore in some new direction. He had to prove he was right; there just had to be a massive stash of food somewhere.

Spike grabbed his bag and headed out while everyone else was asleep. He didn't want to explain himself; he just wanted to prove himself right. He headed north. They had not explored the north as the terrain was rocky and uninviting. Shade would probably think he had skipped out on her and the kid. Nobody ever thought much good of him. Shade wasn't too bad though, so he would have to find something.

The sun rose in the sky, bringing the days' stifling heat with it. He trudged on, accustomed to being barefoot he barely noticed how hot the hard-packed earth was. As he squinted against the glare, he could make out hills on the distant horizon. It looked a long way off. Sweat ran into his eyes and stuck his shirt to his back. He stopped to remove his back-pack, pulled his shirt over his head and used it to mop up the sweat stinging his eyes, and then he tied his shirt onto the top of his head. His stomach growled. Controlling his instincts to rummage through his back-pack and wolf down whatever first came to hand, he rationed himself and selected a piece of jerky that he could gnaw at slowly. Even though he had taken a lot of the food he was not sure how long it would have to last.

The day faded to evening. The terrain slowly began to change. Pebbles bruised his heels when he came down on them too hard. He took his knife from his pack, slashed the lower part of his shorts off and tied the material around his feet. Finally, as dusk turned to night he stopped, exhausted he could go no further. He unrolled his mat, drank some juice, ate a few handfuls of fried potatoe thins and collapsed. He doubted he could make it much further but the hills looked just as far off as they had this morning.

The days followed each other relentlessly; one day the same as the next except for gradual changes in his surroundings. After three days he arrived at the foothills. Another full day of walking brought him to the crest of the first hill. The view from the top was daunting — more of the same. This time on the distant horizon he could see a smudge of grey in the sky. He rubbed his eyes — could it be clouds? He hadn't seen clouds or rain in what seemed like forever. Be nice to be rained on for a while. As he looked below him he could see a river winding it's way along the valley floor. If he walked along the water's edge he wouldn't have to go up and down all the hills. Maybe the main Network villages were on the other side of these mountains. If it rained where they lived then they'd be able to grow things and have food all the time. It made sense; they had to be where the clouds were. It gave him a thrill of hope, the first he'd had in a long time.

He started the descent to the valley floor, the branches underfoot made his feet ache and the slope was steep enough to be scary. He was used to flat land. A few times he lost his footing and had to grab a tree to regain his balance. Trying to keep his eyes on the ground to watch where he was going, branches scraped at his sunburnt blue skin. He wished he'd waited until daybreak to begin his descent. With the deepening twilight it was getting harder to see. He didn't want to end up lost. When he looked up he realised that at least he'd broken so many branches that the path he'd taken was obvious. As his foot came down on another branch it rolled and suddenly he found himself tumbling down the hillside, he hit his head hard on a stump before finally smashing into a rock, his knee taking most of the impact. He rolled over and grabbed at his leg. 'Ahhhhh!' He yelled in pain and frustration into the silence of the deepening twilight. He wasn't going to make it through the hills now. He would be lucky if he could stand, nevermind walk. He would have to go back. He tried to move his knee. 'Crap!' He pushed himself into a sitting position and then used an overhanging branch to pull himself upright. The world swam before him. He closed his eyes and waited for the dizziness to pass. Then he tried to put his weight on his injured leg. Pain shot through his body and everything went black. He slumped back to the ground.

When he woke, it was dark. His knee throbbed, his head ached and he was parched and starving. He rummaged around in his pack until he found a juice and a packet of pre-cooked sausages. He consumed the lot, not caring that everything was lukewarm or that he had downed too many of his rations at once. His stomach cramped in rebellion at the onslaught of food after too many hours of emptiness. He gasped, trying to subdue his uneasiness and not jump at every little sound the night offered up. It was pitch black — there was no moon and the tall, dark trees obliterated whatever starlight might have been scattered across the night sky — there wasn't enough light to navigate by. There was nowhere for him to go. Waiting for dawn was his only option.

His injuries and exhaustion got the better of him. He drifted off into a restless slumber.

Spike jolted awake. He shifted his eyes from side to side and breathed slowly in and out, willing his heart rate to slow. Had he heard branches cracking or had he been dreaming? He must have dozed off again. He gazed into the blackness; it was still dark, maybe less so than before but not by much. There it was again, a snapping of dry branches being trampled. What the hell was it? What kind of wild animals were left in the forests? He had no idea. But whatever it was he was at its' mercy. He could maybe throw it a bit of food and try to hobble away but he wouldn't get far. Crap, what was he going to do?

He heard it again, closer this time. He started to dig through his pack, hoping to find some food that a wild animal might like. Damn, his supply of sausages would've been good right about now. But then, if he survived being mauled by the animal, there still wasn't enough to eat? How would he get back to Shade? Why had he done this on his own? He lay back down and closed his eyes. Maybe if he stayed really still whatever it was would not notice him.

SNAP.

That was too near! He opened his eyes and breathed a sigh of relief. 'Oh, it's you! You scared the crap out of me. How the hell d'you find me here?'

NINETEEN

Emi put the Satcomm down with a shaking hand and returned to Sal's bedside. She found Abe holding Sal's head up, attempting to give her a sip of water, as Zoe came in with cool cloths to try and lower her temperature.

'Matthew's on his way, Sal. He'll be here soon.' Emi checked Sal's pulse, which was far too rapid.

Sal nodded. 'I wish I'd listened to…to you and had the…the vaccine earlier. Maybe if I'd had it…earlier then my…my immune system would be able to f..f…fight all the toxins,' she said through chattering teeth.

'Shhhh, it's okay. We didn't know your imprint was worse than most. That's not something I would've ever guessed. Matthew can give you something to boost your immunity and you'll be right as rain soon enough,' Emi smiled down at her friend.

Emi glanced up as Dez ushered Matthew into the bedroom. She moved to give Matthew space and went to stand beside Dez. Emi rested her head on Dez's shoulder as he put his arm around her and held her tight. She took a few deep breaths to try and quell the knot of fear that had developed in the pit of her stomach. Life was so fragile.

Matthew leaned over Sal and started to check her vital signs. He took out a small light and shone it in her eyes, then listened to her heart before gently prodding her stomach. She cried out in pain. Matthew retrieved his portable scanner from his bag and slowly moved it over her abdomen as he read the monitor. A frown appeared on his face. He extracted a syringe from his bag, filled it with a clear liquid and injected the contents into Sal's arm. Her eyes closed and her body relaxed.

Emi looked at Matthew questioningly.

He shook his head.

'Matthew?'

'Her lymph glands are swollen, her kidneys and liver are failing and her heart cannot stand the strain of fighting the toxins. I don't think she is strong enough to win this battle,' he answered Emi's implied question. 'She…doesn't have long. I've given her something to ease the pain but there's nothing else I can do. It's too late. I'm… so sorry.'

Emi turned her head into Dez's shoulder and quietly began to weep. Dez's arms tightened around her.

'But it's so sudden. I mean she seemed fine at the beginning of the evening,' Dez said to Matthew.

'I'm afraid toxicity is like that. The body can fight it for ages and you can go along feeling mostly okay, and then one day something can cause it to suddenly escalate, the body is too unhealthy to cope, and you end up with toxic shock. The tattoo ink has lead and mercury that bond to your lymph glands, dies them black, affects your liver and can even cause brain damage. And that was just the normal ink they used before they made the super one you all inherited. Plus, a toxin in your genes and blood stream is just *not* meant to be there. With Sal's imprint being deeper than most……'

'But…but I thought you could give an injection for toxic shock? Surely something can be done for her.' Dez questioned.

'It depends on the level of toxicity. Sal's is far too high.'

'Can't we take her to the hospital? There must be something with all your medical advancements that can help her…give her time so she can regain her strength and fight off the toxins,' Dez said as his hand caressed Emi's head and her tears soaked into his shirt.

'It's at a cellular level. Once toxins get into the cells …' Matthew lifted his shoulders in resignation and shook his head. 'I'm sorry. I wish with all our advancements there was something more I could do but…'

'Oh.' Dez rested his head on top of Emi's, all the fight suddenly left him, leaving him feeling deflated and empty.

'I'll stay with you all if that's okay? In case she needs anything else for the pain I'd like to be close by.'

'Yeah, thanks Doc,' replied Dez as he led Emi to the bed. They sat on either side of their friend, Emi holding Sal's hand and Dez regularly changing the cloths on her forehead. The dinner party was forgotten. Everyone mingled at the bedside or in the living room, quietly talking and waiting.

At midnight Sal stirred and opened her eyes. 'Emi?'

'It's okay Sal. We're all here, including Matthew. We'll look after you.'

Sal shook her head. 'I'm so sorry, Emi. I…I shouldn't have…said anything.'

'It's okay, Sal,' Emi glanced at Dez and shrugged her shoulders. She leaned against him as he sat behind her and wrapped his arms around her for comfort.

Sal nodded. '…but…but Edward…' Sal trailed off, her eyes closed.

Emi turned her head to look up at Dez. Sal wasn't making any sense. She must be in so much pain she's hallucinating, thought Emi. As far as she knew, Sal had never had a chance to talk with Edward and had only briefly met him at the party.

Matthew tapped her on the shoulder. 'Mind if I sit a while?'

Emi stood up to give Matthew her spot and headed for the kitchen with Dez. They poured some wine and joined the others in the living room.

'How's she doing?' asked Zoe.

Emi shook her head. 'I don't think she'll last the night,' the misery she felt audible through the huskiness of her voice. 'I can't believe this is happening,' she closed her red-rimmed eyes, trying to momentarily shut out the pain of losing another friend. 'It's just…so sudden and…I thought after the vaccine she was going to get better like everyone else,' she whispered, the soreness of her throat from crying making it difficult to talk.

Matthew came out and put his hand on Emi's shoulder. 'She's not got long left now. Her breathing is very shallow. If you want to say goodbye…'

Emi didn't think she had any tears left in her but her eyes pooled once more as she went to say a final farewell to her friend. Despairingly, Emi leaned over and gave Sal a kiss on the forehead. 'I'm going to miss you Sal. I was looking forward to having you here in New York with me,' she whispered before her throat closed up, preventing her from uttering another word.

The others filed in behind her as she fled the room. She was thankful that her friends were gathered around — she prayed she wouldn't have to say goodbye to any of them in the near future.

A while later Matthew returned to the living room. 'Emi,' he said quietly.

She looked up at him with puffy, bloodshot eyes.

'She's gone. I'm so sorry,' said Matthew, his own grief apparent in the drawn look of his countenance. 'I've arranged to have her… body removed.'

Emi nodded.

'Emi…I know it's no comfort but…I'll work on improving the vaccine. Make one that helps those with deeper imprints…maybe something that could even cure the Blues,' said Matthew, his anger at having lost a patient a close twin to the grief he was feeling.

Emi looked at Matthew in appreciation through her haze of pain. He was a good man, a good doctor. If he could make a better vaccine then Sal's death might at least save others. Heaving a sigh she gave Matthew a hint of a smile in acknowledgement. 'Thanks, Matthew,' she whispered, unable to get another word out past the lump in her throat.

Matthew gave her shoulder a squeeze and then turned to gather his belongings. He left when Sal's body was removed. Zoe followed him out. The others slowly departed, worn out after such an unexpectedly emotional evening.

Dez and Emi, left alone, sat curled on the couch with their arms wrapped around each other.

TWENTY

Launch day had arrived.

The Cloud had been checked and re-checked. The engineers from the Fringe had been there all week comparing every minute detail of the structure to the original drawings. The workmen had also been going over every last connection. The pumps were online, the solar panels were able to rotate to follow the sun, the condensers were all in place, and the wind turbines, which would blow the clouds in the direction they were needed, were fully operational. Only time would tell if their calculations were correct. Once the water was drawn through the entire system, would it be able to produce enough cloud to cool the earth and result in rain was the question in most people's minds. They had tested the first segment of the structure and all had gone well. Now they were going to start up the whole system.

The delegates from New York arrived. Edward brought Peter and Elizabeth with him as well as Matthew, Jax, Zoe and Emi. Jon and Amy managed to get a lift and Abe was there with the girls. Liz and Tom arrived by Hoverboard and any Network members who were near enough and could escape their job were also present. The excitement in the air was palpable.

'Good morning everyone,' said Edward as he mounted the raised platform to address the crowd gathered in the field beside The

Cloud. 'Today is an auspicious occasion. We from the Fringe have been waiting for this moment for…a very, very long time. Those from the Network have not had so long a wait but I believe their excitement is no less than ours. The co-operation with which everyone has worked together toward our shared goal has been inspiring. It's something I wish our ancestors had learned to do long ago; if they had we would probably not now be in the mess we're in. However, moving forward I hope for better things. From my vantage point I would say our future looks very bright. Working together in unity has brought us to this point and we from the Fringe are very grateful to those of you from the Network for all your hard work and your willingness to drastically alter your lives to bring us to this point. I would especially like to acknowledge Dez for his leadership in overseeing the building of The Cloud in its various locations around the world. He's dedicated the last couple years of his life to making sure today could happen. And now, I would like to invite Dez forward to launch The Cloud. Dez, if you will?'

Dez moved forward through the cheering crowd, his head in a daze. He could hardly believe that Edward was asking him to launch The Cloud. He'd felt certain that Edward would have retained the distinction for himself. Maybe he'd misjudged the guy. He climbed up to the platform and shook Edward's hand. 'Thank you, Edward. I'm honoured. Good morning, everyone. This is it, the moment of truth. As Edward said, the Fringe have been planning for this moment for a long time and those of us from the Network have sacrificed the last couple years to making it happen. Working together as we have, has finally brought us to this point. This is the moment that we ensure the survival of the planet and the human race. Well, here we go.' He turned to pull the lever and punch in the codes that would start the flow of water from the river and set the solar panels in place.

There was a roar and a hum as the water flowed into the pipes and the solar panels and condensers became operational. The vast array of panels spun in their frames to face the morning sun. The audience watched in awe — it looked like everything was working as it was expected to. The crowd erupted into a crescendo of noise as they turned to embrace, shake hands, or clap each other on the back and cheer at the success. Soon the condensers would emit vapour into the sky and the turbines would blow the artificial cloud in the direction needed. Some days the cloud would be directed toward the west, where it would build up against the mountains and water the plains below. Other days they planned on creating cumulus clouds that would not produce rain but would block the sun to help cool the earth's temperature. Each day would be different — The Cloud monitored to best utilise the climatic conditions of the day. But today the crowd was not concerned with these details. The plan was coming to fruition, giving them hope that the future would be better than the past.

Edward and Dez shook hands once again and turned to survey the rejoicing crowd, united for the moment in their shared achievements. Dez scanned the crowd until his eyes locked with Emi's. There were tears pouring down her face. He cocked an eyebrow questioningly. Emi shook her head and grinned up at him. Nothing wrong then, just the emotion of the moment!

Edward held up his hands to silence the crowd. 'We've laid out a picnic lunch for everyone in the marquee,' he said, waving his hand to indicate the enormous, white tent under which tables of food were laid out, protected from the scorching sun. 'Please, find a place at the tables or on the blankets put out in the field to the rear of the marquee. Enjoy! Thank you for being here to help us celebrate. This will be a day to remember in history,' he concluded. 'Shall we lead the way, Dez?'

Edward and Dez helped themselves to food, grabbed a beer each and laid claim to a picnic table. Soon Elizabeth, Peter, Emi and the others joined them.

'I'm such a baby,' declared Emi, brushing the last of her tears from her cheeks. 'The energy in the crowd and watching all the solar panels come online at once was unbelievable. I just couldn't help myself,' she said as she sat down next to Edward, across from Dez.

'Tears of happiness are more than acceptable on a day like today.' Edward put his arm around her shoulders and drew her into his side. 'I hope to bring many more tears of joy to your eyes.'

Emi glanced across at Dez who was looking daggers at Edward. She gave him a nudge under the table and minutely shook her head. She turned her head to grin at Edward. 'That was the cheesiest line ever, Edward,' she said as she playfully ribbed him in his side.

'Yes, I suppose it was. Sorry,' he laughed as he grinned down at her. Their faces were so close together it almost looked like Edward was about to kiss her there in front of everyone.

'I forgive you, but honestly, you really need to work on some better lines,' Emi said as she leaned forward to get her wine, forcing Edward to loosen his hold.

He let his arm drop from her shoulders. 'However, I do sincerely expect this to be the beginning of a much better new world order.'

'Here, here,' said Peter and raised his glass in a toast. 'To a new world!'

They all raised their glasses, drank to the new world they were creating and the awkward moment passed, almost unnoticed.

Dez stood up abruptly and went to get himself another beer. He found Liz refilling her wine glass. 'Hey, Liz, how are things going in Sector D?'

'Pretty good for the most part.'

'And Tom, how's he? Do you think he's okay with you being leader?'

'I think so. It's hard to tell with him. He's always been moody so it makes it difficult to figure out what he's really thinking. But I think he's actually less moody since I became leader…and his uncle died.'

'Well…that's good.'

'Yeah, I guess. He still goes off by himself quite a bit. But I don't like to ask and he doesn't volunteer. Always comes back with game. But I feel there must be…'

They parted as others came to fill their glasses. The celebration was in full swing as people tucked into their picnic lunch, mingled and chatted. There was laughter and smiling faces everywhere one looked.

'You know he's one of the few who decided to keep his imprint. I think it's from his mom. At least it looks like hers from what I can remember. He won't have it off. I guess it's all he's got left of her.'

'Hmmm. That would be hard to have removed,' said Dez, his thoughts going to his own mother. He still missed her warmth and support and her zest for life even when times were tough. 'Besides, having the vaccine is not mandatory. It's his choice.'

'Yeah. I learned the other day that his mom…that…Kay, our village healer, said the pregnancy had been fine and then she miscarried, lost a lot of blood and died. Remember I told you that Tom's mom had bruises like fingerprints on her breasts?' Liz paused and took a big breath. 'Well, Kay also found that…she had bruising on her belly.'

'Bruising?' Dez's eyebrows drew down, his expression, grim. 'From internal bleeding, do you mean?'

'No. From being kicked, repeatedly, in her, in her ….' Liz couldn't go on. She stared at Dez, the misery naked in her eyes.

'Oh!' Dez was at a loss for words. The implications to hideous to contemplate. Tom's erratic behaviour suddenly taking on a whole new meaning.

'Yeah, explains a few things.'

'I'll say,' Dez paused, his mind churning, he inhaled suddenly, choked, then exhaled slowly through pursed lips. 'Liz?'

'Hmmm?'

'I…do you…I can't believe I'm going to say this out loud…'

'What?'

'Sam, before he died…I thought he wanted to sit up…you know to help…but now, looking back, he was really agitated. I have wondered if he was trying to say 'set-up'… you know, like he wanted us to set-up something so we could kill the Blues and not have to live in fear anymore…but now…I wonder if he was saying…set-up…like the raid was a set-up?'

'The raid…a set-up…why…by who?'

'Do you think that Tom…that Tom arranged to…to have the Blues kill his uncle in exchange for food?'

'That's a horrible thought,' she glanced at Dez to see if he was serious. 'God, no! Never crossed my mind.'

'Me neither, until just now,' he said as he ran his hand through his hair.

'I can see Tom hating his uncle, but burning and killing a whole village just to…I can't see him…'

'No, me neither…but maybe it went too far…further than he'd intended.'

'Even so, just arranging to have his uncle killed would be pretty horrific.'

'I know. But if his mom died how we think and you say he went off by himself a lot and didn't like to answer questions. And then the raid…it was right after his mom died. Tom must have been beside himself with anger and loathing, wishing his uncle dead. I mean you would, wouldn't you? And I've been going over and over Sam's death and what he was trying to say to me right before he died…and it's the only thing I can think of that makes any sense. I mean if Tom knew his mom was pregnant by his uncle and living in fear of him… maybe Sam saw Tom talking with a Blue…but then…'

They were interrupted as more people came to re-fill their drinks, their merriment at odds with undercurrents of emotion surrounding he and Liz. Dez couldn't bring himself to resume the conversation. But now that he'd remembered the talk with Sam at his death-bed, he couldn't escape the thought that the raid was a set-up and that Sam had been trying to warn him.

'We better get back. Don't want to break up the party,' Liz said, returning to the table, drink in hand, a smile plastered to her face. Dez slowly followed along behind her, trying to regain his equilibrium, his joy at the success of The Cloud vanished behind a haze of new images. His mind swirled. How would he feel, how would he react, if it had been his mother who had been raped and beaten? Beaten so that she died. Not killed by the Blues but by a family member. Someone you had offered food and shelter to. He stopped, closed his eyes momentarily and took a big breath. Now was not the time to contemplate such darkness.

'Now that The Cloud has been launched without incident, I'm planning on a couple of formal celebrations,' Edward was saying as he sat down.

Dez took a sip of his drink and forced himself to assume a neutral expression. The change of topic was jarring.

Emi gave him a quizzical look and cocked her eyebrow at him.

He shook his head and gave her a half-hearted smile before returning his attention to Edward.

'I'll thought to plan one celebration for the Network and those from the Fringe who are working here,' said Edward. 'I'm planning another in New York for all of us who are working there. It'll be too complicated to make it into one big celebration but I'm thinking of televising a live feed so we can be part of each others' festivities.'

'Do you have a date set?' asked Elizabeth.

'In a few months time. That gives us plenty of time for making sure nothing goes wrong with The Cloud, and it gives Charlotte preparation time. Amy and Jon, I was hoping you could do the planning and be the hosts of the one here, but Dez, I think it best if you officiate, since you're the leader of the Network,' said Edward smoothly. It was obviously an order and not a suggestion. 'And Emi, I was thinking you could co-host with me in New York, since you represent the leadership of the Network there.'

'I'd be honoured. Your New York parties are always beyond anything I could have ever imagined,' she replied. Her eyes lit up at the thought. 'Will I get a new gown?' she added with a wink.

'But of course.' Edward leaned into her, his smile reached his eyes as he turned his head to gaze at her. The exchange was intimate, as if nobody else was around.

Dez tried to control the look on his face. He could not afford to alienate this man. He nodded his head in agreement and hid behind his beer. He wondered if Edward felt the undercurrents or was so accustomed to being in control that he gave little thought to others wishes. He was hard to read. God, what a night! He glanced at Emi, who excused herself to refill her glass of wine. She had as little say over her life as he did, but she didn't seem to mind Edward's attention or being in New York.

'The girls have been asking for you Emi,' said Abe as she returned to her seat. 'Any chance you could come for a visit for a couple days sometime soon-ish?'

'I'd love to. I could really use a break,' she replied. 'I could probably just stay on for a couple days if that works for you. I'm already here after all.'

'That'd be great,' Abe beamed. 'The girls will be thrilled. I'll go find them and let them know. I'll come get you when we're ready to go,' he said and excused himself from the table.

Dez noticed that Edward looked a bit put out but had refrained from saying anything. Not wanting to seem petty in front of everyone he supposed. He couldn't control every situation after all. And manipulation worked better if it was subtle; if that's what was going on here. Looked like Abe could manipulate a situation as well as the next man, given the opportunity. He could only assume Abe was trying to give he and Emi some time together but he didn't know what to think of Emi's behaviour. Was she falling for Edward?

Emi was ensconced in Abe's living room, curled up on the woven grass seat of the couch, reading one of the few precious books Abe owned. She had prepped the potatoes and set the table while Abe and the girls had gone to gather some more food for dinner. She was just about to start chapter two when she heard a tap at the door. Opening the door she found Dez on the threshold.

'Dez,' she said, her face lit up in surprise. 'Come in,' she pulled him by the hand and shut the door behind him.

'*What* was all that about?'

'That's not much of a greeting.' Her face fell as she took in the taute stance of his body.

'To hell it's not. I've just been put in my place by your new boyfriend,' said Dez in a controlled voice, an angry glint in his eyes.

'He's not my boyfriend. Not now, not ever.' She didn't need to ask who he meant.

'Seemed pretty cozy to me,' Dez shot back. 'His arms around you, promising to make you happy, and you teasing him back and playfully ribbing him! All seemed pretty intimate from where I was sitting.'

'Well it wasn't. I teased him because I didn't want him to think that I was taking the whole 'making me happy' thing seriously,' said Emi, her mouth a thin line as she defended herself. 'I don't know what that was all about but what was I supposed to do?'

'Oh, I don't know. Maybe sit beside me instead so I can be the one putting my arms around you and then maybe he'll get the hint,' his barely suppressed anger caused his voice to rise an octave.

'I don't think that's a good idea,' she said, trying to keep calm. 'Edward's not someone I…want to cross.'

'So you have implied before. But honestly what do you think he's going to do? Kill me off because I'm a rival for your affections?' he asked as he waved his arms dismissively. 'Or are you just trying to play both sides of the fence…I mean he is extremely handsome and has everything you could possibly want in this god-forsaken world.'

'That was mean,' said Emi. Her own anger was starting to bubble to the surface. 'You know I love you. How can you even doubt? Why do you have to be so jealous?' she asked as her mounting frustration made her voice crack with unshed emotion.

'Why do you have to flirt with him?' he snapped back.

'I *don't* flirt.'

'Looked like flirting to me.'

'Well, it…'

'And you pander to his every…'

'I do not,' she said in a low growl as she clenched and unclenched her fists. She took a deep breath and closed her eyes, trying to form a coherent thought. 'He's a powerful man. He's given us positions of authority, you, me…and I'm trying to…'

'To what? Become his lover? His wife?'

'No…to do my job. To help people.'

'By hosting a party with him as a couple?'

'I don't think he meant it like that.'

'Don't you?' his tone was mocking.

'No, I don't! Besides, what choice do I have? I *never* have a choice. I just play my part and do what I'm told. We're supposed to be saving the planet and the human race…*remember*?' The tears began to well in her eyes but her expression remained hostile.

Dez stared at her. The room was completely silent. Then he shook his head, exhaled and brought his hand to his eyes as he massaged his temples. 'Shit! Emi, don't cry. I'm sorry.' It was if she had slapped him and brought him to his senses. 'I'm being an idiot, overreacting…'

'*That* is the first sensible thing you've said since you got here,' she said.

'I deserved that. Sorry. You're right…I just…don't want to lose you,' he said, the fight suddenly going out of him. 'And, yes, I did forget about the whole saving the planet thing and not having a choice…for a moment.'

'Sometimes I would *like* to forget.'

'Yeah. Sorry. I lost my perspective for a bit,' he ran his hand through his hair.

'That's the *second* sensible thing you've said.'

'It won't happen again. I'll be on my best behaviour from here on out. Promise.'

'I'll hold you to that…maybe I should get it in writing,' she joked to dispel some of the tension.

'Come here,' he said as he gently pulled her into an embrace and kissed the top of her head.

Emi wound her arms around his neck and gave him a kiss with far more passion than he was expecting, given his poor behaviour.

'All right, that's enough. Abe will be home soon with the girls. Shall I pour you a glass of wine? Soothe your ruffled feathers.'

'I think it's you who needs the wine. Soothe your own ruffled feathers. I wouldn't have ruffled feathers if it wasn't for you,' Emi said, still feeling somewhat on edge. 'I was just getting warmed up!'

'Touché! Hmmm, so I noticed,' thinking of her kiss rather than the argument.

'But really we should talk about Edward, and me being in New York and you here and all that, don't you think? I mean a proper talk when you're not being so jealous.'

'I suppose so. Or you could marry me.'

'What?'

'Marry me. Will you marry me?'

'…but, but how? We don't even get to spend time together, nevermind getting married?' she said, her mind reeling with the sudden change.

'Is that a 'no'?'

'What? No, no of course it's not a 'no'. I would love to marry you…I just don't see how.'

'How about if we plan to get married a year from now when things are all settled with The Cloud. If we're married, Edward surely can't keep us apart.'

Emi wound her arms back around Dez's neck.

'Oh, here we go again. Is that a 'yes' then?'

'Yes, of course it's a yes.'

TWENTY-ONE

Spike almost made it back to the abandoned structure he called home. He collapsed in the street as he rounded the corner, his front door within sight.

Shade glanced out the grimy, broken window in time to see Spike as he collapsed onto the dusty street outside the ruined building. 'So, he's come crawling back. Huh,' she muttered as she picked up her water canister and lumbered down the stairs and out into the blazing sunlight. She nudged Spike with her foot but he just groaned and didn't budge. She picked up both his hands and dragged him into the shadows cast by the concrete shell of the building. She grinned as she sloshed water over his face and watched him come to with a start.

'What the…!' he sputtered from parched lips. He brought his hand up to cover his eyes as he squinted into the light trying to remember where he was.

'Here,' she said as she thrust the water canister at him. 'Where the hell have you been? Thought you were dead!'

'Almost was,' he croaked, his throat scratchy and dry. He guzzled the water Shade gave him, taking the edge off his thirst, and poured the rest over his head.

'Don't give a crap either way.'

'I wanted to try lookin' on my own. So tired of everyone bitchin',' he rasped. 'Gimme some more water will ya?'

Shade got up to fetch another canister. 'Don't think I'm gunna be your nurse now you're back.' She passed the water to Spike.

He gulped it back, trying to ease his parched throat. 'I got to the hills, then fell down a fuckin' steep mountain. Smashed my knee on a rock.'

Shade glanced at his leg, which was bound with a filthy bandage. She undid the bandage to reveal his swollen knee. It was a darker shade of blue from all the bruising.

'How the hell d'you get back with a knee like that?'

'That guy who gave me the tip-off before, he found me, left me his pack, had pain killers and bandages and crap in it. I found a big stick. Used it as a crutch. Hobbled back. Took forever. Fuckin' hurts,' Spike grumbled. 'But I think I know where they are. If you help me, I'll show you where our endless food supply is.'

'I'll need food for the kid so don't have much choice do I?' Shade snarled, her resentment at Spike for taking so much of their food seeped through the cracks in her self-control.

'Whatever. Thought you might be a little happy to see me.'

Shade shrugged. She looked at the derelict concrete building, the dusty street and the weeds growing in the cracks of the tarmac and then back at Spike. 'Really, why?'

'Where's everyone else?'

'Gone to see if they can find food. You took so much of it, we're all starving,' she glared at him. 'They're trying to catch rabbits. Ha! Like that's going to happen. One person stays behind in case *you* show up. Lucky for you it was me! The others might of just let you die out in the middle of the street.'

'So you're a bit happy to see me?'

Shade just stared at him, then launched into a tirade about how hard it had been since he'd taken most of the food.

Spike tuned her out. His knee throbbed, his throat was raw and he felt like crap...he didn't want to listen. His mind wandered back to the meeting in the woods.

'How the hell did you find me here?' he'd asked.

'I have my ways. I can always contact you when I need to.'

'And here I've been thinkin' about trying to find you.'

'Don't ever find me or it'll be the last thing you ever do.'

'You threatening me?'

The question was ignored. 'I need you to do something for me.'

'Like last time?'

'No, not like last time.'

'Yeah, I wondered what you got out of that little massacre.'

'What you did served my purposes; so not to worry.'

'Don't see how, but whatever. And in case you haven't been payin' attention...I can't do nothin' for nobody like this can I,' Spike growled.

'Don't worry. I'll make sure you can get out of here alive but in return you'll have to do exactly what I say.'

'Humph. What then?'

'Your timing must be *exact*...and you must make it look like your...normal sort of savage attack but you are *not* to touch *anything* else. Is that understood?'

'Yeah. Easy.'

'This won't be easy.'

'And what do I get out of it then?' Spike dared to ask. 'I need food and lots of it.'

'That can be arranged but you'll have to do precisely what I say. The day of the attack will be of most importance and you must not let on it is anything other than your own…wits…that have been your guide. Is that understood?'

'Yeah, I get it. What d'ya want me to do and how do I get what I want?'

'You and your, um, family, or should I say tribe, will get an endless supply of food as well as some basic comforts if you follow my instructions.'

'An endless supply?' asked Spike.

'Yes, endless.'

'I knew there'd be such a place.'

'There is, but this is not about you raiding for food, it's about an attack, a very specific attack. Is that clear?'

'Yeah, I don't mind killin' for food, 'specially an endless amount. But I'll need my leg to be good first,' Spike said as he looked down at his swollen blue knee and tried to shift his weight. Pain shot upwards and he groaned. 'Have anythin' for pain?' he asked.

'I happen to have an emergency kit with me, yes,' he replied. He threw his pack at Spike. 'You'll find similar packs dropped along the way to ensure your survival as you walk back to your…friends. And don't worry, you'll have time to recover. I'll let you know the day,' he said; then he had vanished into the shadows and was gone.

'Hey,' Shade yelled. She slapped Spikes face, which snapped him out of his reverie.

'What the…?' Spike shook his head and rubbed at his cheek.

'You're not even payin' attention to what I'm sayin'! What the hell's goin' on?'

'Yeah, got tired of your blabbing. I was thinkin'. I was thinkin' that soon you'll be happy to show me just how much you'll like having an endless supply of food,' Spike said with a grin as he grabbed suggestively at his crotch.

'Whatever,' said Shade. 'Don't get your hopes up, asshole. And it don't look like you came back with any food, so what you on about?'

TWENTY-TWO

The celebration had been incredible. More lavish than any other dinner or event that she'd gone to in the city of New York. Everyone was so festive; happy and relieved that the first attempt at controlling the weather had worked. The clouds they'd produced had rained — cool, refreshing, clean water — rain for the fields they'd planted with new crops. It had taken months to get to this point. The celebration was a necessity.

Emi thought the happiest person she knew at present was Jax. He was so thrilled to see all the new crops coming up; types of food he'd never heard of before. He was like a little kid again. Some of the food at the banquet tonight had been from the new crops. To look at Jax you'd think he had personally hand-raised every morsel that people ate. He was in his element, chatting to everyone, asking what they thought about all the new food and receiving nothing but praise.

'Are you enjoying yourself Emi?' asked Edward as he came up behind her.

'Of course. Everyone's so happy. It's impossible to not enjoy oneself.'

'It's certainly a wonderful beginning,' Edward said. He looked at the roomful of elegantly dressed people who were dancing, laughing and chatting amongst themselves and smiled. 'Shall we join the others and dance?'

'Certainly, for a bit. But I think I'll go soon. I'm quite tired.'

'One dance…or maybe two and I'll let you go. I promise,' he said. He put his hand to her waist and led her to the dance floor.

They circled the room, moving effortlessly together. Edward was charming and entertaining. Emi could have happily stayed gliding around the dance floor but her feet really were getting quite sore. She said her farewells and left. The evening air felt wonderful after the warmth of the ballroom. Even with sore feet the walk home would be pleasant. She took off her shoes and wiggled her toes.

When she was halfway down the street, footsteps behind her made her jump.

'Do you mind if I join you?' Edward asked.

'Edward! Oh…no, not at all,' Emi said as she brought her hand to her chest. 'I didn't realise you were planning on leaving so soon.'

'I wasn't, but, well…I didn't want to be seen leaving *with* you as people do like to talk,' he offered by way of explanation.

'So you waited until I had walked down the block and then scared me to death,' she replied teasingly as she cocked an eyebrow at him.

'Sorry, I really didn't mean to startle you,' he smiled down at her. 'Your feet must've been very sore,' he indicated the shoes in her hand.

Emi glanced down at the four-inch heels she was holding. 'I'm still not used to high heels. They're not something one wears when trying to catch a rabbit for your next meal,' she glanced up at him. Her eyes crinkled in a smile at her own quip as she tried to dispel her sudden tension with humour.

'Other than the sore feet we've inflicted upon you, are you happy here in New York?' he asked, his question seemingly casual.

'For the most part,' she replied hesitatingly. 'I love helping. It's quite rewarding…even exhilarating sometimes. But I miss my friends and…the feeling of home, of familiarity,' she glanced sideways at Edward and waved her hand to indicate the tall buildings towering over them. 'This all feels a bit surreal sometimes. Sorry, I don't mean to sound ungrateful and I do get home occasionally to follow up on my research but the time always goes by so quickly and I'm so busy that, well…'

'Would you like to go home for a week or two? It can be arranged.'

'Oh, I would love that,' Emi turned her head to beam up at him. He was so handsome and always so kind to her. She wondered what it would be like to be loved by such a powerful man.

'I can make a Hovercraft available to you whenever you're ready to leave,' he said. 'As long as you promise to return,' he added with a slight catch in his throat.

'Thank you. I have a few loose ends to tidy up on this last project but could be ready by the middle of the week,' she replied as she gave his arm a squeeze of appreciation. 'I didn't think not returning was an option,' she added teasingly.

'It's not. We need you. I need you.'

Emi stopped in her tracks and looked into his eyes. In the light cast by the street light she thought she could detect desire in his gaze — desire under strict control. 'Oh!' she whispered.

They had come to a standstill outside the tallest building in New York City. It was one she had never been in before but was always amazed when she walked by at the opulence behind the glass front doors.

'Can I show you something?' Edward asked.

'Yes, of course,' Emi replied, feeling somewhat confused by the sudden change in conversation. Was she imagining things? This man was so difficult to read. He seemed to give little away of himself and yet was impossible to say 'no' to.

'After you,' he said as a doorman opened the glass door to the elaborate foyer and Edward led the way to the elevator. He pushed the button for the hundredth floor — the penthouse suite. They rode the elevator up and stepped out into luxury like she had never imagined, even after all her months in New York. The hardwood floor gleamed, the city lights twinkled like stars beyond the floor-to-ceiling windows that spanned two stories. There was a full size tree in one corner with lounge chairs beneath its branches — a place to rest or read as if outside but without the intense heat. The living room, dining room and kitchen were open to one another. The dining room held a square table big enough to seat twelve comfortably. There was an elaborate candle centrepiece which almost seemed to beg to be lit for a formal dinner party. And the kitchen was enormous — a dream kitchen for a high-end chef.

'Wow!' exclaimed Emi, her eyes widened in surprise. She clamped her jaw firmly shut to avoid having her mouth hang open in awe.

'Do you like it?' He seemed to be holding his breath as he waited for her reply.

'Yes, of course. And just look at the view, it's simply stunning,' she said as she walked to the floor-to-ceiling windows that looked out over the entire city.

'It's yours.'

'What?'

'It's yours. To live in. I want you to have it. To be happy here.'

'But…but I'm quite content with the apartment that I have now,' she replied in confusion, feeling somewhat like she was about to be ensnared in a trap.

'That may be, but this is better suited to your position as a leader. You are, after all, one of the most influential people in the Network.'

'I'm not sure what to say. I thought I was only going to be here for a year. I was not really expecting all this,' she waved her arm to encompass the suite.

'I want you to stay, to feel part of life here in New York City,' he said. He stepped toward her and put his hands on her shoulders, forcing her to look up at him. Slowly his arms slid around her back, the distance between their bodies disappeared as he brought his mouth to hers with a kiss full of pent up passion. 'Oh god, Emi, you have no idea what you do to me,' he murmured, before moving his mouth to her ear and then the base of her neck.

'Oh,' was all that Emi managed to get out before Edward's mouth descended on hers once again demanding a response.

Emi's head was in a fog while her body was on fire. It felt as if her body was a separate entity — a traitor — as her mouth returned Edward's kisses. If she resisted Edward, would his promise of time back home suddenly evaporate? She so desperately wanted to go back home, to see Dez. What would Edward do to Dez if she resisted his advances? Edward was charming, amusing, kind, but also all-powerful. Her brain went round in circles while her body responded to the sensations being thrown at it.

Emi slowly regained her senses and gave Edward a feeble push away. 'Please, Edward…please, you…this is all…too much,' she said breathlessly.

Edward pulled away, his breathing ragged, 'Sorry, Emi, I didn't…' he paused and drew a deep breath. 'You're right. I'm sorry. I shouldn't have…' he stopped to draw another breath. 'We should perhaps go.'

'It's okay. I just wasn't expecting this,' she said, indicating the apartment. 'Or you,' she added with a hint of a smile.

'No, I'm sure,' he returned her smile and gave Emi one last gentle kiss on the mouth. 'Let me walk you back to your apartment but I would like for you to move in here. It'll be more convenient for you getting to work and it's more suited to your position of leadership.'

'Can I have a bit of time to think about it, or at least get used to the idea?'

'Yes, of course,' he replied, as he led her from the apartment and back out into the street. He walked her the rest of the way home and left her outside her door with a last chaste kiss. 'Good-night, Emi.'

'Good-night, Edward.'

Emi went through the next few days in a daze. Her longing for home was real but now she also dreaded it. What had she done? She felt trapped with no way to escape. Woven into the spider's web and the more she struggled the more she was entwined. What she did, her contribution toward saving the planet and the human race, was important. But so was Dez's, vitally so. Whether she was with Dez or Edward seemed so trivial. In the grand scheme of things, who cared? Yet her gut instinct was that if she said 'no' to Edward that something bad would happen to Dez. She couldn't lose him, couldn't imagine a world, her world, without him. And the planet, the human race, couldn't lose the part he played.

She dawdled over completing the few small tasks she had left on her current project. If only she could delay a few more days maybe her brain would think again and she would find a way out of the mess she'd created for herself. She just couldn't contemplate going back to the Network to face Dez. What would she say to him? What would he say? He would probably prefer she resist Edward and that he end up…what? She wasn't sure, but she shivered to contemplate. Would he think she'd been corrupted by the opulence of New York City? She could see no argument that she could offer to explain her actions. The last thing she wanted to do was lose Dez, or hurt him.

She could see no way to refuse the apartment and also had little idea of how to resist Edward's advances.

A few days later she moved into the penthouse suite.

She was in her new apartment preparing an evening meal for her and Edward when the buzzer went. That was strange. Edward usually used the private elevator that only accessed her penthouse suite, not wanting people to know about their relationship. Thankfully he had cooled his advances. So far it had just been meals together, talking over a glass of wine and a kiss goodnight when he left. Emi had no idea how to put an end to his wooing of her. The only thing she could think to do was delay until she could figure something out. But why would he be buzzing from the elevator in the foyer?

She answered it and the voice on the other end said, 'Hello, Emi, it's Charlotte. Can I come up?'

'Charlotte, yes, come on in,' said Emi. She let out a sigh and buzzed her in.

A minute later Charlotte walked in with an armful of clothes. 'I thought you might like some new clothes for your trip back home. Your ones from here will hardly be appropriate there,' she said as she laid out shorts and shirts on the sofa.

'Oh, thank you. I hadn't really thought,' she said as she picked up one of the shirts and held it against herself. The material was soft, clean and new — nothing like the clothes they could get in the Network — but at least it was casual. 'I really do need to get rid of the last of my old Network clothes. They're pretty ratty,' she smiled in appreciation at the thoughtfulness of her friend.

'You okay? I thought with the arrangements made to go back for a visit you would have been long gone by now,' said Charlotte, cocking an eyebrow at her.

'Yes, I guess so. I had a few things to take care…' Emi trailed off. She wasn't going to fool Charlotte with her excuses.

'Worried about seeing Dez again?' Charlotte tackled the elephant in the room head-on.

Emi nodded.

'My advice would be to not say anything. Don't tell him.'

'But how can I? That would be so deceitful,' Emi shook her head. 'And I feel so on edge. He's sure to notice.'

'Maybe, but I doubt it,' replied Charlotte. 'Just be happy to see him and try to forget about all this for a while,' added Charlotte as she indicated the new apartment and the enormous dining table set for two in one corner.

'I don't know if I can pull that off,' Emi rubbed her hand over her face and exhaled loudly.

'You'll have to. You don't want to make Dez jealous so he does something stupid. Edward is a powerful man, the most powerful man in what is left of the world,' said Charlotte. The warning in her voice could not be missed. She paused. 'If you cross him, Dez will not come out the winner,' she added.

The few words sent a chill down Emi's spine. 'Oh God, Charlotte, I just wanted to help turn our lives around. I wasn't expecting all this,' Emi said. She waved her arm to encompass the apartment. 'I don't see any way out — ever,' she moaned as her eyes fixed on the intimate table setting.

'You'll have to tread water for now. See how things unfold,' suggested Charlotte.

'But keep your cool.'

Emi nodded in acknowledgement. 'Thanks, Charlotte.'

'And don't delay much longer or Edward might begin to wonder why you don't want to go home. To the best of my knowledge he still believes that you go just to do research and have a bit of 'at home' time. Right now he probably thinks you're not leaving because you're so taken up with him. At least you have the advantage of him being fairly conceited and not easily threatened by others,' Charlotte smiled.

'There is that in my favour I suppose,' Emi laughed. 'Thanks, Charlotte. You're a gem. I don't know how I would get by here without you,' she said and gave her friend a hug.

TWENTY-THREE

Dez lay in his bed and stared at the ceiling, not knowing what to do. He'd been tossing and turning for hours. Now that he'd thought that maybe the raid was a set-up he didn't seem able to get rid of the idea. It went around and around in his mind like a form of torture. The idea that one of their own would give away the fact that they had a lot of food on hand for the sake of having one person killed was more than his imagination could cope with. But the more he thought about Sam's death the more he thought that he'd been trying to warn him. He had been so agitated — agitated that he wasn't being understood. Sam hadn't wanted to sit up and help — that would have been stupid — he must have been saying 'set-up'. What else could it have been? And it would explain Tom's erratic behavior since his mother's death and the raid. Maybe he was going off by himself to try and escape the guilt. Had arranging to have his uncle killed resulted in the raid and the slaughter of most of the village at Sector C? The image of confronting, or even questioning, Tom was something he shrank from. But what choice did he have? He had to have answers and he needed to protect the Network — he had to know if Tom was a risk to their survival.

As daylight filtered through the curtains he came to a decision, grabbed his Hoverboard and headed over to Liz's village to see Tom. Even with the speed of the Hoverboard it still took the better part of a day to get to Liz's home. By the time he arrived it was dusk. He almost stumbled off the Hoverboard, his legs tired from manoeuvring over the uneven terrain for hours. He climbed wearily up the two steps to her front porch and leaned against the door jamb for support as he rapped on the door before rubbing his hands across his eyes, trying to dispel the exhaustion. His mind had gone in circles all day as his feet had guided him between the valleys.

Liz opened the door, her eyes widened in surprise at finding Dez on her doorstep. 'Dez, hi. What on earth are you doing here? Is everything okay?'

'Hey, Liz,' he replied as he gave her a crooked half-smile. 'Mind if I stay?'

'Of course not. You look pretty all done. Come on in,' she waved him in as she opened the door wide for him to enter. 'What's up?'

'I've come to talk to Tom,' he stated abruptly.

'Talk to Tom?' Liz's forehead furrowed with concern. 'About the raid?'

'Yep.'

'Oh...far out. Not sure what to say.' She slowly shook her head and offered him a seat.

'Yeah, I know. But the thought just won't leave me alone,' he ran his hands through his hair as he puffed out his cheeks and exhaled loudly.

'It does feel like we're missing a piece of the puzzle. But I don't know what it is,' Liz nodded in agreement.

'You and me both.'

'You really do look pretty done-in. Why don't you try to relax while I make us a meal.'

Liz quietly set about preparing dinner as Dez went to wash and change out of his dusty, sweaty clothes. They sat at the little table chatting about everything except Tom, enjoying the companionship as they ate the rabbit stew, though their minds were heavy with the thought of what tomorrow's confrontation might reveal.

'Do you know what you're going to say?' Liz asked eventually.

'Not really. But I figure the best thing to do is to be honest and direct…and understanding.'

'Yeah. I admire your courage but I sure hope you're wrong.'

'Me too.'

'What will you do if you're not wrong?'

'I really don't know. I can't have someone roaming around free who is a danger to the Network.'

'True!'

'I'll have to cross that bridge when I get there.'

'Just the thought of it makes me feel sick. But as much as I love Tom, you know I have your back.'

'Thanks, Liz. You have no idea how much I appreciate your support. Life is hard…but this is truly a nightmare,' he ran his hand through his hair, his expression grim. 'I better turn in. It was a long, hot day getting here and I need to have my wits about me for tomorrow. Thanks for dinner and the place to stay.'

Liz silently handed him a spare pillow and a blanket as he bedded down on the couch for the night. She headed to bed; chit-chat no longer possible. Tomorrow loomed large; what would the day bring?

Dez woke with the dawn. He couldn't believe he had actually slept. He folded his blanket, placed it on top of the pillow and made himself a cup of tea and a piece of toast. He sat at the little table enjoying the soothing tea and using the few minutes of peace to gather his thoughts. There would be no rest for his mind until he had talked to

Tom — which could make things better or worse. After washing his cup he quietly let himself out into the early morning light. Generally he enjoyed the morning with its cooler temperature and its gently filtered light; but not today. Today he dreaded.

He hopped on his Hoverboard and made his way out of the village to Tom's shelter. He hoped Tom was an early riser. He knocked at the door and waited.

'Dez, hi. What are you doing here?' asked Tom, as he opened the door a crack and ran his hand over his face. He had obviously still been asleep.

'Hey, Tom. Sorry to be so early…but I need to talk to you.'

'Sure, come on in.' Tom opened the door fully to let Dez in. 'Want some coffee?'

Dez nodded, giving himself extra time to think of what to say as Tom made the coffee and brought it to the table.

'So, what's up?' Tom stifled a yawn as he sat across from Dez at the little table.

'There's no easy way to say this — but I have to ask,' Dez cleared his throat. 'It's about the raid…and Sam.'

Tom stared at him blankly. 'What about it?'

'Sam mentioned at the meeting that you were having a hard time and…'

'Yeah, well, that's no great surprise.'

Dez ignored the interruption and carried on. He needed to get out what he had to say before he lost his nerve. 'I mean…your uncle was always pretty mean but I guess he became worse…after…after your dad died…and then with what he did to your mom,' Dez shook his head, '…and, well, I wondered …,' he trailed off. He took a big breath and started again on a different tack. 'Just before Sam died he was very agitated and kept saying 'set-up'.'

'I'm not following you,' said Tom, his forehead furrowed. He sipped at his coffee. 'What's Sam got to do with it?'

'Did you — did you arrange for the Blues to kill your uncle and promise them food in exchange?'

'WHAT?' Tom sputtered as he choked on his coffee.

'Did you…arrange to have your uncle killed…I mean…I wouldn't exactly blame you given the circumstances,' said Dez, feeling uncomfortable in his own skin.

'What? Seriously?' asked Tom. When he didn't get a response other than a remorseful but persistent stare from Dez, he inhaled and then exhaled loudly as he tried to form a coherent reply. 'No. No! I hated him. Kicked him out. He raped my mom…then beat her…caused her death; but him being killed by the Blues was just a…happy accident. I would never endanger the Network like that.'

Dez stared at Tom — he looked directly in his eyes — but he didn't see hidden lies emanating from Tom, only misery. 'Oh, thank god,' Dez rested his forehead on his arms as the emotional relief made his body sag. 'I'm sorry…I…had to ask.'

'What made you think…?'

'Sam. He kept saying 'set-up'. I didn't understand at the time but now, looking back, I think that's what he meant. And then you were seen handing over a buck to a Blue. The fact that you came face to face with a Blue and they let you live. Well, your…circumstances…fit,' Dez shrugged.

'Shit! Yeah, I guess I can see that. But I handed over the buck so that they *wouldn't* raid the village. Made a bargain that they would leave us be if I provided them with what I caught.'

'Oh god.' Dez ran his hand through his hair. 'I got this so wrong. Sorry.'

'Not to worry. No harm done and I can see why you thought what you did. But why would *anyone* set-up a raid by the Blues? Are...are you *sure* that's what Sam meant?'

'No. Not really. But I can't seem to escape the thought,' Dez shrugged his shoulders.

'Well, if not me, then who...and why?'

Dez shook his head. 'I don't know.'

Dez returned to his village none the wiser. He performed his duties, did his job, but his mind was in torment. Try as he might to distract himself, he couldn't forget Sam's 'set-up' now that it was embedded in his mind. Sleep eluded him; he was exhausted.

One night as he was clearing up the dishes from a late dinner, he heard a gentle tap at the door. He dried his hands on a cloth and opened the door.

'Emi?'

'Hi, remember me?' she asked with a grin. 'Can I come in?'

'What? Oh, of course. You can't believe how happy I am to see you,' he said as he threw the door wide and hauled her inside. He slammed the door closed, enveloped her in a hug and buried his face in her hair.

'Hmmm...I'm getting a bit of an inkling,' she replied with a chuckle.

'What are you doing here?'

'Seeing you,' said Emi with a glimmer in her eyes.

'I figured that much. But I mean, did you come to do research? How long have you got?'

'No, I just missed home, and you, so I got a few weeks off.'

'Edward let you out of his sight for a few weeks? How'd that happen?' said Dez in mock incredulity.

'Don't start,' said Emi as the glimmer turned to a warning flash.

'Sorry.'

'But, yes. Although, I should really be in my own valley since I did say I was feeling home-sick.'

'A mere technicality. Surely it can be overlooked,' said Dez, his mouth twitched up in a smirk.

'Precisely. So, am I allowed to get as far as the couch or are guests required to stand by the front door all night?'

'Hmmm. Don't know if I want to let go for long enough to let you get as far as the couch.'

'You know, you're really a terrible host.'

'I beg your forgiveness, my lady. How can I be of service?'

'A glass of wine wouldn't go amiss if you have any.'

'Yes, m'lady,' Dez replied. He stroked his thumb across her cheek and planted a feather light kiss on her lips before turning to get the wine and glasses from the cupboard. 'Come, sit, I have so much to tell you.'

'Good or bad?'

'Hmmm. I'm not sure. Neither, really. Just confusing.'

'To do with what?'

'Well, I thought it was to do with Tom, but now I don't know. I'm at a complete loss.'

Emi sat down on the couch, glass in hand, content to listen as Dez confided in her. She firmly banished Edward and his kisses from her mind. He could stir her senses but he didn't ignite her soul as Dez did. She felt like her and Dez were one — their care for their people, their desire to help save the planet, their shared history. She smiled inwardly. They also stirred each others passions. She wanted nothing more than to live her life with Dez and she was getting tired of waiting. She reached up to run her hand through his hair.

Dez stopped what he had been saying mid-sentence and looked at her. 'What are you smiling about? Are you hearing a word I'm saying?'

She shook her head and gave him an impish grin followed by a lingering kiss.

Dez groaned. 'I was trying to have a serious conversation and then you just tune me out and start taking advantage of me.' He kissed her back. 'What's a fellow to do?'

'Don't hear you protesting *too* much.'

'Hmmm. No, not possible.' He pushed her over, pinning her beneath him. 'You minx.'

She grinned up at him, wrapped her arms around his back and pulled him to her.

Emi had an idyllic time with Dez, which she managed to stretch into an entire month. She tried to banish Edward from her thoughts. She no longer wanted to hide her relationship with Dez. And they didn't. They walked holding hands if they were out, or would sit entwined on the blanket if they took a picnic somewhere. She lost her fear of discovery knowing she just needed to take control of her own life and break it to Edward when she returned to New York. She loved Dez and she was being unfair to Edward in allowing him to think there was any hope. She wanted to start her life with Dez and not have to wait until it was convenient for everyone else.

Dez and Emi talked of their wedding plans and where they wanted to live after they were married. For once they looked forward to their future without dread. It was nice to make plans and feel in control of ones own destiny.

Since The Cloud was complete, Dez felt entitled to be able to work where he wanted. And Emi could continue her research regardless of where she lived. By the time Emi returned to New York she was elated. She was ready to cut her ties with New York, to break the news to Edward and to finally decide her own fate.

TWENTY-FOUR

It had been a long few weeks. But Shade and Spike had convinced everyone that they were sure of where the food was. Neither of them let on that there had been a tip-off. This was the furthest they'd gone — the only place where Network members looked like they were guarding something. It had to be the right spot.

They were gathered at the edge of a forest. It's thin foliage didn't offer much protection but it was better than nothing. Some of the trees were still clinging to life in the parched soil, their green leaves intermixed with the brittle branches of those that were dead. The breeze blowing through the forest was loud enough that it should disguise any sound they made. They were at a spot where the trees almost met the grasslands. Spike was fairly certain he had the right day but they'd arrived later than he'd planned. He glanced up at the sky. It was unusually cloudy but with the long summer evenings there was still plenty of daylight left.

Spike knew what his instructions were but he also had his own ideas. To just kill the guards and leave would be stupid and he wasn't stupid. His plan was to find out what was hidden behind the wall of long grass. He wasn't going to be duped by the guy who'd given him the tip-off. Why rely on that creep to give him food when he could just take it himself. He was positive this was where the supplies were kept.

'All right. Ya ready?' Spike looked around at the group. 'Right, one at a time, and make sure ya ain't bein' watched. Shade, ya wanna go first?'

Shade nodded and peeked out from behind a tree toward where the guard was. He was walking away from her so she ran for cover in the grass then ducked down and waited. After a while one of the others joined her. Each time the guard walked away one more person ran for the tall, swaying grass. Finally, Spike arrived — he was the last.

'Time to spread out. I'll lead this way and Shade'll lead that way. One of ya stop at each guard. We hope to meet up on the other side. We dunno how far we gotta go, so we'll just have to 'ope we 'ave enough of us to kill all the guards. When we're on the other side we'll signal with the horn to start killin'. Don't start early or they might give a warning,' Spike instructed, enjoying the sense of power that being in charge gave him. They were all listening to him for a change instead of berating him.

They moved off through the grass trying to be as inconspicuous as possible. The element of surprise was on their side as the Network would not be expecting a raid way out here. Spike assumed that posting guards must be the normal procedure taken by the Network to protect their main food supply. His heart pounded as he pushed his way through the tall grass, barely containing his excitement at the thought of surprising them. He would outwit them all! His grin caused his snake imprints to slither and dance in anticipation of using his spiked club.

As they moved through the grass, one person would stop behind where a guard was and the rest kept going until they had gone as far as they could. When he had nobody else with him, Spike walked to the next guard and stopped. He crept to the edge of the grass and peered out. They had given Shade a long stick with a bit of material tied to it. The yellow material against the golden grass was not easy to see but since he was looking for it he saw it poke up into the air above the swaying grass. She was four guards away from him. Crap! That meant they would have to kill two extra each. Crap. Nothing he could do about it now.

He blew the horn.

The guard nearest to him had been walking away. At the blare of the horn he turned and, at the same moment, Spike raised his club and launched himself out of the grass. He brought the club down hard on the head of the guard. The man slumped to the ground. Blood from his head pooled in the dirt and turned it to a muddy, brown paste. Spike kicked him to turn him over. Glassy eyes stared toward the sky. Spike grinned. He was good at killing with his club.

Spike didn't have long to enjoy his kill. He looked up to find two more guards rushing at him. He brandished his club and yelled as he charged toward them. They were spread out so he would be able to take out both, one at a time. As the first one reached him he swung his club wildly but the guard ducked. Not hitting anything threw his balance off and he crashed to the ground and sprawled face down in the dirt. Shit, shit and shit! Spike scrambled to his knees and tried to get up but he felt a searing pain suddenly shoot through his arm. Blood gushed from the wound. He was not going down without a fight. He wanted that food and he wanted to kill, a gash to his arm was not going to stop him. He staggered to his feet and lunged at the guard with his club. Spike felt the impact as the spike penetrated the guard's torso. The smell of fear, sweat and blood mixed in the air. As he raised his arms to bring his club down on the guard's head he felt a knife pierce his side. Spike dropped his club, doubled over, and fell to his knees. Shit, the second guard had arrived and he was now outnumbered, injured and had no weapon. He rolled over onto his side just in time to see Shade bring her club down on the head of the second guard. She grinned at Spike, her zipper imprints stretched wide as she lunged at the remaining guard and brought her club down on his head. The guard fell to the ground and lay still.

'Hah, that showed 'em!' she yelled in triumph, her zipper imprints stretched even further apart. 'Ya alright, Spike?'

He looked down and shrugged. All his rolls of fat had protected him from being stabbed to death. 'Yeah, I'll be alright. But what 'appened to the other guards?'

'I killed my one and one other who put up a good fight. Another one just turned and ran but not before I hit him pretty good. Don't think he'll last long. He was pourin' blood. I got a couple good shots in before he ran for it. Chicken shit. Such a coward.'

"Cept he mighta gone for 'elp.'

'Whatever. Doesn't matter. He won't get far and I don't think he'll live long. Besides we'll be outta 'ere by then with loads of food.' Shade ripped the sleeve from the shirt of a guard and tied it around Spikes arm. 'There. Should help stop the bleeding for now. Come on. Get up.'

The Blues slowly re-grouped around Shade and Spike. A few were missing but they'd not expected everyone to live in an attack like this. The main thing was that they'd killed the guards — except for one.

'Lets 'ope the one who got away has a long way to go for 'elp. If not,' Spike shrugged his shoulders. 'Lets go 'xplore,' he said as he pushed his way further into the tall grass. Then he bumped into something hard. 'Shit. What was that?'

Shade parted the tall grasses around them and they peered out into — they didn't know what, but it was definitely not crops or storehouses full of food. 'What the…?' It was just a bunch of posts with coverings on them.

'Dunno.' *What the hell?* He'd done what he was supposed to. He'd killed all the guards — except for the one, but who cared. Shade was good at killing, if she said he wouldn't live long then he probably wouldn't. But where the hell was the food he'd been promised? He'd been duped. 'Ahhg,' he yelled. He shook his head and smashed his club into the structure, the impact reverberating down his arm causing his frustration to escalate.

'Now what?' Shade stared at Spike with daggers in her eyes.

'Dunno.'

'Look, what's that?' asked one of the others.

What looked like smoke was pouring out of pipes at the top of the structure, filling the sky overhead.

'It looks like it's what's making all this cloud,' said Shade.

'I say we smash it,' said Spike. 'They can't make me look stupid and get away with it,' he growled from deep in his throat.

'Who can't make you look stupid,' asked one of the fellows.

'Nevermind,' Spike barked at the guy.

'You're pretty good at making yourself look stupid without any help,' muttered Shade. Her anger at having followed Spike boiled to the surface.

'Shut-up,' snapped Spike, his hand itching to slap Shade for her smart mouth. 'I want to smash it. They promised me food and there's no food here. I say we smash it.'

'Who's 'they'?' asked the guy again.

'None of your business,' snarled Spike. 'Are you with me or not?'

'But it goes on forever. We can't smash it all. If that guy did go for help then…' said Shade.

'I thought you said he didn't have a chance,' said Spike as he turned to look at Shade with loathing in his eyes.

Shade shrugged and stared back at Spike. Hostility emanated from her and her eyes glinted dangerously.

Spike backed down. 'Let's burn the grass and then smash as we go this way and then disappear into the forest,' suggested Spike, his need for vengeance overriding all else since he wasn't going to get the food he so desperately wanted.

'How we gunna burn the grass? All this mist is makin' it kinda damp.'

Shade stooped down and pushed her hand into the base of the tall grass. 'It's still pretty dry at the bottom. It might not blaze but the smoke would keep 'em out for long enough. We've all got our fire-starters. Spread out, light the bottom of the grass, start smashing, keep goin' forward, then head for the trees.'

They all nodded in agreement and spread out through the grass. As they touched their lighters to the grass it began to smoke. They turned into the structure as the smoke filled the air and they began to choke. Clubs raised, they smashed everything as they made their way to the other side. Their eyes watered, breathing was laborious, but they continued to swing their clubs, leaving havoc in their wake.

Spike lunged forward like a crazed man — if he couldn't kill more people or have food then he would at least cause chaos. He'd been deceived. Destroying things made him feel better. He smashed his way through the structure, making sure the destruction was complete as he went. When he finally pushed through the tall grass on the far side he stopped to wipe the sweat from his forehead and eyes with the bottom of his shirt. As he stood back up he noticed one of the guards lying face down on the ground near the tree line. He must have been trying to hide. Maybe he was the one that Shade had injured. He lumbered over and using his foot shoved the guard onto his back. He gasped and stumbled back. The fellow didn't move. He must be dead. Spike edged closer to double check. 'Crap, you're the guy who gave me the tip-offs,' he exclaimed out loud, though there was no one to hear him. He nudged the inert body again with his foot but there was no response. Spike shook his head. *What the hell?* He took one last look. *Maybe he looked a bit different.* It was hard to

288   CHAPTER TWENTY-FOUR

remember, he had only seen the guy a few times and usually it had been at dusk. But still, the resemblance gave him the creeps.

TWENTY-FIVE

'Emi, it's Charlotte, can I come up?'

'Charlotte, yes of course, come on up.' Emi pushed the buzzer to let her into the building, looking forward to visiting with the person who had become her best friend here in New York. She couldn't wait to share all her news with Charlotte. She hadn't seen her, or Edward, since her return but she knew that Charlotte at least would be happy for her.

She opened the door to let Charlotte in and her face fell. Tears were flowing down Charlotte's cheeks; her eyes were red-rimmed and her face blotchy.

'Charlotte, what is it?' Emi reached out to pull her friend into the apartment, enveloped her in a big hug, and nudged the door closed behind her.

Charlotte returned the hug. Reluctantly she pulled away and fished tissues from her pocket to mop at her face and blow her nose.

'Here, let me get you some more tissue. Come, sit, please — what is it?'

Charlotte sat on the couch next to Emi. She closed her eyes momentarily and took a steadying breath as she reached out and took her friend's hands.

'Charlotte, please, you're scaring me,' Emi's voice dropped to a whisper. 'What is it?' she pleaded.

'There's…there's been a raid…at Stage Three of…of The Cloud,' Charlotte stated bluntly. She didn't know how to impart the terrible news.

'But there's no food at The Cloud. Why would they raid there? There's nothing for them to take,' Emi blabbed the first thing that came into her head and looked at her friend questioningly. Her face turned ashen as her blood ran cold. The look in her friend's eye told her there was worse to come.

'No, they didn't take anything. They burned the grass and smashed everything and…'

'But, but…why?…how? What's the point of that?' Emi shook her head.

Charlotte wiped her sleeve across her eyes and took a big breath.

'…And what will we do without The Cloud. I just don't get it. It was so well hidden and it was guarded,' Emi stopped, her eyes dilated as the pieces fell into place. 'Oh, oh no, the guards?' Emi blurted out. Her mind reeled as images flashed through her mind.

Charlotte shook her head. The tears started to trickle down her face once again.

Emi put her hand to her mouth, her eyes wide with fear as she asked the question she didn't want the answer to. 'Killed?'

Charlotte nodded.

'All…all of them?'

'We think so. The grass…it only smoked in some places, but in other places it was dry enough to burn and the…bodies were close to the blaze. We're not sure if everyone died or if some are missing. It's such a mess. It's hard to tell. And we can't identify everyone. They're too…burnt.'

'Oh, Charlotte. What…what are we to do?'

Charlotte shook her head from side to side as if she was trying to banish the thoughts.

Emi leaned forward to embrace her friend. She had never seen Charlotte so distraught. Charlotte's tears soaked into her shirt and glued it to her shoulder. Emi eyes remained dry, her shock too great to let the tears flow. Charlotte took a big breath and gave Emi a squeeze. Emi pulled back to study Charlotte's countenance. Then fear flooded her soul. No, no, no. She didn't want to hear what was coming next.

'Emi, Jax was one of the guards.'

'No, please, not Jax,' she whispered as tears welled in her eyes. 'But he's so young.' Her tears started their silent journey down her cheeks, to drip off her chin and splatter on hands cradled in her lap. But she felt some relief — she had thought Charlotte was going to say it had been Dez who was one of the guards.

'And Emi…'

'Oh, no…please…don't say it.'

'Emi, Dez was also one of the guards.'

Emi shook her head in denial. It didn't make any sense. There must be a mistake. Why would Dez be a guard? He was in charge. He had so much else to do. 'Why?'

'I don't know. Edward did say that as a leader Dez liked to be involved in all aspects of production and what everyone was doing, so maybe it was his turn for a day.'

This time Charlotte took Emi in her arms and let her sob out her grief. Emi's body was racked with despair. Her mind went blank and she could do nothing but moan in her anguish. No, no, no were the only words that went round and round in her head.

After what seemed like an eternity, Emi felt Charlotte gently push her away, lay her on the couch, and then heard her rattle around in the kitchen.

She smelt the warm aroma of brandy under her nose and opened her puffy, blood-shot eyes.

'Here, drink this. It will do you good.' Charlotte held out the brandy glass.

Emi did as she was told, too worn out to argue. 'Thanks, Charlotte.'

'What are friends for? Besides I didn't want…anyone else…to see you like this.'

'Does it matter anymore?'

'I don't know. But I'm pretty sure Edward will be over soon.'

'Oh. Edward. He must be devastated. All his plans in ruins.'

'He's fit to be tied. Keeps smashing his fist into things saying, 'the stupid, stupid idiots destroyed the panels. We're all doomed.' I've never seen him lose control like that. I think it's what frightens me most.'

'Yes, I guess we're all doomed.' Emi's hand drifted to her stomach in a protective gesture.

'Emi?' Charlotte raised her eyebrows.

'I…I figured it out just before you got here. Poor little thing, what a time to be born into the world.'

'Oh, Emi. But when…oh no…Dez?'

Emi nodded. 'It was such an emotional visit, we were finally making plans for our future and well…' Emi trailed off. 'And, quite truthfully, I didn't care if I fell pregnant…it would be a way out of the mess I'd created. I felt so guilty about not just saying 'no' to Edward, letting him have…expectations. And I was so desperate to be with Dez. What am I to do? I was just working up the courage to tell Edward. I couldn't stand the deception anymore…and now this.'

'Oh, Emi, I...' was all that Charlotte could say before they were interrupted by the sound of the buzzer.

Emi looked at Charlotte with dread in her eyes.

'You better go wash your face. I told Edward that I would come over and break the news to you, but all the same I think I'll slip out the back way.' She paused on her way. 'Emi, I have to ask...are you sure it's Dez's? It's not Edward's?'

Emi nodded her head. 'I'm sure. I...I never...with Edward...I...'

Charlotte nodded in understanding. 'It's going to be a tough world to raise a child in.'

Emi looked at her friend and shrugged her shoulders in resignation. What was she to do? She was pregnant and alone. Once Edward found out, would he even let her stay in New York or keep her job? The thought of going back to how life had been before was unimaginable.

'Emi?'

Emi looked at Charlotte, eyebrows raised questioningly. What was coming now?

'Emi...they look alike,' said Charlotte as she turned and left the room.

Emi nodded and went to wash her face. She gazed at herself in the mirror. Her face was white, her eyes swollen and red, she looked completely drained. How was she going to face Edward? What was she to do? Life was so unfair. Charlotte's words rang in her head. It was true that they looked alike — if you didn't know that they weren't related you would mistake them for siblings, or cousins at the very least. But it seemed so heartless and she had never seen herself like that. Oh God, Dez, she thought. But there was no answer.

The buzzer rang again, this time more insistently.

Emi went to the intercom to answer.

'Hello, Emi. Can I come up? I wanted to check that you're okay.'

She buzzed him in without saying anything. The intercom was too impersonal for so much emotion. May as well get this over with. There was no future for any of them now anyway, so — she left the thought unfinished, her shoulders slumped. Where was the brandy bottle? She felt the need for another glass.

She was filling her glass when Edward knocked and walked in. His hair was ruffled and his tie loose, the top couple of button of his shirt undone.

'Emi? Charlotte told you?' he said as he noted her red-rimmed eyes and the brandy glass.

Emi nodded and handed him a glass of brandy as she took a sip from her own. The burning sensation as the brandy slid down her throat was soothing. She looked at Edward with eyes swimming in unshed tears.

'Emi, I'm so sorry. So many from the Network…your friends.' He took her glass and put it down with his and then pulled her into his arms.

She let herself be held. His were not the arms she longed for but her choice had been taken from her and nothing mattered anymore. Edward was alive. She was dimly aware that he smelled of a hint of aftershave which she had grown to like. His hand as it stroked her hair was comforting.

After a while he pulled away and led her to the couch. He put her drink back in her hand. 'Here, drink up. You've had a shock. We've all had a shock. It'll do you good,' he instructed as he brushed a strand of hair back from her face.

She sipped obediently and looked at Edward. 'What are you going to do? All your plans destroyed in one day. I can hardly believe any of it.'

'I'll figure something out.'

CHAPTER TWENTY-FIVE

'But…but I thought there wasn't a back-up plan. That if The Cloud failed then we're all doomed.' Emi found it easier to talk about the big picture, even though it was bleak, than about the death of Dez and the others. She needed to make it less personal. She inhaled the aroma of the brandy and closed her eyes.

'And that may be but, Emi…look at me…' Edward waited until she opened her eyes. Her abject misery was clearly apparent.

Emi gazed at Edward as her mind swirled. Edward — he was so thoughtful and caring. This huge crisis and he'd come to check on her and make sure she was okay. She gave him a glimmer of a smile.

'I won't give up hope, not yet.' He put their glasses back on the table and reached for her hands. His hands were warm, the familiarity of them pleasant. 'I know this is impeccably bad timing but things are obviously going to be even more difficult in the time to come and…and I would so love to have your support…to have you by my side.' His speech was halting, yet rushed.

'You have my support. You always have had.'

'I mean…as my wife,' he said gently, his hands tightened their hold on hers. 'Will you marry me? I love you and need you so desperately, now more than ever. I'm sorry for the blunt delivery and the lousy timing,' he shrugged.

The unfamiliar gesture spoke to Emi about just how uncertain he was.

'Well, will you?' he prompted as he held his breath and waited for her reply.

Time had slowed to a standstill but it had all happened so quickly. It was hard to form a coherent thought. Emi's eyes widened but she managed to prevent her mouth from gaping open. 'I…I…' She looked into his eyes. He looked scared — terrified even — not at the state of the world and the current mess they found themselves in, but at being rejected by her. She couldn't lose him too. And she didn't want to raise a child alone, especially if times were to get even more difficult. He would be able to protect her and get things for her and Dez's baby that she would otherwise have to do without. And maybe with her support he would find a way to save humankind and the planet they all shared. She had no choice. She nodded her consent though she couldn't bring herself to utter a word.

He drew her to him. She crawled over and curled up in his lap. 'Is it okay if we get married soon without too much fuss?'

She nodded. 'I don't want a fuss. It would seem…inappropriate.'

'I'll get Charlotte to arrange things. You've had too much of a shock. It'll be easier this way,' he said. The relief in his voice was audible. Now that he had what he wanted and knew where things stood between them he would be able to get on with repairing the damage, making plans and resuming control. He closed his eyes and smiled into her hair.

She nodded her head and snuggled into his arms. His hand came to her hair and stroked it, offering her what little comfort he could. She leaned her head into his shoulder and wound her arms around his neck. She let him pick her up and carry her to the bedroom. He must never find out that the baby isn't his, she thought as she finally allowed herself to give way to him. Her tears soaked into the pillow in the darkness.

Dez groaned and slowly returned to consciousness. His head felt like it had been split in two and his whole body ached so badly he couldn't tell where he was wounded. He tried to move his arms. The effort almost made him pass back out. He rested and breathed. Breathing hurt. He opened his eyes. Everything was dark. Either it was a starless night or he was blind. He managed to bring his hand to his face and felt sticky goo. Congealed blood. His arm slumped to his side. Damn!

The smell of dried blood made him want to gag. He turned his head to try and see something but there was nothing but blackness. Oh god, maybe he was blind. The thought filled him with fear. The smell of burnt grass assailed him. He tried to call out but his throat was raspy, damaged from inhaling the smoky air. Shit, what had happened? He thought he could remember being hit by a spiked club, wielded by a girl from the Blues, before he turned and ran, desperate to get help. He must not have managed to get very far before his wounds overtook his stamina. Really, was this the end, after all he had been through? He didn't want to die here, all alone, with nothing to prove for his existence. He tried to roll over and push himself into a sitting position but fell back exhausted.

His mind churned as he lay there just trying to breathe. Why? Why had the Blues destroyed The Cloud? It made no sense. There was no food here, nothing that they could possibly want or need. And how did they find the place? It was so far from their normal stomping grounds. They didn't usually travel such long distances to raid for food. Something was wrong but his mind couldn't piece it together. His head throbbed and his tongue stuck to the roof of his mouth. He reached down and unclipped his water canister from his belt and brought it to his lips. He slowly trickled some water into his mouth to ease his parched throat. He tore at his shirt and sacrificed a few more drops of the precious water to wipe his face and clean the congealed blood from his eyes. As he gently rubbed at his eyes he finally managed to remove the last of the grunge from his eyelashes and slowly blink his eyes fully open. He could just detect the forest off to his left in the dimness of the night sky. He forced himself to ignore the pain and rolled over on to his hands and knees to crawl to the tree line. He needed to hide until he had regained enough strength to warn the others. He had to warn the others. They couldn't allow the Blues to destroy all their hopes for the future. But there was something else. Sam's parting words of 'set-up' came unbidden into his mind. Set-up! Could this be another set-up? He lay back against a tree and closed his eyes. His mind went over and over Sam's parting words and then his confrontation with Tom. It didn't make any sense. There was a piece of the puzzle missing but he felt it was just out of reach. Then his eyes opened in shock. He didn't think he'd imagined it. When lying in the dirt, pretending to be dead so the guy didn't kill him, the fellow from the Blues had pushed him over with his foot and then declared that he was the person who had given the Blues the tip-off. Why would they think it was him? He must look like the guy giving the tip-offs. Who did he resemble? He thought of everyone he knew but couldn't think of who he looked like, although he felt like it was hovering at the edge of his mind. If only he wasn't so tired maybe he could put the pieces together. He would figure it out later — he and Emi. She could always put things into perspective. He just had to wait until he regained his strength. Had to warn Emi. Emi was his future. Emi…was his last thought as he passed back out.

He wasn't sure how much time had passed when he next opened his eyes. By the lighting he thought it was probably heading toward dawn. It must be the very early hours of the morning. It wasn't quite light yet, but the darkness of the night seemed a bit less. Surely someone would come soon. His shift was supposed to be from 4pm until midnight. But maybe the new shift had come and gone and they had left him here for dead. His head still throbbed but at least he could faintly see his surroundings. All around him was charred grass and drifting smoke. It was amazing the forest had not caught fire. Maybe the wind had changed direction in time that the blaze had not spread.

ABOUT THE
AUTHOR

G.J. Page lives in the Peak District in England with her family. She is passionate about conservation and the environment. This is her first novel for adults.

She is also the author of the popular children's series *The Travel Adventures of PJ Mouse* and *The Animal Pack* series. Her other books can be found online at www.gwynethjanepage.com and www.pjmouse.com.